Acclaim for

BAILEY'S CAFE

"Graceful, sometimes piercing, often spellbinding. Gloria Naylor's is a commanding fictional voice." —*Washington Post Book World*

"Moving...told in contrasting shades of harsh, comic and magic realism... crackles with passion and wit...Naylor writes consummately well of the real world's edge....Brilliantly conceived and fleshed out...it is an unforgettable successor to Ellison's metaphor of the invisible man, and as incandescent." —Richard Eder, *Los Angeles Times*

"A lacy, near-mystical cantata sung by several voices. This mix of myth, history and mysticism...offers a sensibility as rich in potential as that of the Latin American magical realists....Moving and memorable." —Gail Caldwell, *Boston Globe*

"A stunning achievement...*Bailey's Cafe* is a rich medley of dissonant yet somehow melodic tales of struggle and triumph. With lyrical language that brings to mind the mastery of Toni Morrison and a savage humor that rivals Terry McMillan's...Naylor becomes a magician, a practical conjurewoman who pulls off a literary sleight of hand that is dazzling." —*Atlanta Journal-Constitution*

"Gutsy...a collective blues performance in prose—a lyrical remembrance and triumph over personal catastrophe....A sublime achievement." —*People*

"A powerhouse of a novel...It is a book with something of a comic Ellisonian or Faulknerian rhythm, a defiantly hopeful stance. *Bailey's Cafe* absorbs us in the mastery of its telling." —*New York Newsday*

"The narrative of *Bailey's Cafe* is simple and resonant, its dialogue genuine, as though Sadie and Miss Maple and all the rest really are telling you about their lives over a bad cup of coffee. Transforming the lowly into poetry is a tall order, but Gloria Naylor dishes up something beautiful." —*Miami Herald*

"*Bailey's Cafe* has the rhythm of music—and the power of religious allegory. Beneath its symbolic overlay are tales of fractured lives that will move even the most hardened reader."   —*Vogue*

"There's much...in the intense rhythms of Naylor's slow-burning language, which sings of abuse and violence and hate and pure joy, and of the sweetness and power of the human spirit."   —*Mirabella*

"A dazzling novel. When you enter Bailey's Cafe, you won't leave without being touched by the wonder and the horror that lie there—nor can you fail to be impressed by Naylor's ability to show it plain. In this novel, she has hung on to the mystical streak that runs through her work...and settled into her own voice—and quite a voice it is."   —*Entertainment Weekly*

"[A] remarkable novel...Naylor has transcended the realism of her [previous] three novels to find means anew to give voice to the suffering of black women. In *Bailey's Cafe* that voice is poetic and profound."
—*New York Daily News*

"[An] appealing...strong work with moments of unusual power. Naylor manages to avoid being sentimental, and [is] a wonderful storyteller. When these stories touch us, they do so deeply, mainly because Naylor possesses not only great sweetness, even humor, but also a willingness to stare down some very tough issues."   —*Cleveland Plain Dealer*

"Naylor mixes lyricism with...sexual detail to bring to life the blues sung by her various female characters. In the cafe, these women's pain and triumph, often bittersweet, are explored. What keeps the reader turning the page is Naylor's unswerving moral fervor and intelligence. Plus an arresting sense of humor that she wields like a velvet cape over the pain of racism."
—Patti Doten, *Boston Globe*

Gloria Naylor

BAILEY'S CAFE

A native New Yorker, Gloria Naylor won the American Book
Award for First Fiction in 1983 for *The Women of Brewster
Place*. The subsequent publication of *Linden Hills* and *Mama
Day* served to greatly increase her repute and her audience. A
graduate of Brooklyn College and Yale University, Ms. Naylor
lives in New York City.

Also by Gloria Naylor

THE WOMEN OF BREWSTER PLACE

LINDEN HILLS

MAMA DAY

BAILEY'S CAFE

Gloria Naylor

VINTAGE CONTEMPORARIES

VINTAGE BOOKS

A DIVISION OF RANDOM HOUSE, INC.

NEW YORK

FIRST VINTAGE CONTEMPORARIES EDITION, SEPTEMBER 1993

"Mood Indigo" has appeared in *The Southern Review,* Summer 1992.

Library of Congress Cataloging-in-Publication Data
Naylor, Gloria.
    Bailey's Cafe / Gloria Naylor. — 1st Vintage contemporaries ed.
      p.   cm. — (Vintage contemporaries)
    ISBN 0-679-74821-0
    1. Restaurants—United States—Fiction. I. Title.
  [PS3564.A895B3   1993b]
  813'.54—dc20   93-13117
                      CIP

Manufactured in the United States of America

10 9 8 7 6 5 4 3 2 1

For the two Luecelias:

1898–1977
1951–1987

The author wishes to thank the Guggenheim Foundation and
Jonathan Culler at the Society for the Humanities, Cornell
University, for their generous financial and moral
support during the writing of this novel.

hush now can you hear it can't be far away.
needing the blues to get there
look and you can hear it
look and you can hear
the blues open
a place never
closing:
Bailey's
Cafe

Maestro,
If You Please . . .

I can't say I've had much education. Book education. Even though high school back in the twenties was really school, not what these youngsters are getting away with now, and while Erasmus Hall in general, Miss Fitzpatrick in particular, is still talking about the cream that floated to the top and then to the top of that again, school isn't where real learning happens.

I went to kindergarten on the muddy streets in Brooklyn, finished up grade school when I married Nadine, took my first diploma from the Pacific; and this cafe, well now, this cafe is earning me a Ph.D. You might say I'm majoring in Life, standing in front of this grill and watching that door open and close, open and close, as they step in here from all over the United States and some parts of the world.

A few of them actually think wanting a cup of coffee brought them in, even though they soon find out we make lousy coffee. The grinder's broken and I can't ever be sure what size grounds I'm getting one batch to the next. I brew it for them anyway. And covering up its taste with the food is out of the question: I picked up my cooking skills from the navy mess, where you're taught a little more grease and salt should answer any complaints.

Then there's the few who think it's Nadine's peach cobbler that keeps bringing them back. I admit it's close to spectacular. But she only makes it when the mood hits her and will only dish it up and serve them when the mood hits her again.

And it can't be for the company, like others think. Our customers are all so different I've yet to see anybody get along in here. But that door will still open and close, open and close.

They don't come for the food and they don't come for the atmosphere. One or two of the smart ones finally figure that out, like I figured out that I didn't start in this business to make a living—personal charm is not my strong point—or stay in it to make a living—kind of hard to do that when your wife is ringing up the register and it's iffy when and how much she'll charge.

No, I'm at this grill for the same reason that they keep coming. And if you're expecting to get the answer in a few notes, you're mistaken. The answer is in who I am and who my customers are. There's a whole set to be played here if you want to stick around and listen to the music. And since I'm standing at center stage, I'm sure you'd enjoy it if I first set the tempo with a few fascinating tidbits about myself. (Nadine, nobody asked you.)

I grew up in Flatbush believing that Brooklyn was the capital of the world and that all colored people except for my family were rich. I wasn't a stupid child; Brooklyn had Ebbets Field and the Brooklyn Royal Giants, and since baseball, good baseball, was all I cared about, that settled that for wherever anything else important in the world could possibly happen. And my eyes certainly didn't deceive me: liveried coachmen, sable wraps, and brownstone mansions meant rich, while getting up at five in the morning to stoke the furnace, start breakfast, and lay out the morning suits for people like that meant you weren't. And that's what my parents did as butler and cook for the Van Morrisons, who were as colored as we were; and all their friends sure looked as colored as we were, and while I couldn't vouch for their homes, there was no denying the silk gowns and beaver top hats as they stepped out of the polished carriages that pulled up in front of the house for one of Mrs. Van Morrison's balls.

Those were the only colored people I ever saw until my father started taking me to baseball games, and then I just figured that the hundreds of other Negroes around me were like the Van Morrisons' friends, only dressed down for the occasion. I didn't figure they could be like us, because there were no other colored servants in our household or in the neighborhood. Mrs. Van Morrison's personal maid was a full-busted Swedish girl whose cousin doubled as coachman and gardener. They both ate in the kitchen with us and complained as loudly about Mrs. Van Morrison as my mother did. That left only Bella, a Polish woman, who came in three times a week for the laundry and heavy cleaning. The other homes in the neighborhood were owned by white people and they all had French, Swiss, or German servants. So I think I had it figured out pretty good for a five-year-old: there were rich white people, poor white people, rich colored people—and us.

If my older brother hadn't been so much older than me, he probably could have explained things to me a little sooner than I learned them myself. But with a twelve-year difference in our ages, he was already on the road before I started kindergarten—

—To discover his fortune: my mother

—A shiftless bum: my father.

My folks didn't see eye to eye on much, beginning with their firstborn son and ending with the Van Morrisons. My father would have cut his own throat for Mr. Van Morrison. My mother hated Mrs. Van Morrison with a quiet passion that's peculiar to women: it burns low, slow, and long. If a man disliked someone as much as my mother disliked that woman, he would have just hauled off and punched him in the face and let the consequences be damned. But a woman can drag the whole thing out—over years—and pick, pick, pick to death. I used to think my mother didn't just up and poison Mrs. Van Morrison because we ate whatever they had left over from supper, but now I know that she relished hating that woman and would have done anything to keep her alive and well so the whole thing could go on and on.

I wondered which was the greater or lesser sin: Mrs. Van Morrison not deserving Mr. Van Morrison because she'd been a woman of loose virtue, or because she tried to keep him from hiring my parents. Granted, for my mother, loose virtue could have meant anything from Mrs. Van Morrison's former stage career—

   —Opera: my father
   —Burlesque: my mother

to a brief association with a London bordello—

   —As interior decorator: my father
   —Interiors, period: my mother.

But even my father admitted that the mistress of the house was less than thrilled when her husband insisted upon taking my parents on staff. And my mother got that one nod from him because it helped him prove how wonderful Mr. Van Morrison was, a real race man.

He had made a small fortune as a tea and spice dealer, rolled that into a larger fortune through some shrewd real-estate investments, and split off part of that into railroad, steamship, and oil stocks. No, he couldn't have booked first-class passage on any of those railroads and steamships, but the value of his shares kept going up enough to afford him his own private Pullman and yacht. But he was a plain man who didn't go in for any of that showy stuff. A trustee of the Tuskegee Institute, he'd put money behind the Niagara Movement, what they're now calling the NAACP, as well as some settlement houses for colored orphans in the Tenderloin district. That's how he met my folks; they were living in that part of Manhattan, my father being between jobs and volunteering to teach the settlement kids baseball.

It seemed like a good arrangement: my parents wanted to get themselves and my brother out of those slums in the west fifties, Mr. Van Morrison needed to start staffing his new home on Lafayette Avenue, and he felt why not give his own kind a chance at fresh country air and a living wage? Shows you how long ago it was, when Brooklyn was considered the country.

And it was giving them a chance, to live and work in a house like that. You'd never know it now, with Negroes doing all kinds of domestic work, but back then colored people had a hard time even getting jobs as servants if you're looking at the finer homes. A female might come in on day work as a charwoman or laundress, and a male, if he was lucky, could get taken on as a coachman. But if you're talking about a staff cook and housekeeper or a valet, a gentleman's *gentleman*, Europeans did that—and only certain Europeans.

Wealthy Negroes held the same kind of attitudes as wealthy white people but even more so, feeling that they had more to prove. According to my mother Mrs. Van Morrison didn't want them as servants because it cheapened their appearance to the neighbors.

—It don't matter what color hands is peeling these potatoes; none of them neighbors is about to sit down and eat with her.

My father's version was that Mrs. Van Morrison worried about the second child being born. Servants with large families were a nuisance. My mother wasn't buying it.

—Two children in twelve years. What does that make me, some kind of rabbit?

My father, a dark-skinned man, would actually blush as he put his finger to his lips and cut his eyes toward me.

—Woman, remember yourself now.

If he'd only known, when he wasn't around and my mother and the maid put their heads together over a cup of tea, I heard much worse than that.

I really don't know if I was or wasn't the cause of Mrs. Van Morrison's reluctance to keep my parents on staff. I do know they worked for those people for twenty-five years, retired with a sizable pension, and were later mentioned in Mr. Van Morrison's will. And the few times over those years that I had reason to run into Mrs. Van Morrison she was always nice to me. A tiny tiny woman who favored shades of beige lace for her dresses, but her voice was round and full, making me think that singing could have easily been somewhere in her past. She would put her jeweled hand on my shoulder to ask me about my studies. That's what she called them, studies, while I mumbled something about school being fine before she'd pat me and move on. Good, keep improving yourself.

The truth was, I didn't like school and it was never fine. When I wasn't being punished for getting into a fight, I was punished for sleeping in class, and when I wasn't being punished for that it was for sneaking out early. Now, all of those strappings were justified—except for the last. I wasn't so much sneaking out of school as sneaking *into* the ballparks. A fine distinction that my mother had a hard time appreciating.

Over the years I've tried to figure out what it is about the game that hooked me so early. My father being such a big fan probably helped. He'd been a bat boy for the Cuban Giants and wasn't a bad fielder himself. I think he would have gone out barnstorming with them if he hadn't met my mother and started a family. In those days, he'd say, in those days they *really* played ball.

He had stories about them and the Philadelphia Giants and other Negro independents I took to be a little bit of an exaggeration. No human being could shut out both ends of a doubleheader with the last throw a fastball that went by with so much heat it busted a seam in the catcher's glove. But I *got* the glove, my father said as he dug into the bureau and pulled out a catcher's mitt. There was a slight tear in the seam and scrawled across it in fading ink was the name—
Smokey Joe Williams.
But did it really happen because of a pitch? And at the bottom of a doubleheader? A shutout doubleheader?

———

You don't say your father is a liar. And when I was coming up you didn't even *think* that your father was a liar. Good thing too, because in 1917 I finally saw an aging Smokey Joe Williams pitch.

    —Not at the top of his prime, my father sat in the bleachers muttering and shaking his head.

I was there with my mouth so wide open I could have swallowed flies. That tall, swaybacked man had them fanning left and right, and not just any them—the New York Giants. He ended up fanning twenty of them before the game was over and losing 1–0 on a tenth-inning error.

I had to hear about that error all the way home.

I still hear about that error in my sleep.

I thought it was a great performance. And knowing now what I do about baseball, it was a little bit more than that. Something happened when those colored players were out on the field, and I guess I went to so many games trying to figure out exactly what it was. Sometimes it was exhibition games against the white teams, like the one where I first saw Smokey Joe, but most of the time it was them against each other: the Homestead Grays, the Pittsburgh Crawfords, the Baltimore Black Sox, the Chicago American Giants, the Newark Eagles, those amazing—and still-amazing—Kansas City Monarchs.

I didn't question why Negroes had separate teams; watching their games and then the white games, it was pretty clear to me. The Negroes were better players. And just like us at school, who wanted to team up with the pee-pants who had snot running out their noses? No, winners stay with winners. But they could have been a little more fair-minded and let the likes of Honus Wagner or Ty Cobb on their teams.

Even my father would have agreed that the Flying Dutchman could have endured a season that started in February with barnstorming in the Deep South, a game a day, three on Sunday, as he made his way north, sleeping on the bus riding into town, playing a game, riding again to get to the next town just in time for the first pitch, playing a game, riding again before the real season begins in April, which means he can exchange his bed on the bus for a bed in a run-down Northern hotel and the cow turds between second and third for a field line that only slopes slightly in second-rate parks. Still a game a day, still three on Sunday, but more and more dark faces in the crowds, who cheer his speed and don't sit in deadly silence when he comes in on a two-out hopper and whips it across to first base, so there's less of a worry that retiring the home team to come back then as third in the batting order, once with a line-drive single, again with two batted in will mean pop bottles filled with piss thrown at his head; less of a worry that if he's too good a crowd could turn real ugly, if he's too good he might not make it out of town that night; so the Northern games are where he goes all out and hopefully gets himself voted into the East-West Classics and his team into the Negro World Series, which makes it September but not quitting time because with all of this the pay hasn't been too great and there's always winter ball in Florida for the tourists or maybe Cuba, leaving just enough time to start preseason barnstorming again in February.

Yeah, the Flying Dutchman would definitely have been good enough to join one of those teams; they grow 'em tough up there in Mansfield, Pennsylvania. He could have made it with no rest—in body or mind— and still brought in a batting average of .327 while transforming himself into a golden shield between second and third bases. He'd been just like Pop Lloyd in that respect. And it leaves me confused, why these news-papermen look back at Pop's career and call him the Black Honus Wagner; all things being equal—or in this case unequal—the highest compliment to pay the Flying Dutchman is to call him the White Pop Lloyd. And I'll even bring Ty Cobb into that club, although he'd play dirty and spike a man in a second: he's the White Oscar Charleston if there's ever been one. Those other players, now, those others just couldn't have made it. And no, I haven't forgotten the Babe. Too temperamental. He couldn't have gone two seasons in Josh Gibson's shoes and held on to his record, and so as far as I'm concerned, the title of a White Josh Gibson still goes unclaimed.

And today? You can just forget it today. They've gotten so soft and ridiculous they'll be wanting their mammies in the dugout to suckle them between innings. Only way to explain the hoopla over this new kid, Jackie Robinson. (Just let me make this one last point, Nadine, and then I'm getting on to our own long and blissful twelfth inning.) To hear these people talk, you'd think Jackie Robinson grew up like a mushroom in the jungle somewhere and Branch Rickey was on some kind of rare-species hunt and stumbled over him. Well, if Rickey was after the rare, he didn't find it in that player. Robinson is a dime a dozen in a long-established *league*. The Negro American League, to be exact, whose teams play against the Negro National League. Organized baseball, just not recognized baseball.

I'm the first to admit the Dodgers needed all the help they could get; nobody was going out to Ebbets Field to see that mess Rickey called a defensive lineup, and it got me so I was becoming embarrassed to say I was from Brooklyn—white baseball or not. When you love the game, you love the game, and mutilation is mutilation. So, yeah, he's desperate enough to bring in a colored player, but dammit, bring in a colored player. Try to get your hands on a Josh Gibson, a Satchel Paige, an Oscar Charleston. And this is where the Negro race gets on my nerves—because they're screaming, Hallelujah! and running in droves to see a rookie play with a team so mediocre they end up having to name him Rookie of the Year when he *barely* made it into the Kansas City Monarchs (don't take my word, read the papers), and I guess that's why he's acting like the Negro leagues didn't exist for him. Rickey was his Savior. But the fans know better, especially the colored fans, and still they're killing themselves to see Robinson at first base.

———

If they're so anxious to see colored and white as teammates, all they have to do is keep on doing what they've been doing—going to the Negro games cause The Star Spangled Banner is played to the tune of a cash register and with gate receipts as high as they've been, the Negro owners could have pressed for a whole *team* entering the major leagues. And like I said, when you love the game, you love the game. And don't tell me some of these smart white boys coming up wouldn't have tried out for a place on one of the best teams in the major league. They'd be hungry and ambitious enough to know that they couldn't call themselves a real pitcher until they took the crown from Satchel Paige. And then all these folks yelling, Hallelujah, would have had their eyeful of integration; but there would have been some colored people owning teams and colored people managing teams and colored people coaching teams. And yeah out on that field—but above all, in the owner's box—would have been colored and white together—the American way.

It's not gonna happen now. The best I can see for baseball is the same old way. The Rickeys of the world calling the shots because a hundred Jackie Robinsons isn't gonna really integrate baseball and baseball is *not* going to help integrate America. Having Jackie Robinson out there with Pee Wee Reese is the same as having my mother and Mrs. Van Morrison's maid trading gossip in the back kitchen. We all ate together—Marie, her brother, and Bella—but that wasn't bringing about no real change because Mrs. Van Morrison's neighbors wouldn't dream of eating with her, while Mr. Van Morrison wasn't about to sit in anybody's boardroom. And until that happens, real power getting shared at the top, nothing but a game of smoke and mirrors is going on at the bottom.

I know my position about that Second Coming out at Ebbets Field doesn't sit well with most people, but I call 'em as I see 'em. And if you've got a problem with how I feel, well, there are other cafes. It's never been my ambition to win a popularity contest. If it had been, I wouldn't have married a woman even I have a hard time liking. (I told you I'd be getting to you, darling.) But liking Nadine has nothing to do with the fact that these have been twelve wonderful years.

We're the right kind of fit, me and my woman. I can talk a blue streak and I believe that she hasn't strung more than six sentences together in her whole life. Nadine doesn't have to go on and on about anything. She times what she has to say and makes those one or two words count. I'd get plenty of care packages while I was overseas, but short short letters. Some of the guys got mail from their girlfriends and wives that it would take 'em a whole hour to read, telling them everything Aunt Tessie, Aunt Muriel, Cousin Joe was saying, describing how the snow looked outside the window, what the dog was doing—that kind of stuff—along with the usual how-much-I-miss-and-love-you's. And even those women who weren't too flowery with the words would fill up the page with *x*'s and hearts. I dreaded mail call cause it meant I was going to get ribbed. Deenie doesn't waste words and so she wasn't gonna waste paper. My letters came in these little thumbnail envelopes that weren't much bigger than the stamp. How the guys would laugh. But like I said, she has perfect timing. And going into the third year of my stint in the navy, when I didn't think none of us were gonna survive now that we were *winning* the war against the Japanese, and my nerves were wound so tight I feared popping loose like a lot of good men around me, I got this one-line letter: If you don't make it home, I'm marrying the butcher. Love, Nadine.

I knew she wasn't kidding. My wife doesn't kid. There was no way to imagine her smiling as she wrote that letter, because Deenie rarely smiles. It was one of the hardest things I had to get used to when I first met her. She looked like an African goddess, plunked right down on the third row of bleachers at a Brooklyn Eagles game. A full, round face holding an even rounder set of eyes, all of it as dark as that gorgeous unruly hair. She had it in one thick crown of braids that circled her head. When my eyes moved down, the scenery got even better: one of those gazelle necks, a compact chest, an invisible waist, and then what can only be described

as a Bantu butt. I can't remember anything about her legs or the turn
of her ankles; my journey ended at that butt. Only a fool keeps on
traveling when the road's brought him to paradise.

I did a lot of dreaming between the fifth and sixth innings. You do a lot
of dreaming when a face and body like that is sharing the same plank of
wood only ten feet to your right. Luck was with me and the Eagles were
in fine form, sending them long and deep into left field, giving me plenty
of reason to turn my head in her direction and reassure myself that no,
I wasn't imagining it, those lips do look like that, those eyes do look like
that, and yes, the butt was still there. I did think it peculiar she was
watching the game so quietly. I took it that she must be a Grays fan and
it was certainly one of those days they must have wished they'd kept
themselves in Pittsburgh. But even when they threatened to make a small
rally at the top of the seventh with two men on and Josh Gibson, of all
people, up to bat, she wasn't smiling and cheering like the other Grays
fans. Little for them to be happy about later: two ground fouls and a
foul tip meant even the mighty Gibson could be put out.

That game was doomed to be over at the top of the ninth and I was
wracking my brains over how I was going to meet this strange girl without
appearing to be a masher. I'd already made sure there was no wedding
ring, and surprisingly she must have come to the ballpark alone. A kid
no more than thirteen was on her right and the fella in the plaid suit on
her left was pushing seventy. And if it turned out she did happen to be
into geriatric papas, I wouldn't have no problems beating him up. And
I was even willing to tie one hand behind my back to make it a fair fight.
But Mr. Plaid Suit went on about his business and I was left to follow
her at a distance as the crowd made its way out of the park.

Tall as she was, with the pink ribbons in her straw hat and the wind
fluttering the pink swiss dots in that voile dress, she was easy to follow.
I had to hold myself back from grabbing each fella by the scruff of the

neck who had the nerve to turn his head and watch her as she passed. One jerk almost walked right into a pole and I couldn't resist a snide Good for you, even though he was no more guilty than me of absolute awe over the motions of that unbelievable rear end. No idea that kept popping into my head for introducing myself would work if this was a nice girl. Nice girls who looked like that had heard it all before and weren't about to take the bait from some strange man. And how I wanted her to be a nice girl—because I had made up my mind to follow those swiss dots out of the ballpark, onto the elevated train over the East River, and even up into the Bronx if need be. And when you're from Brooklyn, that's the same thing as committing yourself to the ends of the earth.

She stopped at a peddler's to buy a raspberry ice. I hate ices; they break me out in hives, which has little to do with the fact that I stopped and bought one too. Only three feet away now; my hands were shaking and my heart was pounding so fast I couldn't hear the traffic on the street. And something told me then, in that way you just know things, that if I didn't make my move at that very moment I would lose her. I cursed myself for all the naps I'd taken during elocution classes. Mrs. Fitzpatrick had warned me I would rue the day when I sneered at learning to round my vowels properly. I could have been standing there right now, putting her under my spell, as I talked about the wonders of raspberry ice, delving into the origin of raspberries; the origin of ice in general; the origin of summer, which made the need for ices all so possible and her obvious delight in them all so understandable. Nothing directed at her specific person more closely than that, not even turning my head her way—it would label me a masher—but just standing there, you know, elocuting out into the air, would be enough to get her attention, dammit.

My throat was so clogged up I wouldn't have made it through all of that anyway, and she was about to walk off from the peddler's cart. One run behind at the bottom of the ninth, so you make an all-or-nothing play for the home team. When this girl walked out of my life, what on earth

15

was I going to do with this melting raspberry ice? Since I knew the answer was Absolutely nothing, I dumped it right down her back. She spun around and called me a clumsy fool. I smiled broadly and agreed with her. Then she smacked me in the head with her straw purse. The courtship was on.

My first big letdown came when I found that she didn't care much for the movies. I really didn't either, but I kept looking for ways to get her alone in the dark. And I'm a little ashamed to say that after discovering she was, indeed, a very nice girl it became exciting to try and make myself her one exception. I think that's why it took me weeks to realize that Nadine wasn't much of a talker. All of my conversations had one slant, which only required a firm no from her. And even after I'd given up and moved on to other subjects, the sound of my own voice was so pleasing to me I only needed one or two sentences from her to let me catch my breath before I started off again. But the problem was that when I came to the real amusing parts of my life's story, she didn't laugh. And I can remember pausing—to let her laugh. I remember the pauses getting longer and longer—to drop her a subtle hint or two. And longer and longer, until I worried that she might be retarded.

—You don't laugh much, I finally ventured.

—I laugh all the time, she said.

But she was just being mean, because she didn't. And I knew it wasn't me; I'm a very captivating fella. And besides, what about all those times at Coney Island?

We practically lived at Steeplechase Park. Nadine was from the Sea Islands and she'd always agree to see me if I offered to take her out by any kind of water. One of the nice things about Brooklyn in those days was that I had a lot to choose from. When my money was tight we'd promenade across the Brooklyn Bridge, pretzels for me, a fruit ice for her. And if I was flush, Sunday suppers at the old Iron Pier on Brighton Beach. Coney

Island was the best cause there was always something to do there if you had a little or a lot. And Nadine didn't much care as long as she could smell or glimpse the water. Seeing how she grew up on an island, it was odd she didn't know how to swim, and I'd have the hardest time just getting her to wade near the edge of the beach. She'd spend hours on the boardwalk, though, and that's how I learned she rarely laughed at anything—it wasn't me.

Steeplechase Park had a bit of amusement for just about everyone's taste—except Nadine's. Did she want a fast and furious ride? we could get on the steeplechase horses; she wanted slow? we could get on the carousel. She wanted high and exciting? the roller coaster; high and soothing? the Ferris wheel. The human pool table and two-headed baby for the bizarre, the strolling minstrels for the ordinary. If she liked dark, loud, and scary, there was the Fun House. If she wanted dark, quiet, and romantic, there was the Tunnel of Love; but I already knew not to bother wasting a ticket with this stone-faced girl on that one. Why on earth did she always agree to come when *nothing* about it pleased her?

—I don't know what you're talking about. I enjoy myself every time we're here.
—Nadine, you haven't smiled all afternoon.
—But what does that have to do with being pleased?

At home I had a whole notepad filled with columns of female names, and at least two of them were still speaking to me. I didn't need to be spending my time with this nut case. Unrequited lust can only carry you so far. *What does that have to do with being pleased?* Just that it's something everyone in the whole universe understands—like slitting your throat with a knife. Go to Upper Borneo and smile; they'll say, He's happy. Go there and slit your throat; they'll say, He's dead. It is basic. It is simple. And I was out $2.15 while this dimwit wouldn't even ride the bumper

17

cars with me because it was too tight a fit. But Nadine was still leaning against the boardwalk railing—on her third cherry ice—patiently waiting for me to answer. Like I was the dimwit.

—I'm more than my body, she finally said.

Now there was a piece of wisdom. She certainly was. She was also that vast empty prairie between her ears. I had been more considerate to this girl than to a dozen of the others rolled up together and had gotten no appreciation. No effort on her part. Wronged and wounded, that was me. Misused. Abused (yeah, I could feel the blues coming on). And with me definitely the offended party in all of this, why was I also feeling just a tiny bit guilty?

—Nadine, I am deeply hurt by what you're implying. I have only thought of you as a lady. And I have never, *never* had anything but the most honorable intentions in mind.
—Good, she said. Then I accept.
—You accept *what?*

A man palsied with fear is an awful sight. The sea breezes were chilling the circles of sweat spreading under the armpits of my shirt. My mind went totally blank except for the message my throbbing temples sent racing across it: Please, God, oh, God, no, God, please. I didn't mean what she thought I meant and if she means what I think she means, I need a way to find out if that's what's really happened, and if that's what's really happened, then I'll have to fight my way out of it, yes, there must be some way I can get out of it; but these next few minutes are going to be the worst of my life (I had yet to meet the Japanese) and what's the most that she could do, huh? what's the most? hit me? she's done that before; call me a slimy double-dealer? well, let her say it; cry and wail? well, let her cry; the cops'll come by, I'll get arrested, but then I'm only sentenced to thirty days.

———

I summoned up the courage to stare her down. I was going to the slammer like a man. I saw the same set face. The same quiet attention to her cherry ice. But looking deep into her eyes, I saw that she was laughing. Down at the bottom of those dark orbs, she was bent over double and howling. She laughed and laughed and laughed.

—I've never seen a man more scared.

To put it mildly, I was crushed. And, taking pity on me, she tried her best to stop. Calmly finishing her ice, she disposed of the paper cone in the trash. I saw that a giggle would burst through from the bottom of her eyes every now and then, but she was getting herself under control. As angry as I was with her, I knew she'd only gotten even.

—Let's do the Helter-Skelter now, she said.

She held out her hand to me. I took it. And to this day, I've never let it go.

Sure, she taught me a lesson, and a whole different way of looking at her—and women—which doesn't negate the fact that my wife is still a little strange. While most of what happens in life is below the surface, other people do come up for air and translate their feelings for the general population now and then. Nadine doesn't bother. You figure her out or leave her alone. Falling in love with her, there was no question that she was going to be a part of my life, but if I could have gotten a handle on her at times I'd probably have liked her more. I knew why I finally married her; I just didn't know why she married me.

I wasn't what you'd call promising material. My job as an indoor aviator at the St. George Hotel was about what Miss Fitzpatrick had predicted for me: We are on the verge of unimaginable changes in this country. There are several men in your race who will rise to the top. You won't be one of them. My elevator only ran between the lobby and tenth floor. The penthouse elevator was in the rear, and true to her words, I didn't stay long enough to be promoted to that. After marrying Nadine, I quit to become a Fuller Brush man. I bought into all of their flimflam about early retirement and Cadillac sedans because I knew I could talk to anyone about anything. And a little common sense meant that you started with the dirtiest house on the block and you're sure of a sale to build on when you got to the next house. Nadine had told me that it would be smarter to work it the other way around. But who was listening to her? She was too mean to even buy from me when I was practicing my sales pitch.

War broke out in Europe and saved us both from starvation. It's odd how events can be going on three, four thousand miles from you, deciding your fate on the very ground you stand on, but the dominoes taking as long as they do to reach home, you never make the connection. I can vaguely remember reading in the early part of '36 that German troops had reclaimed some of their land on the west bank of the Rhine. Like most people, I scanned the headlines before going on to the sports page. And since I always picked up the afternoon paper to read while I took a bite of lunch between rounds with my suitcase and brushes, I'm sure I glanced right over the news that six years later I was being called up to ship out from Camp Smalls and head to the Pacific.

Nobody missed the meaning of Pearl Harbor. Those headlines were three inches tall and they yelled that the dominoes had finally come home. I was proud to be assigned to the messmen's branch because the talk at Camp Smalls was all about Dorie Miller, another messman, third class, on the USS *Arizona*, who had carried his captain and other wounded men to safety before manning a machine gun and shooting down six enemy planes at Pearl Harbor. The navy gave him credit for four planes. The newspapers gave him credit for nothing. No surprise to me. I had already learned from baseball who does and doesn't exist when it comes to my country needing heroes. Dorie Miller was the Satchel Paige of the war in the Pacific. But we all knew his name, which is what really counted, since we were the ones who were being sent over there to face those same maniacs.

We weren't getting into Tokyo

I told Nadine I didn't know when I would be back. But I told her I would miss her dearly, think of her every moment, and carry her picture next to my heart. She told me nothing. I promised I would write every chance I got. I promised that my wedding vows would remain as sacred as the day I made them. No shore leave. No women. No wine. No song. She called me a liar—and a pretty lousy poet. Then I stopped all that crap and told her the truth: I knew this would be the most exciting thing to ever happen in my life. And that was when she finally told me that she loved me.

We weren't getting into Tokyo

—Who you gonna kill?
—We're gonna kill Japs!
—Louder
—Japs! Japs!
—Louder
—Japs! Japs!
—Who you gonna fuck?
—We're gonna fuck Japs!
—Louder

The first thing you learn in basic training is to march in time. It makes no difference if you're headed for the cockpit of a plane or the cramped engine room of a cruiser. Navy doctors. Navy dentists. Painters. Metal-smiths. Warrant officers assigned to intelligence, who would spend the war at the Navy Department in their dress whites, learned to march in time. Though there wasn't anybody at Camp Smalls slated for those jobs when I was called up. I marched beside many Fisk and Howard men and a few Yalies too, but they were going to be regular seamen or steward's mates just like me. Those types mostly hung together and I didn't like

21

'em cause they beefed too much. They came in acting like Jim Crow was something new, like they got drafted from Mars somewhere. They had been living with segregation, and so how did they figure the navy expected them to die without it?

If anything, I'm a realist. It was the spring of 1942 and America was what it was. Cockeyed and mixed-up, new and still growing, with all its faults, I had no place else to call home. And the law was the law. I could either learn to bake bread and peel potatoes or spend the summer of '42 in jail. I opted not to go to jail and ended up spending the summer on Guadalcanal. And that's where I discovered that Japan was what it was.

We weren't getting into Tokyo

From the moment my left foot sank into the level sands of that calm beach near Lunga Point (and I remember it was my left foot because the right was bracing me in the supply boat), I stopped calling those people Japs. There wasn't any fighting that day. And my specific job was only to haul supplies through the coconut groves and set up base. But swinging my right foot out of that boat was to land me at war in the entire Pacific.

No vet ever says he went to war in the Gilbert Islands. He might have fought only on those islands, at Makin or at Tarawa, but he went to war in the Pacific. Cause any man who's ever been at war will tell you, you can feel everything that happens on the earth where you are. It's one of the shittiest feelings you can imagine, the way it cakes around the soles of your boots as you first haul ass on up that beach toward those muddy coconut groves, ignoring your stinking sweat as you keep falling and dying at that very moment twenty-five miles away in Tugali, a thousand miles away in New Guinea. For the next three years me, the Brits, the Aussies, the Dutch, and the Filipinos were at war in the Pacific against the Japanese—and only the Japanese—

We weren't getting into Tokyo

—as inch by inch, island by island, we were pushing them back. And they told me I was on the winning side, long before the A-bomb was dropped. But believe me, I understand about that bomb. Cause even with every Medal of Honor they gave me, every victory broadcast, every assembly called to hear the latest greetings from my supreme commander, I wasn't gonna win a war from the sea or in the air, I had to win it on land—

We weren't getting into Tokyo

—the enemy's land.

I don't expect my unborn children to forgive me. But they have to understand how beautiful it was. The end of the world is blue. And it wasn't about saving my life; I was willing to give that up for them—not my country, them. Without them I knew there would be no America. But when the sun rises at the end of the world, the sky and the sea are so blue they only deepen to swallow those streaks of red-gold. Yeah, I know I'll be judged a coward. But I couldn't march into Tokyo. I feared for my immortal soul.

They had taken Guadalcanal. I was taking it back. I was trained to kill. They were trained to kill. And I fought them like a man. They came at me wading across the Ilu River with rifles. I cut them down with my own. And they kept coming. I cut them down with machine guns. And they kept coming. I finally stopped them with antitank canisters from guns meant to rip open steel. Their bodies covered the sandy banks of the Ilu; the treads of my advancing tanks gummed up with their flesh as I felt their heads popping under me like scattered coconuts. They lost Guadal-canal—fair and square—but for six months they still kept coming. I blew them back up into the jungles; I drowned them in Ironbottom Sound. What kind of people were these?

They ate their own dead in New Guinea. And I stepped over clumps of jungle ants finishing what they left. Shit ran down my legs from dysentery and I shook until my teeth ached at night. But even with the damp rotting the clothes from my body and peeling the skin off the soles of my feet, I pushed them north to Buna, where they burrowed, like moles, into the ground. They became one with the very earth they fought to hold. In Buna. In Bougainville. In Tarawa. In Guam. Closer and closer to Tokyo. I couldn't uproot them from the sea: three thousand rounds of artillery. I couldn't uproot them from the air: six thousand tons of high explosives. I blasted those fucking islands into the middle of nowhere, and the earth still crawled with them under my feet. They dug and hid beneath sand. They dug and hid beneath coral. And at Iwo Jima they dug beneath hot volcanic ash. No victory without land. And the land I walked on was killing me. I slung aside my guns and picked up gasoline. I poured it into those holes and roasted them alive. I stood east of the stench from their burning flesh drifting up into the westward trades.

And it was west to Tokyo. But Lord, there was still the Philippines. Corregidor. The Rock. I was getting tired of these bastards. They wanted this lousy, stinking land: I'd bury them in it. I sealed them up alive in the ground. They blew the tunnels open. I sealed them up. They blew them open. And finally they blew themselves apart. Scalps, arms, and legs raining down with bits of gravel from thirty feet in the air. Leyte. Mindoro. Luzon. Seasick from the monsoons. Knifed by cogon grass. I started jumping at the sound of my own heart, trudging through the dark ruins of Manila. I kept jumping at the sound of my own heart, even in my dreams. Like the bombs overhead, pounding, pounding, pounding. I left one out of seven Filipinos sprawled in the streets of Manila, liberated from the Japanese.

I'm a soldier. I follow orders. But I beat them and they don't lie down. I win and they don't lie down. They rise shrieking and laughing from the graves of Guam. Pitchforks against machine guns. Empty bottles against grenades. Baseball bats against Sherman tanks. God, I am so sick of killing the living dead. What kind of people are these? The people waiting down there in Tokyo.

The city lies below my B-29. I'm a soldier. I follow orders. I spray napalm from the air to send rivers of fire running through the streets. I burn ammunition factories. I burn shipyards. I burn schools. I burn hospitals. I burn homes. And they still keep coming.

One last island before Japan. But in Okinawa I couldn't stop the shakes. I chewed up the palm of my hand and spat out the blood to keep from dozing at night. I could stop myself from sleeping, so there would be no dreams. But I had to breathe. And it was in the air, flowing from its source just three hundred miles away. The divine wind. Kamikaze.

The wind fluttering the edge of her flowered kimono, unraveling the baby's swaddling band as they hurled down the jagged cliffs of Saipan. And only twenty-four years on that island. I packed dirt up my nose and panted through my mouth. But I could still hear it. The divine wind. Kamikaze. I jammed empty shell casings into my ear canals.

Saipan. A family picnic. All bathed. New clothes. A hundred hands pressing a hundred grenades to a hundred navels; the explosion of a hundred entrails. And only twenty-four years on that island.

One thousand and five hundred years in Japan.

I could still feel it on my skin. The divine wind. Kamikaze. I took my trembling hands and plastered my body with mud. It wasn't enough. I rolled in the mud, howling up into the hills of Okinawa. Begging for any god to take it all away. I couldn't set foot in Japan.

The very young, the deformed, and the old were waiting for me in Tokyo. And you gotta understand how blue it was. How beautiful, soul-wrenching blue. And you *gotta understand we were winning the war. There'd be no judgment passed on me for what was to happen in Tokyo. I wasn't a coward. I could go in and do my duty. It became just too unbearable to know I'd be doomed to come out alive. Take. This. Cross. From. Me. And yes, I offered any god who would answer even the rights to my unborn children. And the only god to answer claimed them.*

Pika-don. The earth melted open and gave birth. My salvation rose like the head of a newborn. Tears streaked down my face. Its own face gleamed brighter and its breath burned hotter than the sun. It set the sky on fire as its typhoon winds swallowed the puny kamikaze. I was saved. Hiroshima in exchange for my soul. Count the bodies. I'd left more dead in the streets of Manila. On the hillsides of Okinawa. Pika-don. Just count the bodies. But then Nagasaki—where it turned to claim our children. The unborn children.

My seed rained on that city from black clouds, withering the camellias, curling the leaves of oaks, scalding the feathers of songbirds. My seed flowed with the inland tides, sweeping heaps of trout and salmon into piles among the rotting sea turtles. So gentle those tides, as the seed seeped out into the North Pacific, moving slowly, spreading east, nurtured within warm currents across the curve of the earth. It was a long journey. Across a new age. Most of us had shipped back home and I was pocketing my discharge when I saw a few of those seeds finally hitting the rocky coast of San Francisco. A heavy fog was misting around my face as the churning surf sprayed them up into the air. A cool breeze was blowing over my shoulders— steady and heading due east. I felt their hard shells sting my cheeks as they blew on past. It was too late to mourn. Too late to wish there might have been a different prayer. Right here on this soil, we'd be forced to watch them grow. To watch them lead. My prayers had saved me, but the one god to answer went on to spawn for this country the sons—and more sadly, the daughters—who could have marched into Tokyo.

It seems as if I stood on that wharf for years. Behind me all of San Francisco was going crazy with victory celebrations. The boys were home. People danced in the streets with beer bottles and champagne. Church bells were ringing. Firecrackers were exploding, a little too loud for my taste; but the Roman candles whistling and sailing across the top of the hills were pretty with their trails of red-and-silver smoke, and when they landed they wouldn't leave craters in the ground. The fellas couldn't understand my staying down by the water. I had to come on up—it was a wide-open town. Anything you wanted to eat. Drinks on the house. And even the hookers weren't charging. A smart move for the professionals, because right then most women were ours for the taking.

But the surf beating over and over against the edge held me. The fog had thickened so that I could no longer see the water, but the sound was there: sushing . . . sushing. What do we do when the party is over? I knew life was going to be very different (*A different prayer, could there have been a different prayer*), and I felt it just wasn't worth it. Before Hiroshima it had definitely been worth it. I still believe this country had even been worth Hiroshima happening, but at the very moment of Hiroshima happening, it all stopped being worth it. You get a man like that, with thoughts like that, staring out over the edge . . . The only world worth existing for me in that white shroud was the sound of the surf, and I already knew what the surf was bringing . . . sushing . . . sushing . . . A hand reached through the fog and touched my shoulder.
    —There's a customer waiting, Nadine said.
Startled, I turned around and she was standing in back of me. And in back of her was this cafe. The scarred old counter. Peeling linoleum. A haphazard line of wooden chairs and tables at the front window. Greasy white smoke clouded around us from the hot grill. I stared at the spatula in my hand and I could hear the sound of the hamburger sizzling on the grill. It was burning, and without thinking I flipped it over. We were in business.

I never changed the name of this place. When I found myself in here from that wharf in San Francisco, the name Bailey's Cafe was painted across the front window in those same red letters trimmed with gold and I saw no reason to remove it. Because of that, folks think my name is Bailey and I see no reason to tell them otherwise. These people aren't my lifelong buddies; they don't need to know my name. Some of them think Bailey is my surname and they'll call Nadine, Mrs. Bailey. And she'll answer to that as much as she'll answer to anything. Nadine isn't particular about what they call her as long as they don't expect her to get up from behind the counter too often and serve 'em. Not that my wife is lazy; she's helped me make a lot of improvements over the last three years. She sewed the red-checkered curtains herself and went out and found the brass rail to hang 'em on. The double-door Frigidaire was her idea and so was the jukebox.

It's just that Nadine feels that folks shouldn't get the wrong idea about this place. If we start serving 'em too readily, they'll begin thinking we're actually in the business of running a cafe. Forgetting how it happened they stumbled in here, they'll start looking for us when they're hungry. And then when they don't find us, they'll start asking questions. Hey, why wasn't this place here last month when I came by? I could see if you'd just closed down—but the whole damn building was gone. Life's too short to spend time trying to explain the obvious to the idiot. If they can't figure out that we're only here when they need us, they don't need to figure it out.

I guess whoever Bailey was—if there was a Bailey—he knew this place had to be real real mobile. Even though this planet is round, there are just too many spots where you can find yourself hanging on to the edge just like I was; and unless there's some space, some place, to take a breather for a while, the edge of the world—frightening as it is—could be the end of the world, which would be quite a pity.

THE VAMP

—I need a menu.

—We've got no menus.

—All right, give me a hamburger. Hold the fries.

—Hamburgers only on Tuesday.

—Some roast beef, then. Make it lean. And . . .

—No roast beef till the weekend.

—So what can I get *today?*

—What everybody else is having.

—I don't eat corned-beef hash.

—That's what we got. And warm peach cobbler.

—I'm not eating no hash. How's the peach cobbler?

—Divine.

New customers are a pain in the butt until they get into the rhythm of things. Fried chicken Mondays. Hamburger Tuesdays. Hash Wednesdays. Pork chop Thursdays. Fish on Fridays. And a weekend open house: breakfast, lunch, dinner: your call.

Since they're only getting one thing a day Monday through Friday, and anything they want Saturday and Sunday, why print up a menu? But you'd be surprised how long it takes that to sink into some people's heads. It's been a real lesson for me in human nature. During the weekdays some act offended that they've only got one choice and want to argue and get all loud, like somebody's keeping 'em from going to other cafes. Or they could come back on the weekend, when we'll give 'em anything they want. But the weekends bring in another type of character, who don't believe it when you tell 'em it's really *anything* they want. They sit there confused and silly, craning their necks all around, asking over and over for a menu.

Then there's the weekend joker who's gonna test the house policy. Instead of asking for what they'd really like to eat, they start auditioning for the Texaco Star Theater.

—Anything I want? All right, peanut butter and fried pickles on a club roll.

—Sweet pickles or dill pickles? I ask as their grin starts fading.

And after rummaging back in the storeroom, that's just what I bring to their table, along with my souvenir baseball bat. Josh Gibson signed that bat for me after an East-West Classic, and they can see his name real plain as I thump it against the table leg while I explain the check. If they eat the peanut-butter-and-pickle sandwich, it's on the house. And if they don't eat it, I'll make sure they pay me for my trouble.

Usually they eat it. And the next time they come back in, they act like people.

Any of my customers can tell you, I'm not a nice man. But I'm good at my word and I call 'em the way I see 'em. On one hand, this summer isn't gonna be so bad, cause it's mostly my seasoned regulars. On the other hand, it means they know enough about each other to keep a running feud going on. Everybody wants me to throw the other body out of here. Like this place is their personal discovery and only for them and their kind. I know more about some of them than they know about themselves, and they all boil down to only one type, or they wouldn't be in here in the first place. You can't tell them that, though. And when things get too heated, I just turn my back and lean over the grill like I'm doing something miraculous with a chicken, Monday, or a hamburger, Tuesday. But I can recognize their voices with my eyes closed.

Meet Sister Carrie. Cornerstone of the Temple of Perpetual Redemption:

—Lord Jesus, it don't make a bit of sense, all this riffraff and scum in here. I can barely swallow my food looking at the likes of them. Lord Jesus, please, protect my Angel from the filth and abomination taking over this world.

Sister Carrie is one of those who can't come in on the weekends. Tell her she can have anything she wants and she starts shaking like a leaf. She'd starve before she'd answer you. A woman afraid of her own appetites.

—Now, I could see, Bailey, if this wasn't a respectable place. If this was one of those *dives* on the other side of town. But you're right around the corner from the Temple. But, Lord Jesus, I never know when it's safe to bring my Angel in here. Never knowing what she'll run into. And if any of this filth and scum tried to proposition me or my Angel, if this filth and scum ever . . .

Now, meet Sugar Man. All-around hustler and pimp:

—No need for that dried stick to be cutting her eyes at me. Five-alive, she can rest easy. I only mess with women like her in my nightmares. Bailey, give me a plate of that hash, and make it *steaming* hot.

He's a little man, Sugar Man. Dresses to the nines and practically lives in a 1936 Duesenberg. Another weekday player who comes in and orders the only thing we have to offer as if it was his choice.

—Five-alive, this is good eating. And tomorrow you *better* have pork chops. You know me and pig meat.

A little man, Sugar Man. Tiny hands with big diamond rings. Tiny feet in alligator wingtips.

—Total her up and give me the damage.

We have to charge him three times what the meal is worth because he'd insist on paying it anyway.

—Good, now I'll be able to breathe with the likes of that out of here. Angel, honey, don't chew with your mouth open. The lowest thing in creation, something that lives on women. And somebody tell me, what decent man would wear a *purple* suit?

Sister Carrie and Sugar Man aren't as far apart as they sound. If you don't listen below the surface, they're both one-note players. Flat and predictable. But nobody comes in here with a simple story. Every one-liner's got a life underneath it. Every point's got a counterpoint. Here, I'll show you; let's just take 'em one key down:

—*You gotta help me, Lord Jesus. Remove this burning from me. Remove these evil thoughts. Wipe out Satan. Wipe him out. I ache and touch, Lord Jesus. I ache and squeeze. I ache and dig into the heat. I bring up my fingers, wet, and give glory to Your name.*

—*Five-still-alive. And they blame me. The fucking depression. One fucking relief check. And they blame me. They were gonna sell it anyway. One fucking relief check and five of my sisters sitting on gold. They were gonna sell it anyway. I just knew the highest rollers. And they blame me.*

And when you take these down to even a lower key you'll hear about:

her Angel, Lord Jesus, who can't be trusted. All of the care given the child, all of the teaching, and the betrayal is still coming. The girl wants to sin. She can see it in the breasts that keep pushing up over her brassieres. She buys them tighter and tighter, but the flesh keeps spilling out in defiance. The nipples so large and hard, they show through her dress. Inviting trouble. Wanting trouble. Cover yourself. People are staring. Wash yourself down there. Again. Again. She can't let her smell like a bitch in heat. Like the bitch she wants to be.

And Sugar Man working hard to protect his women. All women really need protecting. It's a rough world out there. He knows; he moves in it. Most men aren't worth shit and will take advantage if they get half a chance. Just get in there, grab the jelly roll, and run. Women aren't made up to handle the streets and think that way. Women need pretty things around them. A nice place. Nice clothes. The right man to take care of 'em. They're soft and need you to hold 'em. They need your shoulders to lean on when they have to cry. And when they get confused, they need you to be strong enough to guide 'em. To even give 'em a light spanking. Sure, a little like children— but a whole lot like angels.

—Lord Jesus.
—Five-alive.

That's just two of them, and they're only minor voices. But I think you've got the drift. Anything really worth hearing in this greasy spoon happens under the surface. You need to know that if you plan to stick around here and listen while we play it all out.

THE JAM

Mood: Indigo

What can you say about Sadie? Haven't see her any this summer, but she was a regular here for a while. Would take the single table at the far wall opposite my jukebox and away from the windows. She looked sixty one month and about seventy the next. They age fast in her life. And everybody in here would have an opinion about that life. I don't think they should get in on this one, though, and I can hear 'em already: There he goes, wanting to hog up the whole thing and we've just gotten started. But it's not about my liking the sound of my own voice this time; it really isn't. It's just that . . . Damn, how can I even say it? She was a . . . lady. Yeah, through it all, with it all—a lady. And Nadine would back me up on this one; only customer she ever served twice in a row.

—A little tea, please.

It was more than Deenie liking to hear the way she asked; it was her bringing the mug and Sadie's fine-boned right hand wrapping itself around the handle with the left one taking the napkin and spoon from her. And

39

somehow, by the time Sadie had made the distance from Deenie's tray to the table, the thick mug had lost its cracks and stains, hitting the tabletop with the ring of china, while the bent tin spoon and paper napkin became monogrammed silver and linen. Kind of an amazing thing to watch.

—A little tea, please.

Especially since those hands were shaking so badly she always ended up setting the mug in a pool of spilled hot water. On a good day she could lift it up again to put the napkin under it to help blot up what was wasted. On a bad day she couldn't.

You see, Sadie was a wino. And Sadie was a twenty-five-cent whore. And one night Iceman Jones took her out back to dance under the stars. Yeah, I see I'm gonna have to bring this one on in by myself. It calls for telling straight out, the way it was. Pure, simple, and clean.

Unlike other cities, the South Side of Chicago has always been the South Side of Chicago. Colored settled there, stayed there, and made it their own. It was old and run-down when they found it, and it grew older while they were there. But they gave it whatever they had. Some years that amounted to more than other years: wartime, when jobs went begging and they weren't too particular about who was hired; the union times, when it was a choice between bringing Negroes in or fighting them as scabs. Those wooden shacks got painted then. And coins were put away in Mason jars for a child's schooling. The smartest child's, cause there was no way to put away enough dimes for all of them. But the point was for at least that one child to get a chance. And colored folks lived that way: hanging on during the times with no chance for the times when there'd be *a* chance.

But like in any city, there are those who fall through the cracks of the upswings and downswings. The ones who kind of give up trying for themselves and their children. Sadie's daddy was like that, before he became Sadie's daddy. And he told Sadie's mama, before she became Sadie's mama, that the living was good and the living was easy, as long as it stayed them two. That sat just fine with Sadie's mama; she'd been hoping to meet a man like him. And that's basically what the both of them were: easy-living folks. Party folks. Would stay one place until the landlord had the sheriff put them out, and then go on to the next place. They'd make ends meet, one way or the other. If his luck was running bad in the crap games, he'd work a piece of job every now and then— as a bootblack or shoveling out stables—to sandwich between whatever they could borrow from the latest set of friends. And she'd pick up a few cents from the dance halls and stretch out what he brought in by hustling the greengrocer or the butcher. Even if she'd been the type of woman to consider it, any sort of hard work was out of the question— housekeeping or laundry—because her body was weak from all those abortions. If she caught it in time, she and a friend would do it themselves. A couple of folded towels and a little peroxide on a coat hanger. But if she was too far along, there were some pretty bad fights between them two because he had to come up with the money for a professional. A couple of folded towels and a little peroxide on some forceps.

Sadie heard it so much from her mama that she thought it was her name when she was little: The One The Coat Hanger Missed. Not that the woman ever spoke to her, or hardly ever looked at her, unless she was drinking—and then only to curse her for the daddy's face she wore. But she'd hear it when one of the men her mother brought home for the night would ask about the sleepy child. She'd hear it when yet another

GLORIA NAYLOR

streetwalker would pat her cheek as they moved around that circuit from
boardinghouse to boardinghouse, when she spilled her milk, when she
forgot to tiptoe in the morning, and when she stroked the hair of the
drunken woman sprawled over the dirty dishes on the table; she'd hear
it after she was slapped and shoved away: The One The Coat Hanger
Missed. It took her until she was about four years old to ask, Mama, do
I have a name? And she learned it was Sadie, because that's what the
woman kept screaming each time she brought the leather strap down on
her back, shoulders, head—Yes, Sadie. Sadie. The landlady heard all the
racket and had to come up to pull her off the child. But Sadie had been
taught her name and something a lot more important: the only way out
of this was to love.

The mama had just about lost most of her mind when that beating
happened. Four years' worth of drinking pure absinthe when enough
corpses hadn't yet piled up on skid row for the government to outlaw
the stuff; she was finishing a quart bottle every other day and it was
rotting her brain. And with those two-dollar hustles on winter streets
that can get as cold as only Chicago knows how, she had just about
ruined her looks. No point in talking about the things that could still
have been deep inside. Faith had walked out with the daddy on an errand
for a pint of milk when she was seven months pregnant. Hope had
followed a few weeks later when he never came back. Charity had
amounted to what she considered her goodness in not cutting the squalling
throat of his newborn bastard. And that about summed it up, except for
the little bit of breath in her body.

Since Sadie was so young, she didn't know she was loving this empty
woman in order to survive. Her four-year-old, five-year-old, six-year-old
world was really very simple: her mama did these things because she was
her mama. Her seven-year-old, eight-year-old, nine-year-old world was
when it started to get confusing, because then she could compare her
bruises to the unmarked face of the blacksmith's daughter, her mother's

high-pitched threats to the voice of Mrs. Johnson when she called her own boy in from play. There was a difference. And listening to the other children—who complained about being punished when they weren't good—she knew the difference had to be her fault. So she became very good.

Now her mama could drag in from the streets and drink herself into a stupor across a clean table; the dishes were all washed and put away. And she always found the sheets on her bed freshly changed if she dragged in a man or not. The child discovered ways to make absolutely no noise. Sadie became so good at being quiet in the morning, the woman would have to clear her bleary eyes and open the shutters to find her: under the shelves of the cupboard, a soda cracker softening in her mouth before she dared chew it; in the middle of her pallet, legs clenched tightly together to hold back her full bladder since a creaky floorboard separated her from the chamber pot.

And when very good didn't work, she tried very very good. There wasn't a speck of dirt in any of the rooms they boarded in, and they moved often. Sadie scraped the soles of her boots with sandpaper before she'd let herself into their room. The floor she kept bleached would have left telltale prints if she didn't. In the summer she could make it by on bare feet, but she found the winters were just too cold even with her woolen stockings on. Her head got stuffed up with snot, and when her head got stuffed up, she could hear her breath rattling through her chest and nose—much too loud for the mornings. A ten-year-old, eleven-year-old, twelve-year-old world of pressing threadbare petticoats until the creases reflected light; of darning cheap stockings with stitches finer than the ones put there by machine; of not polishing shoe tops, glossing them. A ten-year-old, eleven-year-old, twelve-year-old world of slicing tough brisket and the knife not clinking on the plate, of spooning corn gruel into her mouth without a trace of milk on her lips. A world of May I, Please, and Thank You; speaking quietly, walking softly. A perfect little lady.

Very very good was to say, I love you, Mama. And very very good was to be deserving of the love she believed was waiting in return. Waiting, you see, until Sadie, somehow, managed to be good enough.

She couldn't reach for any more than very very good with what she found around her to work with. But she could dream of reaching further. And her thirteen-year-old world was full of those kinds of dreams. There was to be a trim white bungalow with a green picket fence, and she would keep the front yard swept clean of leaves and pick all the withered blooms from their fence full of roses. She would go to the academy, learn French and elocution in a starched white collar and black ribbon tie, become so expert with the typewriting machine she'd be the first colored woman hired as a typewriter in the biggest insurance company on State Street. Mama would come down to meet her for lunch. And she could say, Mama, I'm doing so good here, they're going to give me a raise. And Mama would bring one of the tiny red rosebuds from their yard to pin it on her collar, saying, I knew you could do it; I'm so proud of you, Sadie. You're a good girl, Sadie. The setting might change to a suite of rooms with a view of Lake Shore Drive or a town house on Michigan, or even just a newer boardinghouse where the wallpaper wasn't slick from grease and the sink full of cockroaches. And they might be meeting for dinner instead of lunch. The secretarial academy might be Oberlin or Fisk. And she'd gone on to become a teacher or nurse. But the dreams always ended the same way: Mama, I'm doing so good here. Yes, I'm so proud of you. You're a good girl, Sadie.

Dreams of love. Dreams that spoke louder than the whispering of the neighbors when her mother took her into the streets: I've been selling my tail all this time to feed you till I'm sick and near death. Now you better kick in too. She could have gotten a higher price for her if some of the men with those particular tastes had believed she was that young. But Sadie being a busty girl and carrying herself so stately and quiet, they put her age at twenty or so. And with the mama saying it was her daughter and herself looking so beaten up and haggard, they figured Sadie was lying when she told them she'd just turned thirteen. Yeah, I like it when you scream, the very first one whispered and kissed her neck, his hands holding each side of her rigid head. I like it when you scream. Then, pulling on his pants, he discovered that the wetness covering his groin and stomach wasn't sweat. His dark hands fell limp between his knees and tears stood in his eyes as he stared at the naked girl curled up in pain on the cot. He sat there a long time, now able to make out the shapes of the tintypes nailed on the wall, the rag doll propped up in the corner. His head kept moving between Sadie and the sheet tacked up between the two cots in the room, trying to fight the bile rising in his throat. Finished yet? he heard from beyond the sheet. He left a bloody thumbprint as he yanked it down and grabbed her mother, shaking her until her teeth rattled:

—*What kind of woman are you?*

Same words from another man, six months later, but this time one with watery blue eyes. In a back room no bigger than theirs, but a whole lot filthier, smelling of dogs and cats. And this time she had an answer because she was a whole lot drunker: The kind with double the money to pay you. A couple of folded towels and a little peroxide on a pair of forceps. Then Sadie's nose full of ether and with a scalpel he went back into the girl to earn the extra fee. I did it for you, she told Sadie later. Your life woulda been pure hell ever having to take care of a child.

But this last year she was to have with her mama turned out to be the best. They were spending much more time together now, sleeping the same hours of the day, and Sadie even saw her smile. She was a smart child and she picked up things quick: the telltale signs for a man who was carrying a disease or a grudge against streetwalkers. The suits that gave away they couldn't pay what they offered. The shoes that gave away they were working underground for the morals squad. And seeing that her quickness pleased her mama, she worked at it even harder. And this fourteen-year-old world she found herself in gave her new dreams to reach for.

There was to be the same suite of rooms overlooking Lake Shore Drive, because Sadie had picked up a john who was old and very ugly. Maybe even deformed. The type that was the most grateful. But this one was also very rich. And he took her to this party and there were other old men there, just as deformed. One by one she took them, all day and all night, never resting, one by one. Two by two. Three by three. And she left there able to stop at the flower shop for a bunch of orchids, the fishmonger's for oysters and shrimp, just from the tips alone. And she made her mother the most wonderful lunch: the orchids in a cut-glass vase; the real money piled up in front of her plate, enough for six months' rent on their flat. Enough for the doctors and the medicine her mother needed to stop the shaking. And she would say, Mama, I did so well there. The things that used to make me gag, I tried real hard and didn't gag this time. I made them think I liked it. I even took it in the behind, Mama. And I didn't feel dirty with any of it, really I didn't. And Mama would take one of the orchids and pin it on her collar and say, I knew you could do it. I'm so proud of you. You're a good girl, Sadie.

Dreams that drowned out the sound of the wailing and screaming of her mama's losing battle with invisible monsters that crawled out the absinthe bottle. The hawking coughs. The pus-filled urine hitting the sides of the chamber pot. The smell of licorice and fever pouring out in night sweats. Look at what I come to, trying to feed you. Just look at what I come to.

They buried her in Potter's Field, two of her drinking buddies, the old woman on the first floor who made a hobby of funerals, and Sadie. The grave diggers had an easy job of it with the heavy rain. As the cheap pine box was lowered into the pit of dirty water, the county chaplain's prayer was tinged with his resentment for having to be out there in the cold and damp. He gave it all of three sentences: Lord, we commit this soul to Thee. Ashes to ashes. Dust to dust. And he flung a handful of wet dirt down into the grave. Turning his collar up against the icy rain, he jerked his head for the others to follow suit. Each of the women hurried forward to throw in her handful of dirt. Sadie just stood there. Her face was unreadable as she watched the rain washing chunks of soil down the sides of the muddy pit. The chaplain nudged her forward. She took just a step and stood there, so very intent on the soil sliding down the sides of the grave. The old woman who made a hobby of funerals took this as a sign that things would finally get juicy and started to cry. That set off the two other women, each now trying to outdo the other. Sadie's eyes were vacant and dry. The chaplain danced from foot to foot; he'd had more than enough. He grabbed up a handful of dirt, forced it into Sadie's hand, and shoved her to the edge of the grave. She stumbled and went down on her knees. Lord, we commit this soul to Thee. He raised his voice louder. Ashes to ashes. Dust to dust.

Sadie opened her hand and let the damp soil drop into the grave. Still on her knees, she watched it hit the top of the pine coffin. Yes. It was barely a whisper. She leaned over the pit to get a closer look as she picked up another handful of soil and threw that on top of the box. Yes. Another and another. Glassy-eyed, like a robot, she tried to cover the coffin. Yes. Yes. Never above a whisper. Faster and faster. Yes. Yes. Yes. Mud and water flew into her face and onto her jacket as she scooped up fistfuls and fistfuls of soil to fling down into the grave. She fought them when they tried to stop her. Biting and scratching them with her muddy fingernails, using her boot heels to shove dirt into the grave as they dragged her away. Yes—she was crying now, tears tracking through the mud on her face. She was still crying when she got back to their boardinghouse. But, reaching the front steps, she knew from ex-perience that sinking her teeth into her bottom lip until she tasted blood would stop the sobs. She sat down outside their room to remove

GLORIA NAYLOR

her muddy boots, careful not to let them drop too loudly. Every speck of mud was gone before she put them back on and dared to open the door.

There was no fifteen- and sixteen-year-old world. Making it alone. Food to buy. Worn clothes to replace. Room rent to pay. But night remained day, and day night, in the work her mother's friends helped her to find. You're too good for this mess on the South Side, Sadie. So she started out cleaning the gold spittoons in one of the fanciest whorehouses downtown on South Dearborn. They told her she was lucky to get it. The two sisters who ran it were from an old Kentucky family and they would never have hired a colored maid who they thought might have been out on the streets. And looking around at the deep Persian rugs, velvet draperies, and gilded mirrors, Sadie thought she was lucky too. Meticulous as she was about her dress and her work, she moved up quickly there. Within a year she was part of the live-in staff and they let her darn the tatted lace on the cambric sheets and hand wash the negligees. Then she got to carry up the brandy and whiskey to a girl's room when a customer ordered them because nothing she saw behind those closed doors seemed to unnerve her. She could maneuver the heavy silver trays without rattling the glasses, keeping her eyes veiled and her hands steady as she served them, even the night she was called up to pour for an alderman and his German shepherd.

She finally became the personal maid for one of the house favorites. It brought bigger pay but longer hours. A tall, green-eyed blonde who insisted on Sadie changing her entire hairdo between each customer. And since this one was especially good with getting a hard-on out of the drunks, there were more trays to carry up during the night, more torn and whiskey-stained gowns to right before she could get to bed herself in the mornings. It's a shame you're a nigger, Sadie, the blonde confided one slow evening, or you could make out really well here. But Sadie

48

wasn't dreaming of being taken on as one of the house whores; she was standing by the back gate on Saturday mornings, waiting for the wood wagon to come.

He was the color of his horse, a sort of matted chestnut. And when he lifted up the heavy cords of firewood, the muscles bulged and danced under his shirt. A strong man, although his hair was streaked with gray. For a while they never spoke beyond a good-morning. He didn't seem curious about why she was always out there. When you're doing business with a place like that, it's best to ask no questions. Besides, any help who wanted to keep their job inside knew to answer none. Sadie pretended not to watch him as he piled the firewood in the shed, rang the back bell for his payment, and went on his way. She'd have her head turned as if something at the far end of the street had her attention. It was turned just that way one morning he was leaving when she said, My name is Sadie. His only answer to the back of her neck was, Well, have a good day, Sadie. As his wagon pulled out from the gate, he glanced back quickly at the face behind the wrought-iron bars. That gal has strange eyes, he thought. But every Saturday after that it was, Good morning, Sadie. And she lived through each week of nights for the sound of her name in his mouth.

She'd sweep the blonde's curls into a pile on her head and pin them in place seeing a trim white bungalow with a green picket fence, starched curtains at the window where she waited for his wagon to pull up after his day was over. She'd powder over freckles on the bare cleavage and shoulders as she picked withered buds from a yard full of roses. She was baking bread for him and roasting chickens as she mopped up spilled perfume and capped jars of rouge. The mingled smells of stale cigars, day-old sweat, and heated groins were the freshness of sunshine and wind on her backyard line as she changed the sheets in the mirrored room. If I didn't work in here, she thought, he would believe I was good enough to tell me his name. After all, it had been three years. And she lived in dread that he would stop bringing their wood before she learned it.

But in fact he was there for the regular delivery on the very day the federal marshals were closing the house down. A righteous wind had up and started blowing through the country. And with the First World War in full gear, the fancy whorehouses were falling like dominoes all over the big cities.

—Damn fools, the blonde told Sadie, there's no way for them to nail a Vacate sign on every woman's pussy.

But when the sign was nailed beneath the brass knocker on the front door, the kitchen and parlor help were already packing their bags. The Kentucky sisters tried to tell them there was still two weeks' worth of work left in just the clearing out. But colored people had learned that with the law at the front door, it was best to leave as quick as they could through the back. Hang around too long and the blame might be put on them for the whole idea of the place.

When his wagon pulled up that Saturday morning, Sadie was out there as usual, only this time she had her paisley satchel with her. She found the courage to look him full in the face for the first time in three years: I didn't want to leave without knowing your name. And then she dropped her head, which relieved him because he'd never liked her eyes. He took in the rest of her, though: the neatly braided hair, the slender neck, full bust, narrow waist, those tiny fine-boned hands that she clutched in front of her. You got any people? he asked. She shook her head no. He didn't say anything else to her until he had unloaded the wood and rung the bell for his last payment. I could use me a wife, he finally said. I can't have children, she answered. He motioned for her to climb up beside him in the wagon. Well, at my age, I probably couldn't give 'em to you. She sat down beside him, her satchel on her lap. And your name? Sadie asked. Daniel, he said as they pulled off in the wagon together. The whole conversation took all of five minutes, but it was about the longest one they would have during their entire marriage. She went off with a man older than enough to be her father, and she ended up living with her mother again for the next twenty-five years.

Daniel's drinking was quiet, though. Everything about the man was quiet, so Sadie suited him just fine. She knew how not to be there. And his house was kept so clean it was eerie. Not a trim little bungalow with a green picket fence, a three-room shanty hemmed in by other three-room shanties near the railroad tracks. The yard couldn't even grow weeds. Whatever soil there might have been was lost under layers of coal soot mixed with the gravel and rocks sliding down the grading from the tracks. And a little bit more would slide each day as the 7:20, 11:55, 3:12 eastbounds and the 5:15, 8:40 westbounds thundered past. The floor planks would start vibrating and the dishes rattling on the shelves to announce the trains approaching before the piercing whistles and clouds of black smoke invaded every corner of the house. The smoke clouds left behind a dark rain of cinder and coal dust to be breathed into their lungs. The rest was left to settle wherever it could: the tin roofs, windowsills, doorsteps, lines of laundry.

Sadie couldn't do anything about cleaning the roof, but with the places she could reach she ran a race against the 5:15, 7:20, 11:55, and 3:12. As steady as a clock: Daniel gets his breakfast, his lunch pail is packed, and he's out of the door. The 5:15. Sweep down the front porch and railings. Set the fire going for the laundry kettle, making sure the lid is on tight. The 7:20. Boil and stir the sheets, pillowcases, shirts, pants, and leggings. Wash down the outside windows. Do the breakfast dishes. Wring out the sheets, pillowcases, shirts, pants, and leggings. Empty the iron kettle. Throw the wrung clothes back in, making sure the lid is on tight. The 11:55. Wipe down the rope clothesline. Hang up the washed clothes, praying there won't be too strong a wind. Finish the kitchen. Do the beds. Mop the floors. Bring in the damp clothes from the line. The 3:12.

Wipe down the rope clothesline again. Rehang the few pieces still too wet. Start heating the flatiron to press the others. Press a piece. Chop the collard greens. Press a piece. Set the dough to rise. Press a piece. Bring in the rest of the clothes. Fold and put away the laundry. Pluck the chicken. Finish up the dinner. Go spread lime in the outhouse. A quick sweep of the front steps again. A quick wipe of the outside windows. Daniel comes home. The days it wasn't laundry between the 5:15, 7:20, 11:55, and 3:12, it was sewing. And the days it wasn't sewing, it was firing and scraping the cast-iron pots. And the days it wasn't that, it was working on her *garden*. But each day all activity stopped when Daniel came home.

He thought Sadie cleaned too much; the neighbors were beginning to think her peculiar. Talk had it that this new wife of his was putting on airs. All of them could live with the grimy windows that got done maybe once each spring. With kitchen curtains grown dingy and gray from the black clouds of soot. With the gravel banked up against the rusted tin cans and scrap metal in their yards. It's not that they didn't clear it all out every now and then. It's not that they were a bunch of pigs who didn't care. If they could live with all of it, what was she trying to prove? Sadie worshiped the man who had given her the closest thing that she would ever have to what she'd dreamed of. And she was trying to prove that she deserved it.

So she would grit her teeth as the 8:40 P.M. screamed past and not jump up to take in her geraniums before coal dust settled among the blooms. But those times after Daniel had drunk himself to sleep, she would slip out with a kerosene lamp to gently wipe down the velvety leaves. She needed to be inside anyway when he was drinking because it was the only way she could find out what was really on his mind. He spent six days a week hauling odds and ends. Furniture. Scrap metal. Rags. Firewood. A white man's mule, he'd tell Sadie. He hated the work he did, and he hated even more talking about it. They ate their dinner totally in silence, unless it was one of those rare times he had a question to ask her or she had a repair for him to do. She'd know when it had been an especially rough day for him after she'd cleared the dishes. He'd work his toothpick around in his mouth and announce to the air, I think I'll have a taste. Then she knew to take the new bottle of whiskey from the cupboard and set it in front of him with a clean glass. It was always a new bottle. He never stopped until it was through.

Sadie would fade into the corner chair as he drank while staring into the air. At first she'd tried reading; she liked picture books because her schooling didn't amount to a hill of beans and she could fill in the missing story herself. But the house was so quiet he could still hear the pages turn. Noise, was all he had to say. She'd close the book in her lap. But she found that sewing worked, and it was a way to get the leftover darning done. She'd time biting the thread to the click of the bottle's neck on his glass. The silence in the room was always shattered with the passing of the 8:40, and if he'd been at it long enough, she found out all she needed to know. As the vibrating house settled, it might be one sentence, sometimes two, rarely more than three. And he always spoke them to the air: My name ain't *nigger*. So he hadn't moved his wagon fast enough for a policeman that day. Pissing in my pants. Blood running down San Juan Hill. Flames. So he'd been decorated in the Spanish-American War. The Ninth Cavalry charging with Teddy Roosevelt. And later his buddy got pulled off a troop train in North Carolina and lynched. One sentence, sometimes two. She sewed them together over twenty-five years to form the story of a bitter man who could once ride a horse like a god and had to become a mule to keep his family from starvation. There was the first wife, who died. The second wife, who ran off with his cousin. And the two daughters, who never wrote.

His drinking also let Sadie know what he thought of her. And she found out it wasn't very much. He mistrusted her eyes. There was something, something, just hanging on the edge of them he couldn't put his finger on. Her cleaning irritated him—her way of saying that where he'd brought her to live wasn't good enough. The prim way of eating. The prim way of wiping her mouth. All of it saying that *nothing* around her was good enough. And he suspected that she couldn't have children because she'd caught some white man's disease in that white whorehouse. And if he ever found out that was the case, that she was carrying some white man's disease into his bed, he would beat her senseless. As Sadie pieced together all of this information, she didn't confront him with it either to deny or explain. He never remembered the next morning what he'd said anyway. And he certainly couldn't remember over years of such mornings.

The hurt she felt over learning of his feelings was a small hurt compared to some others she'd known. She could bear that as long as he let her stay there. And she made his life much too comfortable for him not to. They both discovered that the week she was sick, the week that led up to their one and only fight. The lesions the scalpel had left in that back room smelling of dogs and cats would flare up now and then. The older she grew, the worse the pains became. She stayed in bed all day and night this time, turning her head away from the grime building up on the bedroom windows. Daniel still had to work while fixing his meals and hers. He had to empty her chamber pot and even started using it himself because he couldn't stand the way the outhouse started smelling. He was tracking cinders in from the front porch and they left a gritty feeling on the floor that set his teeth on edge. Flies were attracted to the dirty dishes piling up in the basin and they lit on his food and buzzed around his head. Now when he woke up after drinking, he'd find the overturned bottle and glass on the sticky table. He started thinking maybe he should stop. He started thinking the place was disgusting. He'd bathe Sadie's head with cool towels, asking her if today was the day she felt well enough to get up. Finally one day she did. And she found her geraniums dying.

She grew the red geraniums on the back porch in any sort of container she could salvage: Mason jars, dented tin buckets, fruit crates, a few real clay pots that she scraped from the house money to buy. They were the reddest flowers she could find, hardy enough to thrive through the soot and vibrations. She used garbage peelings and horse manure to enrich the soil she took from public lots on the other side of town. And she nourished the new blooms with water that she'd soaked eggshells in. The flowers that couldn't fit on the porch sat on the railings, hung from the eaves on ropes, and lined the back steps. Each spring, when they came to full color, Sadie had the garden she needed to round out her dream. But they were all brown-spotted and parched the day she got out of bed.

Her voice shocked Daniel: I asked you to water these. She turned those strange eyes on him and he almost started to explain before he caught himself. This woman needed to know her place.

    —I ain't your hired help. And I been meaning to get rid of them anyway.

And to make good his threat, he bent down to pick up a pot. Later he would say that she shoved him, but it was the surprise that she would even put her hand on his shoulder to stay him that tumbled him over. He hit the porch floor smack on his behind and stared up at her, his mouth dropped into a large O.

    —They leave, I leave, she said.

He jumped up, took a pot, and smashed it in the yard.

    —Woman, this is *my* damn house.

    —They leave, I leave, she said.

She went inside, the screen door banging shut behind her. The sound made him flinch. I oughta come in there to beat you senseless, he yelled while he stood there totally confused. Then he picked up one of the Mason jars and threw it against the house to be sure she would hear it. He tiptoed over to the window to peek in and see if she was packing.

He saw through the grimy windowpane that she was. He made a bad show of hurrying into the house without seeming to hurry. He took the beaten-up satchel away from Sadie.

—They stay, he said.

Without a word she left the bedroom and began to clean up a week's worth of dishes. That done, she went outside to water her geraniums.

After that one fight, she knew there was nothing to fear if she used a few extra cents to buy real kitchen curtains instead of the old sheets she was used to hemming up. A rag rug went down on the floor. A chintz cover was put on the easy chair. She'd hand him the bills and serve up his dinner. He'd get drunk on those nights and talk about fancy-minded South Side trash. Still, buckets of white paint and a borrowed ladder were waiting outside for him each spring. He flat-out refused to build a picket fence to enclose nothing but gravel, but he did take the lumber and fashion her some huge flower boxes, so geraniums were now blooming in each corner of the yard. She went out there herself and painted the boxes green.

The laws of nature finally made her a widow; the man was thirty years her senior. But it was human nature that threatened to take away her home. The two daughters who never wrote managed to show up after the funeral with the deed to that shack. They'd have been hard pressed to find anyone else who wanted it, and they could've rented it to Sadie like she begged them. Just rent it to her, for any price they set, until she could work for the money to buy it outright. No, they didn't want to rent; they wanted to *sell*. They saw no reasons to make allowances for that old drunk's young wife. No shame, up and marrying women even younger than them after he'd driven their mother to her grave. And no telling what kind of money she'd already weaseled out of the senile fool. Buy or get out.

———

Man's law stepped in and said no matter what, they had to give her thirty days. And nowhere was God's law working in all of this, or lightning would have been dancing around those railroad tracks as Sadie sold everything the two daughters couldn't claim: his broken-down nag and the wagon, all of his clothes, any of her spare clothes, the pots and pans, the furniture. She stripped the place bare trying to keep it. It took her ten days to get rid of what had been accumulated in twenty-five years, and it brought the sum total of $97.50. But they were asking $200.00 for the house. And only twenty days left to make the rest of the money. Sadie's head was spinning as she searched through the place looking for anything else she could get rid of. She might sell the bed and sleep on the floor, but with all of the quilts already gone she couldn't even make herself a pallet. And that one chair and battered kitchen table wouldn't bring in more than a dollar, even if she was lucky. In the back of a cabinet she found the cracked sugar bowl she'd used as a bank over the years. She dumped out the handful of pennies, and no matter how many times she counted them, they still only added up to 25. Well, she'd go find herself some work. That was all there was to it. She'd work herself to the bone until she got what was needed to make the deadline for that house. But she looked up, frantic, to discover that the sun was almost setting on the first of the twenty days.

She tried her neighbors first, knocking on each door. A little yard work? Pots to scour? Laundry? Could she mind their children? It was Friday evening and she knew they liked to go out. Some were glad for her predicament: so the high and mighty had been brought down. They rolled the taste of power around in their mouths as she waited anxiously for them to agree about the pennies' worth of labor she'd offered and decided they liked it. The taste was fresh and new, and not wanting to give it up with a *no*, it was, after a long long wait, Try me later. Tomorrow? Yeah, try me tomorrow. And they sat down to dinner, relishing what tomorrow would bring. But some were sorry they couldn't help: if they could afford someone working for them, would they be living in a place like this? And they gave her the directions to houses that they cleaned in themselves, houses on the other side of town.

The autumn light was quickly fading as she started out across town that Friday evening. And it was already dark when she reached the streets where fences of all types hemmed in the green lawns and flower borders. The air was getting chilled and she'd rushed off without the one jacket she hadn't sold. As each door was opened by curious or suspicious eyes, the warmth from the house made her shiver, and her stomach growled as she breathed in the aromas of pot roasts and baking potatoes. Some thought she was off in the head and quickly slammed their doors. A few told her to return on Monday at a decent hour—with references. But it only took one to call the police, and she was warned to get off those streets and go back where she belonged.

She got lost trying to find her way back toward the railroad tracks and ended up on streets where the lawns were even greener and larger, the fences all wrought iron and looming high over her head. The lighted windows of the stone mansions watched her with unblinking eyes as she ducked her head and tried to walk faster. Sadie knew not to even bother knocking on these front doors. She fought back despair, trying to calculate as she trotted along: she would have to double her efforts tomorrow to make up for this wasted day. Or maybe she could make it up over the next nineteen days. Nineteen days to make over $100.00. How much a day? But that math was too difficult without paper. She'd sit up all night if need be and do those figures when she got home.

She was concentrating so hard, she almost collided with the two women leaving through one of the wrought-iron gates. It was only as she skirted around them, mumbling an apology, that she noticed the black sedan idling at the curb. But it was laughter of one of the women that made her stop. *Damn fools*, the echo hit her, *there's no way for them to nail a Vacate sign on* . . . The blond hair was streaked with silver and swept up with pearl-studded combs and topped with a black cloche. The pearls were real and so was the mink stole. The wedding ring was platinum. And the green eyes were still beautiful, the makeup expert enough to mask the spreading crow's feet. Those eyes were startled as Sadie reached out to grab a sleeve under the mink-covered arm.

—I'm Sadie, she said.

The eyes were totally blank and beginning to grow frightened, and as the red-painted mouth was opening in protest . . .

—I'm Sadie, she repeated. Who does your hair now?

It took less than a second: the recognition, the mouth arching up in a smile, the eyes demanding applause for the lighted windows of the mansion, the Vassar-bound daughter beside her, the smooth idling of the black sedan, the husband behind the wheel. On the heels of that second, the daughter was speaking, Mother, who . . . ? Nobody, the blonde said as she shook off Sadie's hand and herded the girl toward the car.

—I need work, Sadie called behind her.

Without turning her head she answered, I'm sorry; my staff is full. The heavy door opened and those long legs swung in. Sadie took a step forward, her voice louder, her meaning clear:

—I'll still come tomorrow. I need the work.

But her last glimpse of those green eyes as the car pulled off told her there was no danger in her threat. He was a john, Sadie, the eyes said. A smart john who knew we make the best wives. Sadie risked standing there to watch until the car reached the end of the long block. She shivered and clapped her chilled hands together for warmth, clapping until the taillights of the sedan disappeared.

It was well after midnight when she finally reached home. And she was already gone on the morning of the nineteenth day by the time the 5:15 screamed past. She made the going rate of $2.00 for cleaning a house that Saturday. She'd raise it to $2.50 after she brought references, the woman told her, because after all, she was taking a chance. And the woman was so pleased with how thorough she'd been that she didn't deduct for the lunch she gave her. Sadie put the crumpled dollar bill and four quarters into her cloth change purse. Did anyone else in the neighborhood need help today? Yes, she knew it was almost dark, but she needed the work tonight. Well, maybe the old woman at the corner who kept all those cats. Lord knows, that smelly place could use a good cleaning any time of day. Sadie picked up another $1.50 for that. And no worry about deductions; she was afraid to eat the food offered her there. Well past midnight again, she limped into the house and emptied the change purse on the table. Two crumpled dollar bills, four quarters, four dimes, and two nickels. She was too tired to add up how much she was behind. And she'd forgotten to calculate the Sundays anyway. No one worked on Sundays— except in the defense plants. Yes, that's what she would try.

Sure, they could use her, she was told the next day. Fill out the application, give them a week or so to run the security check, and she'd be manning a machine by the end of the month. And, no, it couldn't be sooner than that. These things take time, but she'd be making good money once she started—over $30.00 a week. An advance? Was she out of her mind? Get the job first before she started thinking of ways to waste the money. Sadie filled out the application as best she could, hoping something would happen and they would rush it through.

She still made 25 cents on Sunday, picking up litter for one of her neighbors who got tired of her asking, and she added that to a dime she'd found in the gutter. Two more coins for the growing pile. She drank her dinner of hot water and sugar as she pulled out pencil and paper to calculate what was yet to be earned. She had seventeen days left to make $98.40. With $5.79 a day she'd make it with 3 cents left over, so she rounded it off to $5.80 a day. After the first day she'd have an extra 4 cents. And then she'd have the extra penny each day thereafter to buy a little more sugar to heat in some water. And after that first day, if she couldn't make the extra penny she wouldn't worry about it. After that first day, it was really only $5.79 a day. She checked and double-checked. Yes, $5.79 a day. She repeated those numbers over and over under her breath. She repeated those numbers the way some people pray.

On Monday, pocketing her $2.00 for another day's worth of cleaning, she heard of a laundry near the South Side that ran an evening shift. The owner agreed to pay her in cash after each shift since she was willing to run the steam press for half pay. Can't get good steam-press help, he said, since the Chink laundries got big enough to hire their own kind. Just watch your fingers, he told her. She scalded them anyway. But she finished the shift and assured him that, no, the burns didn't hurt. She'd be back on time the next evening. Another $1.75 was snapped shut into the change purse. Sadie knew she was still short for that day, and it was close to midnight again. The other workers left on the last trolley as she sat on the bench, pretending to be waiting for a ride home so she could think.

She didn't believe she'd be able to make that long walk back to the railroad tracks. And maybe if she slept on the bench, she'd have enough energy to work faster tomorrow—do two houses—before she came to the laundry. That would just about make it happen—two houses and the laundry. But they didn't like it if you finished your housework too early. They might not want to pay for a full day. She didn't see why—a day's worth was a day's worth. It was up to her how fast she worked; the house would be clean. They could go around with white gloves in any place after she was through. But she was still short for today. Today she still needed . . . Sadie's thoughts were broken when the man cleared his throat. She was startled to realize that a dark figure was bending over behind her.

    —Out a little late, ain't you, sweet pea?

Her hands gripped the change purse in her jacket pocket as she jumped up from the bench. With her heart pounding she could finally make out the shiny buttons and cut of the soldier's uniform. He stood there smiling, his white teeth in sharp contrast to his ebony face. But she still kept her fist balled around the change purse and inched away.

—Hey, I'm not gonna hurt you. Miss your trolley?

She shook her head no as she inched farther away. The soldier looked down the length of her body, his eyes resting on her full bosom—

—I didn't think so.

Sadie began walking down the street. He fell in beside her. She ignored him, but she didn't tell him to go away either.

—I'm shipping out tomorrow. So tonight's for a little fun.

They came up under a street lamp and when she finally saw his full face clearly, her first thought was the first words out of her mouth: You're young enough to be my son. He broke out in that wide grin again.

—Yeah, but I like 'em experienced.

She lost him by cutting quickly through a back alley that led to another set of deserted buildings. *Don't worry, he won't follow.* She remembered those words. *They'll never follow into a dark alley, unless it's two of them. They'll think your fancy man is waiting.* But they're not called fancy men anymore, Mama, she thought; now they call them pimps. Another alley between the shuttered warehouses led her into the heart of the South Side. The raw burns on her hand were aching as she hurriedly walked through streets that with all of the changes had not changed. The music pouring out of the saloons was different, except they weren't saloons. Linoleum had replaced the wooden planks and sawdust; tall glass mugs instead of pails of beer were handed over the stained oak counters. The ghosts of the ragtime professors bent over their piano keys lived on in the red-and-blue lights speckling the walls from jukeboxes, but the beat was fast, fast, with trumpets now screaming at the same pitch of the 5:15. It felt like a Saturday night because of the soldiers, hundreds who were shipping out and using the sidewalks of the South Side for one big party. The uniforms had gone from the color of dried dung to that of dead olives, but the bodies filling them were still dark and young. Sadie kept bumping into groups of them, corner—Hey, sweetie, where's the fire?—after corner—If you slow down a little, Papa'll buy you a drink. *A woman is a woman*—she also remembered those words—*and a woman is a whore unless she knows how to walk after midnight.*

She stopped to catch her breath at a traffic light. Leaning against its iron post, she felt her head spinning as her eyes dimmed and she feared she was going to faint. Her mind was blank as she watched the light change from red to green to red again. She didn't know how many times it had changed before he came up to her. He wasn't a soldier. And he wasn't young. The plain-cut suit was a little frayed at the lapels. And his felt hat had one more blocking left before the garbage bin. He stood beside the post with his hands in his pockets, watching the lights change with Sadie. From red to green to red again. Sadie counted up what she had earned that day: $3.75.

From red to green to red again. She glanced out the corner of her eye and saw he was fidgeting, a nervous smile playing around his lips. One of the shy white ones, she thought. He was just waiting to cross the street, minding his own business, until I threw myself at him. When he pulls his hands out of his pocket, he'll have on a wedding ring. And he'll want to show me the photographs of his children after. He'll *need* to show me those photographs after. Yes, some things on the South Side would never change. From red to green to red again.

—You busy tonight? she asked without looking at him.
—No, he said. How much?
Sadie locked her hands around the cloth purse in her pocket, remembering the smudged paper on her kitchen table.
—Two dollars and four cents.
She jumped when he laughed so suddenly. You're kidding me, sister, he

said. And for a minute she thought he was telling her she'd miscalculated, she was cheating him out of extra money. But no, it was right: seventeen days divided into . . .

—Two dollars and four cents, she repeated firmly. And pay me first.

He shook his head as he took three dollar bills out of his wallet: You're way below the going rate. There was a wedding ring and there were photographs. Take the three, he said. But she insisted on making change and counted it out to the penny. He pocketed the coins before flipping open his jacket to show her the badge. And then he arrested her.

Two weeks in women's detention. And two days left when she turned up the unpaved road leading to the settlement of shanties. Counting anything stopped for Sadie then. She dropped to her knees in one corner of the yard and rested her forehead on the dry soil of the flower box. Blooming was past, and the velvet leaves of the geraniums were brittle and covered with a thick layer of dark cinders and ashes. The unattended screen door had kept banging in the wind until it hung from the hinges. The windows were shrouded in dirt and soot. The trains thundering by became one train. The neighbors trying to raise her up from the ground became one set of arms. Seeing that she wanted to be left alone, they left her. She stayed that way through the night.

My father used to tell me that a star dies in heaven every time you snatch away someone's dream. Dreams had been dying around Sadie all of her life. And the last star for her was dimming quickly inside. The last thing holding her back from falling to her destruction, an endless plunge through the endless space of the black hole waiting to open in her heart. There were no more dreams. So she knelt through the long night hours with her head in the dry flower bed and prayed for a miracle. Let me keep it, she begged; let me keep it.

———

The footsteps echoed loud on the dry gravel in the still of the night. They came slowly from the far edge of the settlement. A pair of knees brushed her bent shoulders and a hand reached down to stroke her hair. The palm was large as a man's, the touch gentle as a woman's. A threadbare blanket was draped across her back and a crumpled paper bag laid at her side. By the time Sadie looked up she was alone, the footsteps no more than a distant echo.

She pulled the blanket around her and reached for the paper bag. The dingy white paint of her house glowed in the dark as the mucus in the corners of her sleepy eyes formed a halo around it. Rainbows streaked the roof and filled the yard with greens, blues, speckled the dead geranium leaves with spots of bright red. The first thing her fingers grasped inside the bag was a piece of fried fish sandwiched be-tween two squares of buttered cornbread. She ate the gift of bread and fish in small bites, as dawn was now threatening to break apart the visions of the night. But then she reached back into the crumpled bag to pull out the stars. Five of them were emblazoned on a label redder than her geraniums. And the five stars became the only ones she needed as she unscrewed the top of the flat pint bottle to drink the sweet wine.

Dawn broke to no avail. The house was still beautiful and it was still hers. She got up off her sore knees, stumbled to the liquor store, and came back with a supply of stars to put her home in order. That day, between the 11:55, 3:12, and 8:40, she got the porch swept, the floors mopped, the windows washed, the laundry done, the pots scrubbed, the screen door hung, the roof fixed, the entire house painted, the yard dug up and refilled with sod, a picket fence built, a brick walkway laid, all the flowers replanted and blooming. She was so tired, she fell asleep right there at the table. Her head throbbed, her throat was dry, and her breath smelled of rotten fruit, but the place finally looked good. She knew she'd been given a second chance and she'd make no more mistakes. She'd make sure that she always had enough money to keep her home.

It wasn't easy, but she managed the best she could. There was only the small widow's pension from her husband being a war veteran and what she could pick up in day cleaning now and then. Soon the day jobs started to fall off because her hands shook too badly to hide and the throbbing headaches kept her eyes teary. Food wasn't much of a problem because she never had much of an appetite. A bar of candy or a handful of Walnettos could keep her going through the day, and every so often she'd crave a slice of cheese. The biggest expense was put out for a room. Even the cheapest places in the worst parts of the South Side were now demanding high rents. That section of town was bursting at the seams from the families of sharecroppers racing north to take new jobs in the defense plants or anywhere else a space was left by a new soldier. People were using the same bed in shifts: one body getting up and going to the factory while another lay down.

But Sadie didn't need anything much larger than a closet: a Murphy bed, a table and chair, a hot plate for her tea. And when the rent on that got raised, she found a cot being let in a hallway. She could sit on that when she wasn't sleeping, and get her tea at the corner drugstore. The people having to walk over her feet to pass didn't bother her, nor did the stench of burnt cabbage and overflowing toilets, the noisy children jumping up and down the steps. Because at night the stars came out and she made a few improvements to her home over the years. A new sewing room to catch the southern light. Nothing too fancy, but she splurged a bit on the double-pane glass so she could use it in comfort during the winter. The imitation Tiffany shades she'd put on layaway at Montgomery Ward's brought a lovely glow to the main room in the evening. And at last she could buy a radio, now that Daniel was gone.

———

She didn't remember when the city of Chicago condemned that tenement. Or exactly what month the widow's pension stopped coming to a dead address. Or when the satchel with her clothing found a new resting place under a cot in the women's shelter. But she did remember the evening she counted out the change in her cloth purse and found she was 10 cents short of the stars. She recounted once more just to be sure, and then without hesitation she went around to the back alley where the derelicts were roasting their dinner sausage over a trash fire. The second one she approached took her up on her offer. And in the far corner of the alley, barely into the shadows cast by the flames, she made the 10 cents. The officials at the shelter told her it would take a few weeks to straighten out the problem with her pension, so her price the next evening needed to go up to 25 cents and she had to seek out a new group of men, because the ones behind the shelter already knew she'd been had for a dime.

The few weeks to straighten out the problem stretched into months. And she lost her bed at the shelter because she refused to go on public relief. She wanted nothing from anyone except what was owed her. Park benches. Railroad stations. Church pews. She'd sit up and doze during the day wherever it was warm or safe; when she was lucky, it was both. She'd keep herself as clean as possible with the public bathrooms, and every week she'd return to the shelter to see if her pension check had arrived. Any stray penny or nickel she'd find on the sidewalks would go into her cloth purse for the stars. Some evenings she would only need to sell herself for 23 cents, some evenings 15. And on the rare times she'd find a silver dollar, it meant four whole evenings could pass without her picking up a man.

She never bought food with even a penny of the money she'd find on the sidewalks. The down-and-outers who moved in that world saved her from starvation. They liked Sadie. Something about her made her different from the other women bumming around with them, and it wasn't only those strange eyes. If it weren't so unthinkable, they might have found the words to say it was because she had *class*. She didn't use filthy language, even when she was drunk, and she stayed either drunk or hung over all of the time. And they found themselves saying Excuse me when a *bitch* or *fuck* slipped from their own mouths. And they didn't get insulted when she quietly refused to sit around and share a good bottle of whiskey with them. She'd never drink anything but Five Star wine and she never screwed for anything but the exact price. It made a few of them a little eerie, and they'd turn her down for the 2 or 3 cents when they'd gladly have taken her if she'd asked for much more.

Somewhere out there are a lot of pension checks waiting for Sadie, but they certainly hadn't found her by the time she found her way into this cafe. She walked in here from the streets of Chicago the same way they walk in from Detroit, Saint Paul, Memphis, or New York. It's the last place before the end of the world for some, and since it soon becomes common knowledge that it's up to Nadine what a customer is charged, Sadie knew it was no handout when my wife decided her cup of tea or occasional dish of cobbler was on the house. Sadie more than paid for it with what it took to turn our thick mugs into fine bone china.

And with all that's gone on before, this is where the story really gets sad. Enter Iceman Jones.

A bear of a man, although he isn't very tall: broad at the shoulders and full in the chest, with thick, round arms and legs. And he has a sort of square-cut face that's always struggling with a five o'clock shadow. Winter or summer, he's in that heavy gray tweed jacket, but even along with the burlap pad he uses over his left shoulder, arthritis has set in from thirty years' worth of toting blocks of ice. IIIceemann, IIIcemann, he calls from the seat of his wagon. He'll rein up his horse in the middle of the street to give those who need him a chance to poke their heads out the apartment windows. It never fails, he says, it's always the woman on the top floor who'll want the biggest piece.

He's gotten so good over the years he can gauge with his eyes the difference between where to hit for a fifty-cent piece or a sixty-cent piece. That sharp pick gets situated at just the right spot; a tap of the hammer, and the right-size chunk breaks off fair and clean. That's the best part of his work for him, the skill his stubby fingers can call up to tap off that exact piece. It's like cutting diamonds, and the way the ice can sparkle on the edges when it catches the sun, sometimes he could believe he's dealing in jewels. But it ain't an illusion that can last too long, he says. Cause then you gotta put on that shoulder pad, grab them tongs, and haul that sucker up them steps. It don't take long for that icy water to start seeping into your shoulder bone. And wouldn't ya know it? That very one on the top floor who asks for the biggest piece is the same one who wants you to wait while she empties her drain pan. In all the time it took me to make it up six flights, she couldna reached under the icebox and emptied that pan? And then he'll smile and shake that bear head, making you think that he could be a little bit at fault himself for that melting ice. It's a warm smile.

Iceman Jones became a regular here around dinnertime, after his wife died. He said my music suited him, none of that be-bop de-bop that gets your stomach jumping too much to digest what you ate. It's music you can talk over, and Jones likes to talk as much as he likes to listen. He has a great time on that counter stool when misfortune brings Eve and Sister Carrie in here on the same day. And Carrie, knowing he's a churchgoing man, will try to get him in on her side.

—And the Bible says it, don't it, Brother Jones?

—Yeah, the Bible says it, Sister Carrie.

And then he winks at Eve. In his line of work he's learned a lot about getting along with people, and from having the privilege of looking inside so many iceboxes, which tells a whole story about somebody's life, he's also learned that most things aren't what they seem.

It was spring when he first met Sadie. Like everybody else, he'd seen her before at her single table against the far wall. And like everybody else, he'd heard the talk about what she was and had his own opinion: A real pity, she musta been a fine-looking woman. And then one day last spring she dropped her teaspoon as Jones was walking past to get to the counter. He stooped to pick it up for her, and as she reached for it with her quivering hand, he looked her full in the face. He met the eyes of a four-year-old dreaming to survive. She gave him a soft Thank you, and his own hands weren't any too steady as he took his seat on the stool to order his dinner. He wasn't as talkative that day, and he picked at his food.

Jones was a man with a life as simple as you could make it: a mama and daddy, three brothers, two sisters. They were poor but they ate. They were close but they fought. He dropped out of school. Sowed a few wild oats. And at twenty he took a job on an ice wagon that was worse than some, better than others. Later there was a wife, one son, and one daughter. They were still poor but they ate. They were close but they fought. The children grew up, got high-school educations, moved away. The wife died. He grieved. And the last letter had brought news he was due to be a grandfather. He had his lodge, his church, and his handful of friends. And the two evenings a week he didn't eat in the cafe, he liked puttering around the kitchen with concoctions of stew or baked beans. Jones couldn't imagine, didn't *want* to imagine, the type of life it must have taken to freeze that look in a grown woman's eyes.

Without appearing to, he began studying the woman herself. The steel gray hair was frizzled from not being oiled and pressed, but she kept it neatly parted and braided. No disputing it was a wino's face: the puffy eyelids, the drooping lips. But her skin stayed dry and ashy, which meant she was no stranger to water, even if she couldn't find lotion. The two dresses she changed up each day, rough and dry, but clean; a pair of men's socks; rubber-soled loafers. He wondered how she managed to keep the loafers polished. There must be a tin of Kiwi down in that satchel, as well as a bar of soap, because the only body odor was of fruit gone bad. He'd been let into fancy apartments where women weren't as tidy about themselves, and this one lived in the streets.

She knew he was an iceman. He knew she was a twenty-five-cent whore. That took care of how they earned their money, but neither of them knew the other's name. So the next week Jones introduced himself. Sadie had few occasions to tell anyone her name, and when she did, she always turned her head to the side as if expecting a blow. An old habit that went way back to how she'd first learned it. She didn't stop him when he pulled up a chair to her table, but she didn't have much to say, either, as out of the blue he started telling her about his day.

He began with the way the sun looked coming up over the East River, where he bought his ice from the warehouse. He bought by the pound, sold by the piece. And somewhere in between the meltdown, he managed to make ends meet. He described the sounds of his horse's hooves on the cobblestones and paved roads. The thumping of the wagon's wheels. Not too many horses and wagons left. If he stayed in this business, he'd probably get a truck, but he had a sneaking suspicion that by the time all the horses were gone all the iceboxes would be too. He had stories about the people he'd met: the cheapskate who told him it was a sin to charge as much as he did since it was only frozen water and, after all, water was free; the old spinster who wanted just a sliver each day to keep a favorite parakeet on ice. He carried Sadie through the sights and sounds and smells of his day, amusing her as you would a child. And almost, almost, making her smile. When she got ready to leave, he stood up and pulled out her chair.

Sadie allowed Iceman Jones to come as far as the picket fence that night. Under the stars she stood with her hand discreetly on the gate latch so he'd understand this was where she wanted to visit. There was a gentle wind that fluttered the voile curtains in the lighted kitchen window and brought the aroma of her chicken casserole. It was still too early in spring for the geraniums to be blooming, but she pointed out the mulched beds that would soon bear her Martha Washingtons and trailers. She'd thought about roses, she told him, but believe it or not, even the American Beauties don't get as red as these, and roses are finicky, they wouldn't hold up with the trains. And did he know the ones lining the fence had leaves that smelled of mint and lemon? Oh yes, when he came back to visit in the summer, she would show him. That is, if he was coming in the summer. She felt her face grow flushed, thinking she might have been too forward, and was glad for the darkness to hide her embarrassment. Well, she would have to go in now. But it was so very nice of him to stop by.

Every time Jones saw Sadie, he'd pull up a chair to her table and tell her about his day. It got so she would finally smile, her right hand fluttering up to hide her mouth. Sadie's teeth were in bad shape; the sweet wine had rotted some of them through, and lack of a dentist had taken the rest. She forgot all about them, though, the evening he came in with the story about his one and only sale that day. It really was a story, moving close to shades of a lie. Only worked one hour today, old girl. He'd taken to calling her that, making it sound like the caress he meant it to be. And it wouldna been a whole hour, except I turned up Lenox instead of heading straight for Amsterdam. See, the fire trucks were blocking off most of Amsterdam from 123rd to 125th and I could see the smoke, but Nell had already smelled it and she was getting skittish. I doubt if she's got enough juice left in her to be a runaway, but I wasn't taking no chances. And wouldn't you know it? The hydrants had broken down and they couldn't get but a trickle of out 'em, and the building just a-blazing.

Now, they'd gotten all the people safe, but they didn't want the thing to spread. And here's the fire chief racing up and down the streets in his automobile, shouting—Water! We need Water!—when he spots me in my wagon. I'm as civic minded as the next fella, but I told him Nell wasn't gonna make it. So we unhitched her, hitched my wagon to his automobile, and pulled it on to the fire.

Sadie's hand started fluttering to her mouth. And I called out from behind the counter, Jones, you're supposed to be a Christian, and lying like that. Bailey, if I'm lying, I'm flying, he said. Then he looked at Sadie and winked. Well, all right, I didn't have quite enough ice in my wagon to put out all the flames. So me and the firemen stood around that building and spit out the rest.

Her laughter was like music. And the whole cafe stood still. In the presence of something that beautiful and rare, you're afraid to move, afraid to even breathe. But seeing that she'd become the center of attention, she smothered it almost as quickly as it was born. Talk resumed at the other tables, dishes began rattling, but none of us, especially Jones, would ever be the same again. He sat there staring at Sadie, and since she only knew to read silence as disapproval, she ducked her head and mumbled into her tea, I'm sorry, I just thought it was a funny story. It was meant to be, he said. Jones didn't come into the cafe at all the next week. Or the next.

Sadie pulled the two rockers out on the front porch. The weather had turned warm enough to sit out there under the stars. She hoped he didn't mind that she had yet to invite him into the house, but the quilted pads she'd sewn herself made the wooden seats comfortable enough for them to talk for hours. And how that man could talk. The deepness of his voice made her peaceful inside, and he was kind enough to mention the few changes she'd made, things you wouldn't expect a man to notice. Yes, she did fix her hair a little differently now. Just thought she'd try bringing the bangs to the side. Her forehead was way too large to sweep it up off her face, but some older women did look pretty with those new French rolls. What did he mean she wasn't that old? Look at all this gray up there. She was old as Methuselah's mama. It wasn't a very good joke; she didn't have much practice. But there was laughter on her front porch. For the first time, there was laughter.

Jones came back in the third week and took his regular seat at the counter, looking for all the world like somebody had stepped on each of those bear toes. Sadie wasn't in that evening, which seemed to irritate him even more. He jerked his head toward the empty table. Guess she's out there earning her twenty-five cents.

—Not always, Jones, I said. We both know sometimes it's only a
dime.

He gave me a real hard stare and I gave it right back. He blinked first. His voice was soft as he dropped his eyes. Has she been by any, these past weeks?

—She's been in, I said.

He started rolling his water glass between his huge palms. It just makes you worried and all, her living in those filthy alleys and God knows where else. It's kinda dangerous out there for somebody like her; the world ain't what it used to be.

—But she's been in, I said.

Finally he raised his head: Did she ask about me?

—No, she didn't.

It was to be a special evening and Sadie was nervous. Maybe he wouldn't like the place. Maybe he'd think she was showing off. But you should use your good crystal for company, and it wasn't like she'd bought the whole set outright. She'd laid away a piece at a time over the years: the juice glasses, the water glasses, the wine goblets, worrying that Waterford would change the pattern before she'd gotten them all. And the candles on the dinner table were a real nice touch, because the candles made the edges of the goblets sparkle like diamonds. And he'd appreciate that

*because he'd once told her that he felt like a diamond cutter with his ice. And it's
not that the room was totally dark with nothing but the candles; she had all the
lamps on, the imitation Tiffany shades polished and polished again, to give the
room a real comfortable feel and keep him from getting any ideas. The first time
the man's in your home, you don't want him thinking you're forward. No, her
good china, her good glasses, and a very simple meal: baked chicken, spinach, boiled
potatoes, and a store-bought cake for dessert. She knew men—start too soon with
homemade cakes and then they start getting nervous. A knock on the door. She
did a quick check in the mirror and hurried to let him in.*

She took her regular table and it was one of her bad days. Her hands
wouldn't let her raise the teacup so she could use her napkin to blot up
the hot water she'd spilled. And there was a bruise on the side of her
temple. She told Jones she had slipped and fallen. He wanted to take her
to a doctor but she said she'd be fine; it was nice of him, though, to
offer.

—The streets are no place for you, Sadie.

—I don't live on the streets, she said.

He figured the Five Star was close to running her crazy. And when she
was ready to leave, he grabbed her hand: Don't go out there tonight.
Now, she looked at him like *he* was crazy.

—But it's time to go, she said.

—Don't go out there tonight. Here, I'll give you the quarter.

She snatched her hand away and gathered up her satchel.

—I don't take charity.

Jones was stunned and told her with anger that some women would
rather beg—or even steal. It was a queen who held on to the back of
the chair and glared down at him.

—Those women aren't me.

Seeing that she was turning away, he grabbed her hand again.

—All right, my money's as good as the next man's. A quarter for
your time.

She backed away from the coin he'd thrust into her face: I thought we were friends.

—We are, he said.

Jones took her tiny fingers and wrapped them around the quarter.

—I'm not buying your body, I'm buying your time.

And, still holding her hand, he led her toward the rear door of the cafe.

There is nothing in back of this cafe. Since the place sits right on the margin between the edge of the world and infinite possibility, the back door opens out to a void. It takes courage to turn the knob and heart to leave the steps. Jones opened the door, his bulk shielding Sadie from the sight of that endless plunge, and then he turned to look down into her eyes.

—Old girl, I didn't mean to hurt you in there.

—I know, Jones, she whispered.

He held her face between his large, callused palms and traced along her eyelids with his thumbs. She closed them and he leaned over to press his lips to hers. Sadie had her first real kiss. If she smiles now, we can do this, he thought. She opened her eyes and smiled. So it became a full silver moon, streaked with navy blue clouds, the sounds of the river hitting a pier, and the feel of damp wood beneath their feet when he escorted her off the back steps. Then her right hand up on his shoulder, his left around her waist, as the iceman and the two-bit whore began to dance.

She had worried needlessly about the dinner; he was charmed by the place. He told her how happy he was that she'd finally invited him in. He was beginning to think that maybe she didn't like him. Or maybe she couldn't cook. Well, after you finish my food, you might still think so. It was getting easier and easier to feel at home with this man. Would he like a bit of apple cider before they sat down to eat?

———————

He guided her gently through the two-step, keeping time from the rhythm of the waves. Just the sound of their feet sliding along the wooden planks. And the sound of his voice. Old girl, I'm gonna tell you, what you see is what you'll get. I'm pushing sixty, fighting arthritis, but my pension will take care of two.

He carved the chicken; they both liked the wings, so he winked and told her it was a good thing God made 'em in pairs.

The sliding along the planks. The sound of his voice. What I have, you'll have. What I eat, you'll eat. Wherever I lay my head, there's a place for you.

He helped her clear the table and wash the dishes. Insisted on polishing the crystal himself until it shone. The night was warm enough for them to go out on the porch and sit in the rockers. In the still of the night they could hear the new radio playing from the living room.

—And I want you to know, I ain't talking nothing improper. You get my name, such as it is, along with the whole bargain.

Yes, so easy to feel at home with this man. And she would keep him in her home, since it seemed he wanted to stay. Nights just like this, sitting on the porch, stretching into eternity. Nights full of music. Nights full of peace . . .

—So what do you say, old girl? We got ourselves a deal?

Thank God, she knew how to keep a place for him. And thank God, it would always stay that way.

―――――

Sadie shook her head no. It was a deal she just couldn't live with. She moved out of his arms and left him standing in the middle of the pier. At the back steps she retrieved her satchel. Her fingers closed tightly around the quarter in her pocket as she looked up at Jones's sky. She knew this dear sweet man was offering her the moon, but she could give him the stars.

Eve's Song

This summer the talk in here is all about Dewey's upcoming election—and Eve. The Indians closing in on the pennant—and Eve. The first new line of Chevys since the war—and Eve.

Taking them in order of importance for the cook: Cleveland jumps on the bandwagon, getting Larry Doby from the Negro Leagues along with the immortal pitching arm of Satchel Paige. So now the Cleveland Indians are kicking butt all up and down the American League. Surprise. Surprise.

Next—

I knew the clutch wasn't staying in automobiles. Women are driving now. When we went overseas they took our jobs and started making their own money. A big mistake. They talked back enough as it was, and with a lot of them still making good money, they even got the auto makers listening to them. It's too hard for them to work those gears in high heels and straight skirts. So guess what? No clutch.

Next—

Everybody knows I don't think much of Truman since he dropped the
A-bomb. Like I said, I understand what all that was about, but it's still
hard to forgive. And although it's really blaming the messenger for the
message, I'm not gonna be too sorry to see him lose this one. The only
reason he's getting my vote is because the choice comes down between
a man I don't like and one I don't trust. Reading the papers, that puts
me in the minority again. But it's a position I'm used to living with. After
all, I can't find a thing wrong with what goes on at Eve's.

Eve was my first customer. We opened on a Tuesday, and she took that
overdone hamburger I put in front of her without a word. Not that she
ate anything but a small piece of the bun; she's a vegetarian. But I didn't
have to explain the routine to her, like no one had to explain it to me.
Her place, she says, has always been right down the block from this cafe.

Too bad that Sadie couldn't have found that brownstone the way she
found us. And I knew there was no use in directing her there. A woman
is either ready for Eve's or she's not. And if she's ready, she'll ask where
to find it on her own. Not that finding her place is any guarantee of
getting a room. Eve is particular.

   —Particular? Lord, Jesus. They're all sluts and whores and tramps.
   —Come on and admit it, Bailey. She's got a good game going, and
   the nerve to bad-mouth me. Every pimp don't need to wear pants.
   —A house full of nothing but sluts and whores and tramps.

Eve lets out rooms in her house to single women. Sometimes they pay
her, sometimes they don't. I don't know how she decides when to charge
or not. I figure it's none of my business since I'm not a woman and
would have no reason to go there looking for a place to stay. I do know
that charity has nothing to do with it. Eve is not a charitable person.

You can look into her eyes and see that. She wears small rimless glasses that magnify those deep brown eyes. And it's a plain brown face that doesn't scowl but doesn't appear pleasant either. It appears, well, just there. Cut and dried. I've never heard her laugh, never even *seen* her laugh inside the way Nadine taught me it can be done. I'd go so far as to say she's a woman without a sense of humor. She's a stylish woman, though. Tailored silk suits. Oxford heels. But if you look real real close, there's always a faint line of dirt just under her manicured nails.

—She runs a whorehouse. Nothing but a whorehouse.
—Every pimp don't wear pants.
—She'd sell her own mama for a dime.

Eve knows exactly what some people think about her. And she honestly doesn't care. And all that I can honestly say is that the women who come straggling in here and ask about Eve's look just like any other women in the cafe. Some are older than others. Some wear makeup, some don't. Some are very pretty, some are quite plain. The only thing they have in common is that they need a place to stay. And I tell them the only thing I can: Go out the door, make a right, and when you see the garden— if you see the garden—you're there.

But does she know about delta dust? That's what I ask any time I'm tempted to let a woman stay here because of the pain in her story: Daddy beat up on her. Mama beat up on her. And every blessed soul in between. But does she know, does she know about delta dust? Early last summer one came here who'd had Lucky Strike spelled out on the inside of her thigh with a lit cigarette butt. A reminder to get the right brand the next time she was sent to the store. I estimated it must have taken him a good hour to spell out the name of those cigarettes because the letters were so evenly matched and she had full, sorta bell-curved thighs. And she could have used a place to stay too. Had left Mr. Lucky Strike for a new man who'd gotten her pregnant before going back to his wife. From there on in, her story shifted into the familiar key of and-nobody-loves-you-when-you're-down-and-out, so that my mind began to wander: My impatiens needed pruning. They were threatening to take over the back steps, and if you let them alone too long, they crowd out every flower in the yard. But I still let her finish her story—they always need to finish their stories—even though, looking at the flesh that had healed into deep craters with a scaly film, I knew I wouldn't take her in. Although hers was the worst I'd heard, except probably for Esther's, and I'd still kept Esther for other reasons. That kind of woman hated men. And there was no more room available for that kind in my boardinghouse. Esther was enough. Besides, with all that this woman had been through and would still keep going through—they always manage to keep going through it—she didn't know, just didn't know, about delta dust.

A thousand years ago and I can't wash it off; I still find a few grains of it in the bottom of the tub after I've pulled the stopper. I don't know why I keep thinking I can; it's no more possible than washing away my fingerprints or my color. I guess because it's only dirt, and there's something that makes you believe you can wash away dirt. But it's not a part of me—it is me. I became it, on that long walk from Pilottown to Arabi. The walk that took a thousand years. When people ask me how old I am and I say, About a thousand years, they think I'm being coy. But it's the gospel truth.

I didn't have an age when I lived in Pilottown. Godfather always told me that since I never had a real mother or father and wouldn't be alive if it weren't for him, *he* would decide when I was born. And I guess to make his point, whenever I'd ask what day was my birthday, he kept changing it year to year, month to month. As many times as I'd ask, that's as many as he'd keep changing it. He was patient that way, when he wanted to teach me a lesson. One evening, out of spite, I went to him more than twenty times in the course of an hour to ask for my birthday. And I picked the hour just after he'd cooked dinner and washed the dishes, knowing full well he prized that time for reading the Scriptures. More than twenty times, because I'd go back to my room and note it on my slate—and each time it was a different date. He didn't ever slip up and give me the same date twice. I would have taken that as a clue that it was probably the day I was born. The very day he said he found me in a patch of ragweed, so new I was still tied to the birth sac and he had to bite off the umbilical cord with his teeth and spit it out to save me from being poisoned: And going through all that for any she-creature earns me the right to decide when it was born.

By the time my breasts were showing and Godfather stopped putting my underpants on the yard line because of the stains that wouldn't wash out, I figure he'd given me a birth day and year for every box on the Sinai Church calendar. And by that time, I'd stopped caring because whatever my age it was old enough to start making a difference to the men—and women—in Pilottown. The men had only one question in their eyes when they looked at me then, and mine had only one answer: He would kill us both with his bare hands. But the women's eyes held other questions, unnatural questions, as their heads followed us when we rode by in the wagon. Why was he still cooking and cleaning for me? Why had he never married? Why was no boy ever allowed to come and call? Or even walk me home from church? But Godfather would stare them down and mutter softly, It's none of their damn business what goes on in my home. But he did stop bathing me on Saturday nights in that old tin tub, and the dark brown homespun he used for making all my dresses was cut loose and full from the shoulders to the hips. They now hung on me like the ugly brown sacks they were. Did those women understand what they had done with their slitted eyes and evil questions? I was now forced to go through months and months with no one and nothing to touch me.

It was always a silent house anyway, except when he was angry. Godfather grunted his way through speech, and when he was in the pulpit those grunts were just faster paced and louder, so the words resembled rounds of thunder. It got him the reputation for being a good preacher, and it was very effective, those sounds coming from such a large man. The barrel chest, the stalky arms, the salt-and-pepper hair beaded with sweat. But at home he was a looming, silent presence, and I grew up understanding that too much talk—which for a child is little but a string of questions—was to be clamped down with a Hush your chatter, and that to continue beyond his patience was to make him angry.

And his anger was much worse than the quiet—Godfather laughed when he was angry. Suddenly. Unexpectedly. Quick and sharp falsetto bursts that were like shards of glass on my ears. Each burst a little higher in range than the last—each new burst after some ragged interval. So you're caught waiting between them in a leaden leaden silence so heavy your heart feels like groaning under the weight and then the lightning vibrations of that shattering laughter coming from nowhere to send your heart pounding and flying into little pieces. He never hit me with his hands; he didn't have to with a laugh like that. I would do anything to keep from hearing it.

But when the Saturday-night baths stopped, anger was the only thing left in my home to touch me. There was no reason for his callused palms to be on my shoulder as he poured the water over my back. Grim-faced and concentrating as the lye soap was scrubbed in descending circles on my skin until it tingled. My ears and fingernails—a deep scowl as he wrapped the rough washcloth around his pinkie finger to unearth any hidden speck of grime. And so now I had no reason to reach out to him to balance myself in the slippery tin tub, sometimes only pretending to slip just so I could be allowed to reach out for his arms. And to know that just this one time he would permit me.

———

Yes, I fault them—not him—for what happened later. And I thought about those righteous righteous women every time my bare feet split open and bled afresh on that trek from Pilottown. They were so concerned about my age, and by the time I reached Arabi there was no doubt about how many years I'd lived: close to a thousand. And I don't spend a lot of time with the right or wrong, good or bad of what I am—I am. But I wouldn't have needed to leave east of the delta if Godfather hadn't thrown me out of the church. To be thrown out of his church was to be thrown out of the world. The town had only three buildings that qualified as such: the school, the cotton exchange, and the church. He was the preacher in one, the scale foreman and bookkeeper in another, and no one attended that drafty school past the ninth grade. And since *he* had thrown me out, there was nobody who would dare to take me in.

It didn't seem like much when he first discovered me pressed to the ground, my nose buried in the peppermint grass. A border of mint grass grew wild along the dirt walkway to the back porch steps. The strangest thing, that grass, the way it was mixed in all unruly with the tangled weeds and dandelions that passed for a back lawn while it grew straight and neat along the dirt walk. It was thickest and sweetest along that walkway, and that's why I chose to sprawl there on my stomach, so I could bury my nose in it. You see, Billy Boy had an awful smell to his sweat. Always had, his mama said, even from a baby. His nickname stuck from then, and he didn't mind people calling him what they did because he'd kept that baby's brain. And the stomping only made him sweat more, and also something about our game excited him. Maybe he could sense, in his own small way, what it was doing to me. The vibrations of the earth. *Stomp, Billy, stomp*. I can't remember when the game began. It might have started with hide-and-go-seek or tag. Or it could have been just some of the silly nonsense children invent to pass the time. The best toy is your imagination, and with us, the only toy. No, it couldn't have been tag, because that would have meant touching. Yes, it was probably hide-and-go-seek, because then I would have been pressed to the earth, hiding under a bush or rock shelf. And Billy would have been It since kids like him are always It—so grateful to be allowed to join in and slow to leave when the rules keep changing up to keep them from ever winning. And, yes, with hide-and-go-seek you only have to call out, I see you—there's no touching—and I wouldn't have been too afraid to play that game.

So it was hide-and-seek, and I was pressed up under a juniper bush. Low to the ground, trying to blend in, with my brown hair, brown skin, and brown sack dress. And it would have been early evening because Godfather led a prayer meeting at church then, and if he were home he would have found some excuse to get me away from the other children. And it couldn't have been too close to suppertime or I would have known to be up on the front porch waiting for him to come in and ask me what I wanted him to cook for us that night.

So the game first began in the early evening. In the summer. And near the Louisiana delta that means the air is cream and the lingering heat from the sun throbs just under the rich soil. And I felt the warm earth against my warm flesh, pressed so hard into the ground I could hear my heart beating in my ears—beating in time with that last throbbing warmth of the sun in the packed dirt under my stomach and thighs. And then the vibrations of Billy Boy stumbling and crashing through the low bushes as he came closer. So close: the vibrations: the pounding of my heart: the quickness of my hot breath against my arm. And underneath it all —through it all—just a tremor. A slight tremor of the earth moving. And his hulking figure coming through the twilight. Man-size feet carrying that infant's brain. But the tremors stop as he stands still in the clearing to begin searching for us. And the loss of that sensation hits me in the middle, a dull, aching pain. It makes me sit up, flushed, my arms wrapped around my waist—Here, Billy—and his face is all smiles: he's found someone. But I have to be quick: *Stomp, Billy, stomp.* His smile disappears. Blankness. Confusion. *Yes, stomp.* He's so eager to please—Yes, a new game. And he raises his knee high and pounds that man-size foot into the ground, to be followed by the other. First one—then the other. One—then the other. And I hurl myself back on my stomach to press as tight as I can into the earth and the tremors, the tremors on my arms, legs, thighs. I part my thighs ever so slightly and arch my pelvis hard into the soil—there, yes, now I can feel it even down there. So close to the earth—the tremors. *Stomp, Billy.*

A new game that none of the children but us wanted to play. On the edge of the cotton fields. In the crepe myrtle groves. In blind Miss Lemon's backyard. *Stomp, Billy.* And after my breasts began to round out the top of the brown sack dresses, the tremors would scrape the coarse cloth against my small, aching nipples, against the tight throbbing between my spread legs. The earth showed me what my body was for. Sometimes I'd break my fingernails from clawing them into the dirt or bite my arm to keep from crying out. And Billy Boy stomping up dust as I humped myself into the ground—him sweating and baying at the clouds.

It grew to be an old game that even Billy Boy tired of unless I bribed him with a shiny penny or a piece of biscuit and jam. I sought him out and sought out the earth whenever I needed release from the tight silence in my home, tightening to the point of danger the closer I grew toward womanhood. Or when the spring brought a looseness and a new blooming that were equally threatening. And I began to choose more dangerous places, places that made being touched that way all the sweeter: the paved road leading to the cotton exchange, the patch of oaks within sound of the hymns drifting out of the church during evening prayer. Never too close, but never too far away either. In the evening my brown hair, brown skin, and brown sack dresses blended into the dirt. So it was only Billy Boy for them to see, silhouetted against the setting sun; Billy Boy marching round and round in circles, Adam's apple straining, head thrown back to the sky. Not a soul would give it much thought, even later when he'd get so worked up he had to call out my name. In his garbled throat it was—Eeee . . . A crazy man-boy smelling like a goat, kicking up dust, and howling in the twilight.

I started inching my dress up. First just above the calf, wanting nothing between my skin and the vibrations. And by the time Godfather caught us it was only above the knee, the bare beginning of my thighs one with the earth. Billy Boy was pounding up and down the packed walkway; he had learned by then to step over my spread legs. And it was the sweetest of all the times; perhaps, because with memory, it was the last. And I wanted to scream as my fingers dug into the mint grass, pulling it up by the roots. Fragrant roots that I buried my nose into. My throat almost too choked to urge him on—*Stomp, Billy, stomp*. And that's all there was for Godfather to see: Billy Boy parading up and down his back walkway. Me spread-eagled on my stomach with mint grass stuffed to my nose. But as he stood there immobile at the back fence, the evening air bringing him the smell of the earth and the smell of me—it was all he needed. He knew. And he began to laugh.

He said I was going to leave him the same way he'd found me, naked and hungry. And he wasn't one of those preacher men who deal in flowery language—he meant just what he said. The first chores I ever did around that house were to haul the wood and build the yard fire where he burned every one of those brown sack dresses he'd sewn for me. And then he made me strip off the one I was wearing—and he burned that, too, along with the cotton underpants and cotton wraps I used to bind down my breasts. Those underpants would have been ruined anyway, because then he purged me with jars of warm water and Epsom salts. To remove, he said, every ounce of food his hard work had put into my stomach.

———

I had sometimes wondered, you know when children want to scare themselves, what his laughter would have sounded like if his anger was ever totally unleashed? If those shrill bursts of air would just have gotten higher and higher until the world crumbled apart? And I would imagine the windowpanes shattering and the roof caving in—all of Pilottown crumbling piece by piece into the dust if I really, *really* went into his parlor and smeared molasses on the pages of his Bible. But the imagination is no match for reality. I found out how such laughter would be that evening with the embers in the fire burning down and me kneeling in a pool of vomit and shit as his food emptied out of me, because his laughter keened high over my heaving body, spinning and diving, circling the clouds—a flock of wounded doves screaming.

I left from east of the delta to follow the riverbed north. Buck naked and so ashamed to steal, I made the one theft forced on me serve two purposes. A huge sack of King Biscuit flour. I used a sharp stick to tear out a neck hole and two armholes in the burlap, and I mixed the handful of flour left in the bottom into a paste to still my diarrhea. And yet thinking of what he put me through that night before he threw me out, it all pales in light of my journey from Pilottown to Arabi. First Venice. Boothville. Olga. Cajun country. A long walk in a dry winter through the meanest part of Louisiana. The Cajuns were poorer than we were. And when you're talking about white folks who are poorer than colored folks in the *best* of times, and this was one of the worst—you can just imagine.

Finding work was out of the question among people who were desperately seeking it themselves. And those who were of a mind to share what little they had, found it was just too little to go around. And I could feel the sharp resentment for my need bringing that home to them. And those who weren't of a mind were glad for the chance to give me what they had been given—the backside of the world to kiss. Triumph. Empire.

Bayou country. Only dry mud in those swamps, cracked and oozing like the soles of my feet. The alligators too tired to bother with me. Water moccasins curled up and dying. And the dust, the dust. Homeplace. Happy Jack. Diamond. A layer of dust; I kept walking. To keep myself from harm, I stopped looking hungry and tired when I passed within sight of trappers and hunters. That only left crazy, and even the most mean-spirited will leave crazy people alone. I learned to eat what the muskrats ate—hope. And I blessed Godfather every step of the way. If he had raised me with tenderness, I wouldn't have found the strength to do this.

The delta dust exists to be wet. And the delta dust exists to grow things, anything, in soil so fertile its tomatoes, beans, and cotton are obscene in their richness. And since that was one of the driest winters in living memory, the dust sought out what wetness it could and clung to the tiny drops of perspiration in my pores. It used that thin film of moisture to creep its way up toward the saliva in my mouth, the mucus in my nose. Mud forming and caking around the tear ducts in my eyes, gluing my lashes together. There was even enough moisture deep within my earwax to draw it; my head becoming stuffed up and all sounds a deep hum. It found the hidden dampness under my fingernails, between my toes. The moist space between my hips was easy, but then even into the crevices around the anus, drawing itself up into the slick walls of my intestines. Up my thighs and deep into my vagina, so much mud that it finally stilled my menstrual blood. Layers and layers of it were forming, forming, doing what it existed to do, growing the only thing it could find in one of the driest winters in living memory. Godfather always said that he made me, but I was born of the delta.

And when I finally reached Arabi, dead lice and gnats in my matted hair, the flour sack a filthy remnant of strings and twigs, nettles buried into the caked mud on my ankles, I sank to my knees to think. Ten miles outside of New Orleans. By then I'd lived a hundred years ten times over, so there was a lot to think about. I'd paid for this ordeal with a loss of good eyesight and a loss of my sense of humor. I considered neither of those fatal; I'd already clearly seen enough of the world to know there was little I needed to laugh about. And the only road that lay open to me was the one ahead, and the only way I could walk it was the way I was. I had no choice but to walk into New Orleans neither male nor female—mud. But I could right then and there choose what I was going to be when I walked back out.

The year was 1913 and I carried into New Orleans poor eyesight, no sense of humor, and a body of mud. I was ready to leave ten years later with three steamer trunks of imported silk suits, not one of them brown; fifty-seven thousand, six hundred and forty-one dollars, not one of them earned on my back; and a love of well-kept gardens. To some people what I accomplished in that place equals my trek along the delta. I'll tell you right now, New Orleans was child's play. But it was my first real city and there I learned about any city in the world. I wanted out because I was bored. If I could get through all I'd gotten through, then I was overqualified to be the mayor of New Orleans. And much too overqualified to be the governor of Louisiana. And when I kept thinking on up the line, the comparisons were beneath contempt.

And thinking on up the line was to come to the end of the line about what I could do with my potential. It seemed there was nowhere on earth for a woman like me. That's how I ended up here, taking over this brownstone and starting my garden. And over the last twenty-five years the only drawback has been that, sometimes, in this business you could use a sense of humor.

Even the stone wall blooms around Eve's garden. And there's never a single season without flowers. The spring aubrietas and Russian mustard planted between the stones give way to summer pinks that kinda scent the air with clove before the autumn joys take over along with alpine poppies and columbines. It's Nadine who knows all their names, and she clued me in to something else about that wall: They're all wildflowers, she said.

And then there are the flowers around the border of the yard itself that Eve keeps blooming in cold weather: camellias, coltsfoot, winter jasmine, pearly everlasting.

She's got some kind of plan to all of this. As you move in toward the center of that yard, where that large tree stump sits, spring, summer, or fall you're gonna find circles and circles of lilies. Day lilies. Tiger lilies. Madonna lilies. Canna lilies. Calla lilies. Lilies of the valley. They grow in low clusters and on stalks; they vine up the stump of her only tree. Swamp lilies. Peruvians. Casa Blancas. Enchantments. Pink. White. Yellow. Brown. Striped. Lilies-of-the-Nile. Stars of Bethlehem. Nerines. And none of them have a price. But all of her other flowers are for sale.

—*Everything* in that place is for sale.
—When you have a house full of single women there are gonna be gentleman callers.
—Gentleman callers? Lord Jesus.
—And I was taught a gentleman buys a lady flowers.
—Ladies? Lord . . .

The way I see it, her flowers are like my food. She begs no man to buy them. But if they're coming there—and they're only coming because there's a particular woman they want to visit—they either fall into the routine or not. If they don't like the house rules, they can stay away. But she passes no judgment on the behavior of those women once she lets them live there, and she passes no judgment on their visitors.

But Eve insists that her boarders only entertain men who are willing to bring them flowers. If he can't do that much for you, he doesn't need to waste your time. And if he shows up empty-handed, she has her own cut and waiting. I guess those fellas think it's cheaper to buy them from Eve than some other florist. The women living at her place have specific tastes. I know because I've never had them in here except as weekend customers, when they can get exactly what they want to eat. The meals they've requested over the last few years have read like a map of the world, especially the United States: everything from Cincinnati chili to western omelets to New England fish chowder. The only one living there now who's never eaten in here is Esther. And God knows where that gal came from.

SWEET ESTHER

It's the height of summer and I can still get a chill when I think of the first—and only—time I laid eyes on Esther. The dead of winter. I was doing the midnight shift by myself when I looked up and she was over by the door, hiding in the shadows. Scared me out of a year's growth. A little thing like her. That corner of the room was turned into a block of ice. It was hard to believe that someone's hate could change the air that way. The shadow spoke one word: Eve. But there was no way to give her the directions she needed; I knew that once I opened my mouth—to say anything—she was going to leap out at me like some poisonous spider. You see, I was a man. And I was a man who dared to stand in the full light. Nadine had told me she had a feeling she should take the midnight shift to give me a rest. And one day, Lord, one day, I'll listen to my wife.

A flimsy latch and a cold draft saved me from having to fight off Esther. A blast of winter air banged the door open and it brought the scent of the Christmas roses growing in Eve's backyard. She slipped out of the door and followed the fragrance home.

———

This time of year it's impossible to find Christmas roses, except at Eve's. She forces them to bloom in any season for Esther's gentleman callers. And there is a certain breed of man who does go there to see her. Who looks forward to what's waiting for him down in that dark basement. Like they say, it takes all types to make the world. But sometimes you wish it didn't.

⇒

I like the white roses because they show up in the dark.
I don't.
The black gal. Monkey face. Tar. Coal. Ugly. Soot. Unspeakable. Pitch. Coal. Ugly. Soot. Unspeakable.

We won't speak about this, Esther.

I don't. I am twelve years old and glad that it is dark. He cannot see my face when he calls me to come down into the cellar. I always come when he calls. This is your husband, my brother said. Do whatever he tells you, and you won't be sent away like the others. Can you be married without a gown? Without the beautiful white flowers and the veil that sweeps the floor of the church? Without love? Even at twelve years old I doubt, but I believe in my older brother. He is kind to me and calls me only *little sister*. And there is much more food here than at home. My brother has the fat wife and eight children to feed. My new husband has four hundred acres and six men, along with my brother, to help him plow. There are jars and jars of pickled beets, string beans, cabbage, molasses, and whole plums in the cellar. Thick burlap bags of flour, potatoes, and cornmeal that tower high over my head where I kneel after he calls me. All prepared by the bitch, he whispers.

———

I do not want to be like her. I do not want to be sent away. So I will not tell anyone what happens in the cellar. The whispers: spiders scratch and spin in the dark. The bitch lies about him all over the county. To the minister. To the sheriff. To his own field hands. The bitch wasn't woman enough to have his children and so she lies about him out of spite. For revenge. Lies that he is not a man. Lies that he wanted more than was his due when he called her. I do not want to be sent away. So I come down when he calls. And rejoice that it is dark.

We won't speak about this, Esther.

My new house is very pretty. And so big. A room just to eat in, with nothing but a long table and a cabinet filled with shiny glasses and plates. And a whole bedroom just to myself. The first night I am afraid of being in such a room alone. But the mattress is so deep and soft. Goose feathers. I can pretend I am a princess. Only princesses would have a bed like this. Deep pink and trimmed with lace. The black gals. The monkey faces. They can only sleep on the old smelly mattress the fat wife throws away. Too smelly for her babies, she says. I am so glad he does not look at me, or he would not give me a bed like this. The pitcher and basin would not be china with tiny pink roses; the mirror would not be that big. The mirror would not show my face. I lie there the first night and pray to God very hard that he will never look at me.

God answers my prayers.

It is the hag who comes to wake me the next morning. She pours warm water into the china basin and washes me with soap. It is a pink soap and it smells like flowers. I ask her why she is rubbing me with lard. Backwoods trash, she mumbles. This cream costs more to buy than your brother's miserable shack. I am frightened by the way her chin tightens and the long gray hairs on it quiver. I have never seen a woman with a beard. It is the hag who wakes me each morning to bathe and rub me with the cream. It is she who cooks the meals, cleans the house, and washes our clothes.

I work with her. She teaches me. An angry, silent old woman. But she does look at me. If only to tell me I am clumsy and stupid. To warn me that she will take the price of a broken dish out of my ugly black hide. At night when my husband is home from the fields, his eyes avoid mine. He looks into his plate or he looks at the hag. He talks to her about his day. He asks the hag how quickly I am learning. When I will be ready. Soon, she says. And soon she leaves. That is when he begins to call me into the cellar.

We won't speak about this, Esther.

He says they are toys. I have never had toys. At my brother's, I made my dolls from pieces of rags and loose straw from the floor of the chicken coop. But I have seen toys in the Christmas book they send from Montgomery Ward and they are also in a big wooden chest like this. Your toys, he whispers. No doll clothes. No roller skates. No pogo sticks. No rocking horses. Play with your toys, he whispers as the spiders scratch and spin, scratch and spin their webs in the dark. My hands reach into the wooden chest and feel the shapes of the leather-and-metal things. No jumping ropes. No rubber balls. The edges of the metal things are small and sharp. The leather things coil around my fingers like snakes. They are greasy and smell funny. No, they are not toys. I do not know what they are, but I will soon learn what they are for. And I will learn that in the dark, words have a different meaning. Having fun. Playing games. Being a good girl.

I try and try to find a word for what happens between us in the cellar. The fat wife used to say, Every time he puts his hands on me I come up with a big belly. But my husband touches me and there are no babies.

Is there another kind of touch? Should he touch me when I am in bed and not kneeling in the cellar? Would that bring me the babies? I have no one to ask. I am ashamed of my ignorance. I am allowed no friends. And the only woman to visit is the hag. She comes every month or so, and these are the times they will sit up all night and get drunk together. I know by now to stay out of their way. The radio is my only company. He has a beautiful radio: it is large and made of mahogany with shiny brass dials. The songs speak of kisses. For hours I imagine what it is to have a man kiss me. The songs speak of making love. I cannot imagine what that is and I grow irritated by the songs. The music causes me to ache in a way I cannot understand.

I turn the dials until I reach The Shadow. It becomes my favorite program. It becomes more. It becomes my friend because it finally gives me the words I have been seeking. What we do in the cellar is to make evil. I still come when he calls. But now I know that his touching will not bring babies. And as I kneel before him, I dream that the Shadow will come to stop this evil. I listen closely behind the whispers and the spiders as they scratch and spin. I listen for the Shadow's footsteps. For his laugh. I dream that the Shadow will take the toys and do to my husband what he does to me. I dream this for many years. And then I grow up. I still believe there is a Shadow. But I also come to believe that he enjoys to stand there and watch.

We won't speak about this, Esther.

I stay with this man for twelve years because I am a good sister. My older brother gets higher wages with each passing year. I stay even though I come to understand that I am not married. This is not what married people do. My older brother gets peace at home when he buys the fat wife a Bendix washing machine. I stay one year for each year my older brother took care of me against the shrill protests of the fat wife. And each time I am called into the cellar to kneel among the sacks of potatoes and flour, I count the days left to repay my debt. I count the many ways in which you can hate a man. My brother knew. My brother knew.

I thought about killing this man when I was within hours of becoming the next lying bitch to leave. I thought about sparing the other young girls waiting in line to sleep alone in his pink-and-lace bed. The other twelve-year-olds with brothers. But my guess turned out to be right. There are too many of them to kill. And there are just too many twelve-year-olds.

We won't speak about this, Esther.

To this day, I don't. The only person I ever told is Eve. And that is because she already knew. The first thing she offered me was this basement room. And she removed the light bulbs herself. What they'll need from you, they'll need in the dark if they know it or not, she said. Even that type could not bring themselves to return if they saw your eyes. You have the most honest face of any woman I know, sweet Esther.

So they don't see my face. And I never see theirs. But I do like the way the white roses show up in the dark. I can see them clearly, very clearly, as they wither and die. I rarely leave this basement. And I only open the shutters when it is time to clean. I won't let Miss Maple down here. He insists he needs bright light to do the job properly, but he's still a man after all. No, men must only visit in the dark. And they must bring me the white roses. And they must call me *little sister*. Or I no longer come.

MARY (TAKE ONE)

He's come in here looking for his daughter. But no one knows her by that name. His overalls splattered with dried cement, the lace on one of his work boots loose and dragging along the floor. He goes from table to table, asking each man about his daughter. He walks a hundred miles between each table, his knees sagging, his back hunched from the strain. If he comes over here to the counter, I'll tell him that no one knows her by that name.

He's making a mistake with the way he tries to describe her: tall and pretty, fair-skinned. His daughter is more than pretty. She's one of those women you see and don't believe. The kind that live just outside the limits of your imagination. And I'm hardly one of those fellas who go around thinking that light is right. My whole philosophy's been, The blacker the berry, the sweeter the juice; but this gal is from Wonderland.

When Sugar Man first saw her, he just about lost his mind. She swung in here on those high high heels, dropped her suitcase by the counter, wrapped those long, perfect legs around the end stool, and crossed those perfect arms in front of her. A cocoa-butter dream. Curves went into curves went into curves. It was a weekday and so I hoped she was willing to eat the one thing on the menu, cause if she'd wanted something else—and you give a woman like that whatever she wants—I would have had to break a house rule to serve her. And that woulda meant I'd have to do it over Nadine's dead body. And since I love my wife, I was praying hard that my new customer wouldn't make me kill her. It turned out she only wanted coffee. Two sugars. No cream.

—You rang? said Sugar Man, sliding his tiny little self onto the next stool. If that suitcase means you need a place to stay, baby, I've got one that's just the ticket. We can run right over there. And don't listen to my mama; I was putting her in the old-age home anyway. And if you don't like that apartment, I'll *build* you another. As a matter of fact, I'll build you two so you can have a spare.

She rewarded him with a smile. Soft red lips to melt in your mouth. A deep dimple. She ran her fingers up the side of her face to push a curl back under her veil. One of those peekaboo veils that draped from the brim of her hat, leaving you just a hint of one brown eye. Bedroom eyes. Warm and sleepy.

Sugar Man was crushed when he found out she was looking for Eve's. A woman like this could make him a small fortune. He tried to talk her out of it. The place was full of crazies. And she was much too good— excuse his language—for a cathouse. She said she'd heard it was only a boardinghouse. He said she'd heard lies. Then she asked me what *I* had heard. I said that the garden was awfully nice. And I was about to lean over the counter to elaborate when Nadine yelled out that my chops were in trouble. I hurried back to pull them out from the broiler, but Sugar Man kept on insisting that whatever Eve's was, she wasn't the type to live there. And she told him in that sweet sweet voice that he really knew nothing about her. That's true, he admitted, but he was willing to take the many hours necessary to learn. They could start right now with a little spin around the block. Did she notice his Duesenberg parked in front? The fifteen-thousand-dollar Duesenberg? It's hard to miss it, she said. Well, they could jump right in and run by his place to pick up his *good* car.

Sugar Man sure has a way with women but this one wasn't buying. She slid off the stool and picked up her suitcase. It's no secret I'm a rear-end man, and watching her walk toward the door told me why. It's a sin for a woman's body to do that to cloth. Not that I can remember exactly what she was wearing. As the door closed behind her, Sugar Man shook his head and had the courage to whisper what every man in here was thinking: Born to be fucked.

And so when he came in here looking for his daughter, begging any man to help him, close to tears—no one knew her by that name. He tells them he's been up and down the streets of Kansas City. He tells them he's run ads in the papers for months. He tells them that no matter what she's done, he loves his baby and just wants her home. His daughter's tall and pretty, fair-skinned. But his daughter is more than pretty. And his daughter lives at Eve's now, where no man calls her by that name.

It was Daddy Jim who started calling me Peaches. Plump and sweet. Yellow and sweet. Daddy's baby. Daddy's beautiful baby.
—Pride before the fall, Mama warns.
His seventh child. The one daughter. The last is a father's gold. Yellow gold in this baby gal, in my Peaches; he'd roll my cheeks between his fingers until they blushed.
—Color-struck: Mama shakes her head.
He dressed me in sky blue. Made a cotton sling to hang on his chest and took me everywhere. My brothers told me this. I don't remember.

———————

I remember large, dark hands, the knuckles ashy and cracked. Bits of granite and dust under the broken fingernails. A bricklayer's hands. I remember the wall he started building around the house when I was nine years old. And I remember that it was already too late.

But in my teens the wall did keep the boys out. Most of them weren't brave enough to ring the iron bell on the locked gate. And the few who were, their knees gave out waiting for him to take his dear sweet time getting up from the porch swing and reaching inside the screen door to prop his shotgun in full view before coming down the walk to ask them what they wanted. And of the few who made it through all that, fewer still could choke up the breath to whisper that they wanted to see Peaches.

—*Who?* he'd ask as if they were speaking Chinese.

—I want to see Peaches, sir.

He'd wait forever, Daddy Jim, letting them fidget and sweat, pull at their starched neck collars, jam their shaking hands into the pockets of their knickers and out again, into the pockets and out again. And after he had them right at the breaking point, he fired off the last question sharp and loud:

—*Why?*

They'd turn tail and run like crazy. Cause he was really saying, I already know why you want to see my daughter, and you know I know why, so let's see if you got the guts to tell me? And I'd watch the cowards from my bedroom window, laughing. Daddy Jim was something else.

—One dog knows another, Mama says.

But he shouldn't have worried about the boys. He should have worried about the mirrors.

I had a bedroom full of them: one attached to the large oak dresser; two in the doors of the wardrobe; a cheval that Daddy Jim imported from

Belgium; a heavy silver hand mirror that was part of a matching dressing set, the silver brush and comb all with the same engravings of morning glories and vines; the mirror inside my notions box, where the tiny ballerina danced when you opened the velvet lid; the mirrors packed away in drawers from Christmas, Valentine's, all my birthdays—rose tinted one year, petal shaped the next. Everywhere I turned, I could see her. But what was she doing in my room? She was a whore and I was Daddy's baby.

Every mirror outside had told me what she was: the brown mirrors, hazel mirrors, blue mirrors, oval, round, and lashed mirrors of all their eyes when they looked at me. Old eyes, young eyes, it didn't make any difference if the mirrors belonged to men: I saw her standing there unclothed with the whispered talk among my brothers, their smudged laughter about the sofa down the block on which they were always welcome. But there was a difference when it came to the women: the young and unmarried reflected her with an envy so intense it bordered on hate; those older and married, with a helpless fear. Yes, they all looked at me and knew, just knew, what she was. You have to believe what you see in the mirror, don't you? Isn't that what mirrors are for?

Before I was nine years old, my father's friends would sit her on their knees, touch the soft curls on her head, raise her dimpled arms. The gal has promise, Jim. And he would nod, proud. So proud. And upstairs in my mirrors I would try to see what she had promised that would cause the heat to seep up through the rough denim of their pant legs and melt the corners of their mouths.

—What have you promised them? I whispered to her.

—You. You. You.

I smashed the swan-shaped mirror, my tenth-birthday present, after the choirmaster put his hand under my blouse. I smashed it with the metal edge of my roller skate because I could see her small brown nipples tightening as I remembered how it felt to be pressed into the dark corner of the high altar, to have his soft hands squeezing and stroking, his breath warm against the top of my head.

—What have you promised them?

—You. You. You.

I didn't have the words to explain about my fear of her, so Daddy Jim spanked me for breaking that mirror. He had sent all the way to San Francisco for it. I never broke another.

In horror I watched her grow up, and I learned to hate her for breaking my father's heart. Nothing satisfied her, nothing. And I tried everything to make her go away. I brought in straight A's at the academy. I worked part-time at the druggist's. I joined the Girl Guides. I joined the Missionary Circle. I rolled bandages for the resistance in Spain. I sang for the glee club. Sang for the war relief—sang in the church choir. But she was always there, reflected in the wetness of men's eyes. Tormenting me. I wore high-necked shirtwaists and loose skirts, thick woolen tights, even in the summertime, that scratched and left welts on my legs. But I could feel their eyes stripping my clothes away: they knew her promise was there. You. You. No, not me—I wasn't like that. No, never me. So I gave them *her*. Sweet, sweet relief. Their eyes would cloud over, the pupils tiny pinpoints that finally reflected nothing—not her and least of all me—as they groaned and sucked and plunged and sweated. Free, at last, *I* was free as I gave them her. In the cloak closets after school, behind the prayer altar, under the druggist's soda fountain, against the coal furnace in the Girls' Club, in the backs of milk wagons, in deserted streetcars, shadowed doorways. Any teacher. Any janitor. Any deacon. Any porter. Any storekeeper. Any race, any age, any size—any son of any man— had the power to drive away that demon from the mirror. Over and over, they became my saviors from *her*.

Why, baby, why? And I tried to tell Daddy Jim why I followed them everywhere in Kansas City. Did whatever they wanted. He'd find out about some man and go raging out, wanting to fight. But it was not *that* man; I didn't care two cents about—and hardly ever knew the name of—that man. Any son of any man was my savior. Don't lock me in my room, not there, I pleaded; I'll have to find a way to get out again. I tried to stop him from wasting his money on doctors. I tried to stop him from hurting himself by beating me with razor straps, leather shoes, his fists. I tried to stop him from crying. I didn't want to leave home, but I had little choice. I couldn't stand to see my father that way.

—God's judgment on him, Mama says.

Although it was hard for me to keep a job for very long, I never thought about going back home. There weren't many shops willing to hire colored girls, even those from the academy, even those with fair skin. Of the few that did, I had my pick among them and I worked hard. But word spread quickly among the shopkeepers' wives and I was out. If they'd only known, their marriages were safer with me there, doing what I did, than with most of the other girls. Those other shop girls were always scheming to find husbands—their own or someone else's—to take them off their feet. And *a* man in my life was the last thing I needed. From the shops to the factories to picking up bits of day work cleaning house, the story was the same. I was always scraping to pay my room rent. Going with only oatmeal, peanut butter, and soda crackers for weeks at a time. The same woolen wrapper, season after season. And, I guess, I just got fed up with trying to live decently. So the lies began and they were the first step down.

It was a part of town that Daddy Jim would have whipped me blue for even talking about. Twelfth and Highland. Eighteenth and Vine. A part of town that swung. Fast music. Fast women. Those clubs really weren't as bad as I'd grown up hearing: no liquor and opium flowing out into the streets. As a matter of fact, they looked sort of shabby and sad, especially in the daytime. But I could find work when they came alive at night: each manager said he couldn't hide someone like me back in the kitchen. Did I know how to mix drinks? No. Did I know how to dance? No. Did I know how to sing? Yes, I could sing, but not the music they were playing. He'd take another look at me and say he could teach me. So my first lie to each of them was that I wanted to learn.

Some of these men took care of me longer than others. It depended upon how long it took each of them to discover my second lie: that he was the only one that mattered. None of them mattered. The fights would be awful, but the fights were the price I paid to keep a decent flat and warm clothes in the winter. The price for the low life I was living. Sick: I got called that a lot when they found out. A sick bitch. But I already knew that. I had to be sick, because over time, very slowly over time, I was forced to admit that I actually enjoyed being held and touched by some of the men I lived with. I was even starting to look forward to their coming to bed. There are no words to describe how ugly that realization was. I knew *she* was a whore. Had always been a whore. Was probably born a whore. For as long as I could remember, I could see her in their eyes. But now as I looked in the mirror—thinking of how my own body had betrayed me with him—I could see her in mine.

Before, I had only hated her. Now I wanted to hate myself. And I started thinking that I should always have hated myself, I was probably always enjoying those back rooms and back stairs. I was probably always tempting the choirmaster. I was probably always making men in the streets look at me that way, my father's friends look at me that way. I was probably always asking for it, asking for it. I was probably always dirt. Yes, I was sick. Sicker than the angry man in front of me knew. Last night I warmed inside when he caressed my neck and touched me.

But it took a long time to hate myself as deeply as I wanted to hate. It took a long time and a lot of work. Many more lies and another step down. I moved from the men who only took care of me to the men whom I stayed with long enough until they made the mistake of caring about me. I didn't feel bad having to pretend that way. After all, they were lying too, weren't they? There was nothing good to see in me. They were lying about my poetry books, about my singing hymns in the tub, about my laugh and the dimples in my cheeks, about the way I tossed my head. And sure, we had a good time in bed together, I *loved* us being in bed together, but then I was a whore. And it was their own fault when they got hurt.

I would have stopped myself for one or two of them, if only I'd known how. The one or two who I almost believed really cared, with whom I would think that if, indeed, I had been born into a world without mirrors, there might have been a chance for a real home. But it was so mixed up by then. Sometimes I was out there because I was getting too comfortable and it was time to get back at them for lying and move on, sometimes to punish myself for being the piece of filth I was, and sometimes, sometimes . . . When it was dark and secluded enough at our chance meeting; and there was little talk, no questions, so no lies; and he under-stood not to offer me money; and he understood it must be right there, it must be quick, it must be now—sometimes, those times, were the purest joy I had ever known.

Besides the one or two, I certainly would have stopped for the cripple if I could have. The man worshiped me. I should have guessed that feelings like his were dangerous, and perhaps I did, hoping that he would kill me and save me the trouble. He carried a pearl-handled straight razor; he needed it, being a gambler and as small as he was. His build was delicate like Sugar Man's, but the large sums of money he spent on his clothes didn't make him look cheap. That straight razor was the first thing I noticed about him when he came into Piney Brown's. No, that's not quite true, the first thing I noticed was his clubfoot—it's what everyone noticed—but the first thing he showed me was the pearl-handled razor. His way of saying hello. He stroked it like a baby as he asked me if there was room at my table. Any regular at Piney Brown's knew there was always room at my table. And they also knew that I didn't drink or smoke. So his second and third questions told me right away he was a stranger in town. But it was the fourth question that put him into my life: Before we even get started, tell me your real name.

I was to hear it whispered as he dressed me for bed each night. Mary. Always a fresh nightgown. Always white. He started with my bobby pins, removing each one so gently I didn't lose a strand of hair. His small fingers were the comb, his cupped palm the brush, as the loosened curls fell to my shoulders. With each button of my blouse: Mary. He'd raise my right arm and slip it out of that sleeve, bring the blouse around my back, then raise the left arm and slip it out of that one. My skirt was slid down into a pool of bright cotton at my ankles. The hem of the nylon slip was guided up and peeled off over my head. The metal hooks in my brassiere, one by one: Mary. The elastic band of my panties sliding down my waist and over my hips. He'd sit me on the bed before unfastening the garters. My nylons were next. The extended right leg, then the left leg, supported between his armpits as he knelt before me, the nylons forming perfectly even rolls of brown mesh that came to rest at the tops of my shoes. He'd cradle those two feet in his hands, staring at the curves of the rolled nylons, fingering the leather straps of my high heels. I could feel his warm breath on the tops of my feet, the deep trembling. He waited an eternity before finally baring them. His fingers would slip under the rolled nylons, he'd grasp the curve of my instep and slowly stroke the nylons and shoes over the arch, slowly over the toes, his breath quickening, his hands moist as he circled and stroked the fine bones of my feet until stockings and shoes all spilled into his lap.

And he never called me anything but Mary. Never. Not even when Kansas City had to become Saint Louis, and Saint Louis had to become Chicago, and Chicago had to become South Bend, and South Bend—Cincinnati. He made the same mistake Daddy Jim had. One thought a wall would be the answer; another thought distance. Still he never called me anything but Mary. Never. But after he found out about the redcaps on the trains, he knew there was no point in traveling past Cincinnati. Yes, I guess, I should have expected what was coming. The apartment he put me in was too fine: a marble lobby with doormen and carpeted halls. The hours he worked were too long: all-night games into late-afternoon games until his hands shook so much he couldn't hold the cards. The clothes he made me shop for were too expensive; the furniture was too large for the rooms. Everything imported or not at all. Months and months, it went on like that. His working himself to exhaustion, his buying and buying and buying. He didn't question my absences. He didn't curse. He didn't plead. He just took out his straight razor one morning at breakfast, pressed it against my throat, and told me very quietly that the next man I was with, I would have to watch die. He would have done it, too, made me watch that man die. And the next. And the next.

For a solid week I never left the apartment. I didn't even trust myself to take packages from the doormen. I sat on the thick brocade divans. I clenched and unclenched my hands. I listened to the radio. I watched my new television. I paced the blue-and-gold Persian rugs. I read the leather-bound books in the mahogany cases. I sorted and re-sorted the silks, cashmeres, and angoras in my closets. Now realizing all of it had been put there to warn me that there was no place on earth to run. If I'd known a way to stop, I would have. Didn't he understand that? I opened and closed linen closets. Kitchen cabinets. The dumbwaiter.

His closet was as large as mine. All tailored suits and matching vests. Pinstripes. Worsteds. The cambric cotton shirts. The velvet boxes with jeweled cuff links and tiepins. But my eyes rested on the rows and rows of custom-made boots for his shriveled and twisted foot. Thousands of dollars' worth of boots: the calfskins almost uncountable, alligators, eel-skins, suedes: kept in immaculate condition. I had known him to throw out a new pair of Moroccan leathers because he couldn't remove a water spot on one of the toes. I looked at his boots and I looked at my feet. It was all I did for another solid week in that apartment. As soon as he'd leave, I'd open his closet to look at those boots and look at my feet. But at the end of that second week, when I took the beer opener from the pantry drawer and went to the bathroom mirror, it was to stare at my face.

The police thought he had done it. But since I refused to change my story, there was nothing they could do and they had to release him from jail. No one believed that a woman would do that to herself. No one believed that his grief wasn't guilt. But his grief over what he'd lost was very real. First, I took the tip of the beer opener, smiled into the mirror, and traced the path I was going to take: under the right cheekbone— yes, it must be the right—then a straight diagonal across the dimple, all the way over to the left side of the chin. A thin red line was left on my skin for me to follow, so I didn't need to smile again as I grasped the opener in both hands and dug down. But I wasn't prepared for the first bolt of blinding pain; it took precious seconds to catch my breath. And now the opener hanging in my ripped cheek was too slippery to hold firmly because of the gushing blood. I made a poor job of it. I had to resort to sawing my way down, leaving hunks of flesh wedged between the two prongs of the opener. That took so much time that when I'd only reached the bottom jawbone, the pain was so intense I passed out. I awoke to him wailing my name and the ambulance wailing out in the street. And after the sirens had died down, my name kept echoing over and over. It was the only word that man could bring himself to say in my presence again.

I walked out of the hospital free to do whatever I wanted. And since he had started me on the railroads going east, I kept going east. It gave me pleasure to sit on the right side of the train aisle and to watch through the window's reflection as one of them moved hopefully toward the empty seat beside me. I'd show my good left dimple when he asked if the seat was free.

—Yes, I'd answer, and so am I.

He'd almost break his kneecaps hurrying into that seat. So where are you going? I really didn't know where I was going. And hadn't a clue about what to do once I got there. Everything was so cloudy. So confused. But I spoke the truth each time as best I knew it: Wherever women like me go—and I'd turn my full face to him and raise my veil. Sometimes it was embarrassment. Sometimes it was disgust. And many many times, pity. But each time there was *the* question.

I collected a lot of business cards on those trains. Men who promised to give me the name of the right doctor. One was even a plastic surgeon himself. And I'd expect nothing in return, child, he said, absolutely nothing. But how to tell this nice old man I didn't want to fix my face? I'd probably have to end up doing it all over again.

When those railroad tracks ran out of land going east, I changed trains and went south, changed again and went west, then north. I was circling back toward the east again and realized I'd come to the end of the line. That's when I heard of a place where women like me could go. Just get off at that next stop, I was told; you can find Bailey's Cafe in any town. They turned out to be right. And Eve never asked *the* question. Gently she removed my veil, and she lifted my chin in her hands to trace her thumb down along the path I had taken in front of the mirror. I saw only the scar reflected in her rimless glasses as she felt each jagged curve, each section of twisted flesh. And it was only the scar that was reflected in her eyes when she murmured, Beautiful.

It's Sugar Man who finally shows her father how to find his way down the street to Eve's. He's hoping to get a ruckus going just out of spite. Sugar Man can't really describe what goes on in that brownstone since he's never been inside, but that doesn't stop him from making up stories. He fills her father's head with the *hundreds* of men who go there to buy Peaches. She gets a lot of callers, but hardly hundreds. And the only thing they buy is daffodils. Of course, now, he leaves out that he's tried

from the first to put her on the streets. And even kept trying after he
found out about the scar. There's still a lot of mileage left below her
neck, he says.

He presses his case every time Peaches comes in here, but that isn't too
often. She seems to like staying close to the house. And with all the
callers she does get, Sugar Man's never been one of them. He wouldn't
give Eve the time of day, no less the fifty dollars she asks for the daffodils.

—And you ain't a pimp? he spat out.

—The girl chose the flowers, Eve said. And you try growing daffodils
in the fall.

Eve won't let Sugar Man and the father past the front door. Visible over
her shoulder are the eager men waiting to visit Peaches. They sit knee
to knee in the parlor. That side of the room blooms with bouquets of
the yellow flowers. The word didn't take long to spread. The hot one
who moved into the second-floor room takes on all callers. But there are
fewer men now than the week before, who were fewer than the week
before that.

—Leave your daughter here, Eve says, and I'll return her to you
whole.

The autumn wind is chill outside and the fragile heads of the daffodils
wilt easily in the heat of the parlor. And if they go upstairs with a bouquet
that's less than perfect, Eve's taught her to send them back down again.
Look in that mirror good, and accept no less than what you deserve. The
longer the line, the longer the wait; the later the season, the warmer the
house. And it's the same fifty dollars for a fresh bouquet.

—I don't know what she's doing up in that room, Eve says, and
to tell you the truth, I don't care.

———

She spends much more time with each gentleman caller than she spent the week before. And at the time curfew is called, there are still some waiting. But the next evening, if they want to come back, it's the same fifty dollars for a fresh bouquet. Fewer and fewer men, longer and longer waits.

—But whatever she's doing up in that room, she's doing it feeling beautiful.

Winter's coming soon and Peaches will still demand daffodils. More perfect and more perfect daffodils. They will be gotten at no florist for any price. And it will take a special man to give Eve what she'll ask for hers. A man special enough to understand what the woman upstairs is truly worth. The house will be even warmer, but soon he'll only have to buy a bouquet once. There'll be no one else waiting.

—Go home, my friend, Eve says, and I'll return your daughter to you whole.

The man standing in front of Eve is crying, and he keeps calling for Peaches to come down to him. There is no answer from the lighted room on the second floor. He calls louder and there is still no answer. Eve closes the door in his face. He hears the bolt slide shut as the autumn winds blow cold.

—Go home, my friend. I'll return your daughter to you whole.

JESSE BELL

One man's weed is another man's flower. I'd get pretty lonely here after midnight if it weren't for Jesse. The few customers who do straggle in are the type who want tables as far in the corners as possible, or they sit by the front window and stare out into the dark. They come at this hour for the express purpose of being left to themselves, and I oblige them. But this time of the year it's pretty much deserted and it'll stay that way until we move into the holiday season. Christmas Eve, we'll be packed in here, New Year's Eve too. Until then being open twenty-four hours means a long stretch between dinner and breakfast where I mostly do a little reading, rearrange the storeroom, or think about getting out my toolbox and fixing the coffee grinder. Nadine's been after me for months to take that machine apart. I figure she has to find something to nag about since I'm flawless in every other way. Each morning when she gets in I tell her just that, and what she tells me is pretty near unrepeatable. She'd better be careful; it's not too late in the season to trade her in for a newer model.

———

But I was thinking real hard about fixing it tonight when Jesse came in. I owe her five dollars for the bet we made about Truman. Bailey, ain't you learned by now, she says, not to believe anything you read in the papers? Yeah, I have, but a part of me didn't want Truman to win, and now I'm out of a five-spot unless I can get it back in gin rummy. Jesse has shortened many a night for me. We're both native New Yorkers and from the only two boroughs that matter; knowing her has gotten me to expand my horizons and admit that some good can come out of Manhattan. She's one of those Big Apple gals who won't bite their tongues about nothing. Like me, she calls 'em as she sees 'em, if it wins her friends or not. She'll come in here with a pocket full of nickels for the jukebox while I'll pull out her pint of Jack Daniel's I keep hid and pour us both a nip. Curfew starts midnight at Eve's: no more visitors or music, and her boarders can't have hard liquor at any time. A whorehouse convent, Jesse calls it. Right or wrong, Jesse can get you laughing, and she plays a mean hand of rummy.

—How'd you sneak out tonight, Jesse?
—Her faggot watchdog fell asleep.
—Come on, Miss Maple isn't a queer.
—Would you want him to marry your daughter?
—I don't have a daughter.
—Then adopt Maple; you'd get two for the price of one.

There's no love lost between Jesse and Miss Maple. He's been in here complaining about her at times himself. She won't let him change the linens and her room is a mess to clean because she litters the carpet with crushed dandelions. The men who try to visit her get their flowers smashed right in their faces at the door.

—They're only coming to see me because of those lies in the paper, she says.
The King scandal was pretty big, but it was a long time ago too. I try

116

to tell her that maybe some of them just want to keep her company. Shoot the breeze, like us; play a few hands of cards.

—Not in a pussy palace, she says.

But since she lives there and she's not doing nothing but giving out a good dose of verbal and physical abuse to her gentlemen callers, maybe the others aren't doing anything either.

—Bailey, you ain't talking to Shirley Temple, so just deal me my hand. My room is right next to Peaches's, okay?

—Well, Peaches is a special case.

—And then every sleazeball pervert within fifty miles is tripping down to that basement.

—Esther is kind of a special case.

—Mother, what does Eve do? Pay you a commission?

—I wouldn't make much on your flowers, Jesse.

Her laughter is good-natured and comes from deep down. The nice thing about Jesse is that she can take it as well as dish it out. She told Eve she wanted dandelions, and I'm sure Jesse did it to be annoying. Those are the kind of plants Eve usually pulls up as weeds. But then as Eve has often said, Jesse is a special case.

I've gotta find out if the funny farm gives cash rewards. Cause one telephone call to clear out this place would set me up for life. Sometimes to amuse myself I try to figure out who would be worth the most to them: I admit I'd bring in a few dollars turning my own self in, but it's chicken change beside what I could get for Esther down in that basement hiding in closets. The nympho next door to me. Or this faggot with his slip hanging, who's about to make me slap him silly if he don't quit putting starch in my sheets. Starching and ironing the sheets in a whorehouse. Who ever . . . ? I don't care what Eve says, this is a whore-house, and her pruning all the zinnias in the world won't change that.

Oh, Mother, now that's a cold one. I know I owe her, but I don't thank her. And she told me that, too, after I left the House of D. and she got that monkey off my back. Told me there'd be nothing to thank her for when it was all over. Bad as it was, the way she did it, I'll never forget the way she looked the whole time I was retching my guts out. Like it wasn't pain. Like it wasn't real. Like I was a kid or something, complaining about a scratch on my knee. A icy icy mama. The only woman I've met who would be a match for Uncle Eli. Lord knows, I wasn't. And I am quite a woman. Was a woman before I was a girl. But that horrible old man, may he rot in hell, kept at it until he killed me. He was a mur-derer——a cold-blooded murderer.

A murderer is somebody who plots to take somebody's life, ain't they? Well, he took my husband and son. And they were all I lived for. Still not satisfied, he took away my good name. Hope the devil is kicking his ass right now——from east hell to west hell and back again. Him and that whole clan——upstanding Negroes, teachers, office clerks, doctors—— educated folk. Got it so when they mention my name up on Sugar Hill, noses flare out like they smelling something decayed. Oh, yeah, Jesse Bell. The tramp from the docks. That slut who married into the King family. Child, didn't you read about what happened? She went straight to the dogs. I carried a good name. And I was a good wife. I mean, a good wife. But I didn't have no friends putting out the *Herald Tribune*. And it's all about who's in charge of keeping the records, ain't it?

Yeah, I'm from the docks. My people always made their living from the waters around Manhattan Island. And it was a honest living. I grew up around rough men who worked as hard as they cussed and drank. You know what it means to be a longshoreman in the wintertime? It means my uncles and brothers having the skin between their fingers split open

from the cold. Cause after a while it's safer to throw them gloves aside
—they freeze up on you just like the sweat freezes in your mustache
and eyebrows, and if that guide hook in your hands slips, you and the
other men got two tons of scrap iron swinging like a yo-yo coming out
of the hold of that ship. Had a cousin crippled for life that way. Musta
been ten below by the water that December. And the boss man called
for a speed-up, so they're unloading more than common sense allows to
begin with and working faster than anybody would call sane. A small
winch snaps, and that's all you need to get a load off balance and have
a crate of granite blocks coming toward your head. Well, he goes to
guide it away from his crew and that hook shoots through his frozen
gloves like squeezed butter. Edge of that crate snapped his arm clear off
from the shoulder. And they say winter is the best time. Cause in the
summer with everything else you gotta put up with the stink. Press your
nose to a rubber tire, or take a whiff of gasoline sometimes. Now, how
about a mountain of crude rubber or an ocean's worth of raw gasoline?
How about doing it ten hours a day? So your sweat stinks like oil? And
your bologna sandwiches taste like oil? And you welcome the breeze from
the dock tides cause it's bringing only rotting seaweed and dead fish.

And, sure, they knocked off a few stiff drinks after putting in time like
that. It took the taste of the docks out of their mouths and let them
cuss the boss man, so they could go back the next day and do it all over.
Glad for the work a lot of people weren't getting and glad that they were
working like men. Taking it like men. If my people coulda done something
else, I don't think they would have. Nobody messed with colored long-
shoremen. Not even the meanest Irish cop would press them but so far
when he got called into one of their joints to break up a fight. If they
were real real drunk, and there was a whole lotta blood, the cop might
get away with calling them *boys*: All right now, boys. Let's lay off it, boys.
You going before the judge on this one. But if it was just your regular
cut-'em-up and they were still half-sober, that Mick called them *men*:
Now you men know I can't be having this shit on my beat. I'll run your

black asses in, I will. His language had to get rougher to make up for having to address 'em as *men*. Cause that cop knew there was no way he—or a whole police force—would leave that bar the way they walked in if they called 'em anything else. When I was coming up I only heard the men in my family called *niggers* when they were talking to each other. Nobody gave it a second thought, cause it had a special meaning coming out of their own mouths. And the way they figured it, if you ain't paid the dues, you don't join the club.

It takes a real strong woman to make a home for men like that, or you just wouldn't have no home. She's gotta be able to dig her toes in and give it back one for one. And take no junk when her rent money is short; cause the Bell men made a lot and spent a lot—too often on the wrong things, especially the wrong females. Like the ones living at a different address from where he got his light bill. They were men with big appetites. And their women had to know how to feed 'em. A large spread on the table and plenty of loving when the sun went down. Or a ready can of lye and sugar water if he hadn't made it there by the time the sun was up. But Mother always told 'em, You do right by the woman who has your kids. Don't care what you may think of her, them are *your* kids. Now, I can't say the Bell men were always married to the mother of their children, but they sure married them children. Every payday they'd go by and leave something for diapers and milk, a pair of shoes. Help her meet the gas bill if she needed it. Even if it meant being cussed out for their trouble. And even if she had a new man, they'd send the money by me or Mother. They were brought up to believe another man shouldn't be asked to take care of their kids. Mother drummed that into their heads, guess cause she had it so hard bringing us all up without a daddy—or more like, daddies.

I don't know how that old woman did it. People think the docks are awful now, but they're sugar tit compared to her time. Whenever my brothers would start acting up, thinking they gonna bad-mouth her, using their liquor as an excuse, she'd show 'em that big scar running straight across her belly—push her skirt band right down and show 'em: I got this cause I wouldn't take no shit from a man; you think I'm gonna take it from a *boy?* She's talking to something over six foot now, something near about thirty years old and mean drunk enough to chew iron. And Mother could say *boy* and make it sound worse than *nigger*, make it sound like something diseased. They looked in her eyes and they saw the sea. Saw them early dock shanties and what she had to do to survive—and they apologized right quick. It wasn't out of pity or nothing. Power knows power. Women like that breed daughters like that, and the docks were full of 'em for the Bell men to marry. My brothers respected every woman they took up with—any other kind wouldna lasted down there.

It was a big shock when I married into the Kings and went to Sugar Hill. Those women got treated any old way and took it. I don't mean being slapped upside the head or any such thing; they figured that was the kind of treatment I saw around me growing up. Well, I had sometimes, but there are worse things than hitting a woman. Like having your husband call you stupid and lazy in front of a whole roomful of people while you stand there and smile and smile. No, the man wouldn't use the exact words *stupid* or *lazy*, but it amounted to the same thing. And if I could figure it out with my lack of education, surely she could, and still she smiles and smiles and smiles. Yeah, there are worse things. Like having the girlfriend and the wife at the same dinner table. Like the wife knowing about it all the while, and the husband knowing she knows, and him getting a thrill out of it all. Cause the wife's not going to say a word. Cause this son of a bitch is a doctor somebody or a lawyer somebody— or maybe just a man somebody that she feels she's nobody without. Women up there look at other women as nothing unless they're attached to some man's name. And attached they stay, no matter what he does. And personally, I knew a few of them who actually got their butts beaten worse than some women down on the docks. But they got beaten by stone sober men behind stained-glass doors. And with all their money, they couldn't afford to cry.

Let me tell you, that was *not* the case in my house. And I had the biggest brownstone up there, married to a King. Yeah, I was head wife cause the Kings owned most of everything in Sugar Hill. Those who didn't call 'em *landlord* had to call 'em *sir*, cause they dabbled in politics too; and from what I heard knew where a whole lot of skeletons were buried, even in the basement of Tammany Hall. That's what I was used to, colored men that other men respected. And it was why I even considered marrying my husband. But folks wondered—and they wondered loudly—why he ever married me. And that handkerchief-head, Uncle Eli, led the band on that one. Even went so far as to say I slipped some kind of secret potion in his drink when I met him that night at the Savoy. How in the hell you gonna find some juju potion that lasts nineteen years? Nineteen good years.

Weren't nothing secret about my marriage. I got him the same way I kept him—with the best poon tang east of the Mississippi. And just cause it was 1924, don't let people tell you that nice girls *didn't*. They did then, they do now—and I'll bet my grandma's drawers they always will. But it's the smart girls—nice or not—who understand that men have a short memory in that department. So you gotta find ways of reminding 'em of how good it was while promising them it's gonna get better still. And the hardest part is to remind them without saying a word. If you spoke about such things out loud, you would be indecent. You see, the real secret is that men don't give a second thought about marrying girls that *do* as long as they stay ladies.

I can't say I was what you might call a nice girl when he met me. He wasn't my first man, but he wasn't my fiftieth either. He damn sure was my last. And don't think some of his friends didn't try. I mean, some of his so-called best friends. And *I* was the one who always threatened to leave. All that phoniness and crap up on Sugar Hill. Them bad-mouthing me almost from the day I came. But I stayed because I loved my husband, and from the very beginning he understood about her.

What goes on in our home, goes on in our home, he said; I rule here. If only that had been true. Like the rest of the Kings, he feared Uncle Eli. And for the life of me, I couldn't figure out why. Just a tired old man and an Uncle Tom at that. I don't even think he was my husband's real uncle. I don't think he was anybody's uncle cause that woulda meant he had to be somebody's mother's child. A woman wouldna birthed him. A woman woulda seen the hate in his eyes for us the minute he slipped out of her, and she woulda crushed his puny little head between her knees. It didn't surprise me to learn he'd never been married, the things he said about women. And the way you'd catch him looking at them sometimes would send a chill up your spine. The same kind of look you get from those men who buy white roses for Esther.

My husband was different. Way different. He loved everything about women. I mean, even little things like how I managed to get the seams in my stockings straight or how I penciled in the beauty mark over the right side of my lips. He'd watch me trying to arch my eyebrows for a whole hour, just fascinated, you know? Not so much that I was doing it, but that it was being done—this thing that women do. You gotta keep tight reins on a man like that, cause Maybelline made a whole lot of those pencils. So Mama went where Papa went, or Papa didn't go out that night. He'd get tickled over my being a little on the jealous side, and if truth's told, I played it up a bit more than I really was. Makes a man feel special that way. And thinking about it, he *was* special cause I never had a problem about her.

My biggest problem was at the dinner table. A new bride, mind you, so I'm putting on the hog. Frying catfish. Washing and chopping collard greens. Baking biscuits. Smothering pork chops till they cried for mercy. Macaroni salad with *homemade* mayonnaise. And he'd just pick and pick at his food. He'd be smiling all the while, but I could see he was having a hard time swallowing. Now, if I knew anything, I knew how to cook. So I'm trying to figure out what it is until one night I set a platter of buttered cornbread and a steaming bowl of oxtail soup in front of him. He plays around in the soup with his spoon for a while, brings up the oxtail, and asks me timid-like, Wife, what kind of meat is this? I coulda fell off my chair. A colored man, brought up in Harlem, who didn't know what oxtail soup was? Then it all comes out. Uncle Eli never let the Kings eat like that. He called it slave food—that old Tom. Well, Mother, I saw the sorry mess I had on my hands. So I began his education right quick.

The next night I baked three sweet-potato pies. I mean, the heavy kind with lard in the crust and Alaga syrup bubbling all through them. And while my pies are cooling and he's in the bedroom reading his newspaper, I run me a warm bath and throw a whole bottle of vanilla extract in the water. So I'm soaking in the vanilla, the pies are cooling, and we're all ready about the same time. I go into our bedroom, carrying one of my pies, dressed the same way I stepped out of that tub. I made sure it was sliced real nice—six even pieces. And he's looking at me like I've gone out of my mind, but I still take it all real slow. I laid back on the pillows. Took out a slice, without disturbing a crumb, mind you. And wedged it right between my legs. It was time for the first lesson. Husband, I said, pointing, this is sweet-potato pie. Didn't have a bit of trouble after that. Except it was all the man wanted for dinner for the next month.

Over the years there were a lot of good times. And we'd have kept our home together if we had managed to keep Uncle Eli out of our business. Yeah, I got the reputation for being a real nasty bitch. And, no, I wouldn't answer the door when I knew it was him out there knocking. But I knew what was at stake: let him worm in a inch and he'd be crawling around for any kind of dirt in every corner of our house. There was no way Uncle Eli—or even the other neighbors—would have understood about her. But my husband knew right up front, right from the beginning. She was with me that night at the Savoy. When you're into women as much as he was, I guess you understand that somebody else might feel the same way about 'em at times like you do. And I respected my home; I never brought her there although he told me I could. Your friends are welcome here, Jesse, he'd say—even your special friend. But I knew better than that. There's only so much you can expect even the best of marriages to take. My needs were my own. But so was my home.

But Uncle Eli didn't have to know about that to hate me. He did it on general principle. He'd call the other wives *Mrs. King*, but whenever my husband forced me to go to his family parties, it was always, Why, good evening, Jesse Bell. Not that I cared; I was proud to be a Bell. He just had this nasty old way of rolling it over his tongue like it was dried spit. And I'd shoot right back: Why, good evening, Uncle Eli. *Mister Bell* and I are so happy to be here. And my husband would just fall out laughing until Uncle Eli gave him one of those crazy old stares—and he'd shut right up. See, that's how my husband was. He'd talk about being his own man, but he wasn't. Sure, he'd rebel at times. I guess marrying me was part of that. Still, a part of him believed in what Uncle Eli said. All that lift-the-race this and lift-the-race that. To raise something, you gotta first see it as being low-down. And I didn't see a damn thing wrong with being colored. And where did Uncle Eli want us to be lifted up to? Why, white folks. And not even the honest ofays who worked with my uncles and brothers at the docks. Real white men. Naw, he meant the dicty white folks. The ones with money. I got so sick of his preaching. White folks are looking at us. White folks are judging us. They were Uncle Eli's god. And it was a god I wasn't buying. But he was always up in my face, thinking he could tell me how to act and dress. How to decorate my own house. I let it go in one ear and out the other and did just what I wanted to do. But the Kings had always listened to him. And I have to admit they'd gotten very far, believing in his god.

When I had to go to his parties, I went. But I out and out refused to eat there; I didn't care how insulted he got. And he got insulted plenty, but I didn't trust nothing at his table. It didn't look like nothing I grew up eating. When the Kings wanted to grease back, they'd sneak over to our house. And I would put on a spread. Uncle Eli had a natural fit when he heard some of them were doing that. Besides the fact it meant they were eating slave food, it meant they were rubbing elbows with other members of the Bell family. I always had my people over. Big house like that, and only me and my husband. Sure, I wanted company and kept plenty of it. And Mother was always welcome in my home. We'd sit her at the head of the table, where she belonged, and have ourselves all kinds of fun.

And they were parties, do you hear me, nothing but parties. They were *not* orgies. I think that lie, out of all the lies, hurt me the most. What would I look like with Mother in the house—my own mother—and having people running around buck naked and drunk, cutting each other up with knives and ice picks? And them saying Mother enjoyed it, that's how she raised the Bells to be. Every time I think about it, even now, I see red. Please, devil, please, kick Uncle Eli's ass again. Yeah, we played jazz and played it loud, the way it was meant to be heard. And them that wanted to dance, danced. If the truth be told, it was mostly the Kings up there on the floor begging us to teach 'em the new steps to the lindy or the fox trot. After the dishes got cleared, the Bells were just as happy to put a bottle of Jack Daniel's on the table and sit around playing bid whist. And there is no way—no way—you're gonna have a group of colored people, a deck of cards, and a game of bid whist going on (uptown, no trump) without getting into an argument. Somebody's gotta be shouted down for not shuffling the deck good enough. Somebody's gotta threaten to cut somebody's dumb throat for throwing out the wrong card or bidding a book too high. And somebody's gotta be accused of cheating when they're adding up the score. Or what's the point of playing? I had my parties often, and I had 'em loud. But that's a far cry from being a loose woman.

And after my son was born, I only brought in a crowd once a month or so, and I quit having them sit up in my house until two or three o'clock in the morning. It left me too worn-out the next day to take care of him proper. Yeah, after my son was born, a whole lot of things started changing. Uncle Eli almost looked at me like I was a human being when we brought him home from the hospital. All the Kings were waiting in the front parlor, and I was too happy that day to argue when he practically snatched the baby from me to show him all around. Look what Jesse Bell has given us. That old man was so proud. A new King. I was proud too. And deep down I was thinking, Maybe now they'll accept me. Deep down, I was tired of fighting. I knew my son could be a great man cause he had the blood of two good families in him. With the brains of the Kings and the spirit of the Bells, there'd be no stopping that boy. I shoulda listened more closely to what Uncle Eli was saying: Look what Jesse Bell has given *us*.

It started slow at first, you know. And in that quiet, sneaky way that people like them are so good at. I wanted Mother to live in and help take care of the baby. She wasn't getting no younger and I figured it was a way to ease her out of that beaten-up old house by the docks. Uncle Eli wanted a nanny. I wanted him to go to school with the other kids in the neighborhood, so he could play stickball, get into the regular ruckus that boys do, and learn to take his knocks. Uncle Eli wanted a private tutor. Well, we got the nanny—handpicked by him, of course. And we got the tutor, who came through the same route. And Uncle Eli used my husband to do his dirty work for him—after all, wouldn't any father want the best for his son? And the best started to mean that he couldn't spend the weekends with Mother and his other cousins down on the docks. That he couldn't go fishing with my brothers during his summer vacations. You see, the best started to mean anything that had nothing to do with the Bells, and it ended up meaning anything that had nothing to do with *me*. I wasn't fit to decide what friends should come to his birthday parties, what clothes he should take to camp, what books he should read.

You know I didn't take it lying down, but all this didn't come stringed together like I'm saying it; it came in little pieces, one thing this year, another thing the next. I can still hear my husband: Now, Jesse. Now, Jesse. Trying to convince me it was all in my mind. I was being—what was his words?—overly paranoid. Yeah, I guess it was paranoia when my sixteen-year-old son refused to go to Mother's ninetieth anniversary party because he didn't have anything in common with *those people*. And how could she have an anniversary anyway, since she'd never been married? First time in my life I ever laid a hand on him. Straight across the face. It was the anniversary of her life! And if she hadn't been married to her life, his miserable little butt wouldn't have been here. It might as well have been a dead woman ranting at him. I looked into that boy's eyes and saw my words were lost, lost.

It was about then I started drinking real heavy, trying to figure out how it all happened—when had it happened? And no point in going to my husband. When it came to something connected with our son, he was a King first and last. So, yes, I went to . . . her. And I cried in her arms, never talking much sense and drunk lots of the time. She'd really become, as my husband called her, that special friend. And at least she understood why I felt there was a reason to cry when he got accepted into Harvard. Nobody else would have. Not even my own family. They were as happy as the Kings over that one. And that's how they got suckered into that cookout Uncle Eli threw. I warned 'em not to come. I had a bad bad feeling about the whole thing. Why would Uncle Eli invite the Bells to celebrate with the Kings?

Why, to do just what he did. To embarrass them in front of everyone on Sugar Hill. To give the boy a real send-off by killing any last bit of respect he might have had for my side of the family. The radio had been saying for days that it was gonna rain on the weekend, and, looking back, I can see that was part of his plan. So was telling my people to come two hours later than he told anybody else—and telling 'em to bring all the food and liquor they wanted. But see, he'd already rented this big striped tent to set up in my backyard and hired waiters and a cook. They brought in one of those new propane grills, although I had a special-made barbecue pit in the corner of the yard. He coulda easily put the tent over my barbecue pit. But then that woulda meant that when my people finally arrived, he couldn't have done what he did. Cause it did rain that day.

And there's all of Sugar Hill under his fancy tent with their fancy clothes, chitting and chatting, with their champagne glasses. His flunky waiters running between 'em with little bits of grilled mushrooms, smoked cheese, and that kind of shit on silver trays. That sound like a cookout to you? So here come my people with the things they was supposed to bring: a crate of spareribs and about thirty chickens that Mother had cut up and soaked overnight in her special sauce, bowls of potato salad and coleslaw, cases and cases of beer. They stack all that stuff up in the corner of the yard, cause there sure wasn't no room under Uncle Eli's tent. And they're ready to cook—ya know, join the crowd. But it don't take 'em too long to figure out the deal. His hired cook had that little propane grill all filled up with her mess, so they could just get out there in the rain or shut up.

Like I told you, I'm from proud people. And there was no way they were gonna go home with their tails between their legs just cause they'd been set up. They came for a cookout and a cookout they would have. I helped 'em the best I knew how, finding as many umbrellas in the house as I could. But it was kinda pitiful to watch them trying to light up the charcoal on my open pit in all that rain. And the cardboard boxes started soaking through at the bottom and tearing up. Water getting up under the wax paper on the potato salad and ruining it. And the crowd under that striped tent looking out at 'em like they were a bunch of trained monkeys from the circus. My husband told me I shouldn't keep running out there with them in the rain; they were welcome under the tent. And I told him to go to hell. Couldn't he see what was going on?

They never did get that fire lit. But, my brother joked, at least we remembered to bring our own beer openers. And so they stood out there and ate their wet potato salad and got drunk off their warm beer. Mother caught a chill from being out in the damp. The next week it turned into pneumonia. The next month she was dead. My husband said I was out of order, blaming Uncle Eli for her death. After all, she was over ninety years old. And that whole cookout business, why, that whole business had just been a misunderstanding. I looked into that man's eyes and saw that he actually believed what he was saying. And yes, it might as well have been a dead woman ranting at him. My words were lost, lost.

Liquor wasn't enough after that. Nothing was enough to answer the question that kept haunting me and haunting me—when had Uncle Eli killed me in my own home? When? And what had he used? I couldn't stand to have my husband touch me after that. I looked for the answer in her arms, but now even she wasn't enough. But there were hidden places, smoky back rooms, with others like her. No, that's not the truth, they weren't like her. Those others were stone dykes. They tried to dress like men. They tried to swagger like men. And they scared the hell out of me. If I had wanted a man, I knew how to find one—and sure knew what to do with one. I had gone to those clubs looking for women.

Looking for answers. And then one night someone slipped a little paper envelope of white powder in my hand, and I found what I needed.

I'm gonna tell you why people get high: cause when you're that far up there, everything becomes clear. I ain't lying, crystal clear. I mean, you can see *everything* about your life, all at one time. Every face. Every name. Every place you passed through. The questions you been asking, why you asked 'em, what the answers are, what to do about it—all at one time. Cause you high, ya know, way up high, and so it's all laid out before you. All this stuff I been telling you—it wasn't jumbled up like now—it was clear, clear as day—and all at one time. Except it takes more than one ride to remember all that stuff when you come back down. So you go up again to remember a little more. And up again. You see, there's a whole lot going on in even the simplest life, a whole lot to put in order. And then you start thinking that, maybe, if you got a little higher than the time before, you'd have more of the answers in your mind when the ride was over. So you sniff the horse. Then you pop the horse. And after a while the only decent ride is through the mainline.

I'm not making no excuses for becoming a junkie. In fact, I was glad I discovered heroin. Yeah, I was glad—do you hear me?—glad. Cause when that dyke club got raided and Uncle Eli used every bit of influence he had to make sure my name hit the newspapers and stayed in the papers, throwing dirt on everything about my life, just digging, digging, until they dug up my special friend and my husband had to say, *had* to say he didn't know, cause, after all, he was a man and a King and there was his son to consider, so I'm out there by myself, on display like a painted dummy in a window as the name Jesse Bell came to mean that no-good slut from the docks and the nineteen years I'd put into my marriage didn't amount to dog shit; the care I'd given my son—dog shit; the clothes I wore, the music I liked, the school I went to, the family I came from, everything that made me *me*—dog shit; cause nobody was interested in my side of the story, not the reporters, not the neighbors, not the divorce court, nobody, cause everybody was standing around like vultures looking at me fall fall fall, waiting for me to smash my brains on the pavement, yeah, waiting for me to lose my mind; and within a inch of the ground, within a inch of having my head split open and my brains spill out, Jesse Bell grabbed onto the reins of that white horse, letting 'em all see her spread wings as she rose.

It's time for me and Jesse to put the cards away; the sun is gonna be up soon. She's waiting to spin out her last few nickels in the juke. She'd better get back to the boardinghouse before she's missed, although I've got a feeling that Eve knows about her slipping out to visit with me. Little really escapes her.

Looking at Jesse with the blue-and-yellow lights of the jukebox playing across the healthy tones of her skin, it's hard to believe it's the same woman who came in here with Eve's card a year ago. The business card was creased and smudged, curled and ragged on the ends. It looked like it'd been through fifty wars—one less than the woman carrying it.
   —There's no fucking address like this on the block.
She was standing there defiant in a pair of run-down Italian pumps. But none of the customers were going to disagree with her, because there *was* no house number like that on the block. To them she was a woman stating the obvious, so they kept on eating and ignored her.
   —What are you looking for? I asked.
   —The address on this card, goddammit.
She was sweating heavily in a wrinkled silk chemise and the weather wasn't hot. Her nose was runny, her eyes weak and teary. A well-dressed junkie.
   —What are you looking for? I asked again.
   —*This address*, goddammit.
With short, jerky motions she pushed the card across the countertop,

her fingernails broken and filthy. I didn't have to read it. You'll never find it, was all I said before I turned back to scraping the grill.

Eve had given that card to Jesse in the women's house of detention. A revolving door for petty offenses: vagrancy, shoplifting, prostitution, third-degree assault. She goes there once a month under a program set up by the commissioner of correction. It's your typical charity work for bored society women. The haves trip in and mingle for a while with the have-nots. They bring 'em lipstick, combs, toothpaste, cigarettes, and they listen to their troubles. Friendly Visitors, or something like that. Eve joined the group because it's the only way she can get down to the isolation cells. But she usually finds herself making that part of the friendly visit alone. The stench is something awful. Alcoholics. Junkies. Hysterics. The problem population. The women crouch in wire-mesh cages among the watery stools from overflowing toilets. If they're not too sick to care, they push their floor mattresses away from the corners where they have to vomit. Because if they're not too sick to care, they've tried to keep the one sink clean enough to allow them to drink from the faucet.

The only thing Eve brings to the prison is her calling cards. She walks slowly down the dark hall between the isolation cells, looking at each woman. And many times she'll walk back up that hall without having spoken to one of them or handed out a single card. These visits are very practical. And there's no need to waste directions on someone who's just going to spend her life staying lost. For some reason she did stop at Jesse's cell. And no, she wasn't moved by her story. But when she was tired of wallowing in her own shit, come and find her.

And Jesse finally did. She stumbled in here three or four times, yelling about the wrong address, until it dawned on her to simply ask, How do I get to Eve's? I was more than happy to tell her. She had a pretty rough mouth and a lot of the customers were complaining. No, only Sister Carrie was complaining. But when Carrie starts up it can sound like a cast of thousands. And she was the one who finally remembered Jesse's picture from those old newspaper articles and kept at folks in here until they remembered the story too—or, at least, said they did to shut her up. Jesse is still real real sensitive on that issue and Carrie smelling blood will go in for the kill every time she sees her. She'll have her daughter, Angel, hand her that dog-eared Bible from the bottom of her canvas bag and get the urge to start reading aloud, and I mean, loud:

—The thing abominable to the Lord; a wife that committeth adultery which taketh strangers instead of her husband!

Jesse will throw her fork down and start cussing something furious, which only spurs Carrie on. And I'm suspicious that Carrie takes a little poetic license with some of those verses:

—And the Lord saith, Yeah, yeah, you're gonna burn and fry because of vile affections: for even their women did change the natural use into that which is against nature.

Once or twice I've had to keep Jesse from jumping on Carrie. I'm not a churchgoing man and don't want to criticize somebody else's beliefs. But it started becoming clear to me that Jesse's salvation isn't the thing uppermost on Carrie's mind. It's like she wants Jesse to strike her, like it would prove something.

Eve won't put up with it and she can hit Carrie where it really hurts. Carrie is partial to the whore Scriptures. To hear her reading, you'd think loose women were the only thing ever on the Lord's mind. Eve will be at the counter, minding her own business, when Carrie starts up. She's got a high voice that she makes sure gets heard all the way from the window tables. She licks that thumb and starts flicking the pages of her Bible:

—Thou hast built thy high place at every head of the way, and hast made thy beauty to be abhorred, and hast opened thy feet to every one that passed by, and multiplied thy whoredoms.

———

Without turning around, Eve will raise her own voice and talk straight across the counter to the lard cans up on the shelf: Somebody in here likes Ezekiel. Somebody even likes the *sixteenth chapter* of Ezekiel.

Carrie's mouth drops open. She looks at the page and looks at Eve's back. Then she looks back at the page again, hoping some miracle will change it. But since loud is righteous in her book, she gets louder still:

  —How weak is thine heart, saith the Lord God, seeing thou doest all these things the work of an imperious whorish woman!

Eve keeps holding her conversation with the lard: Somebody even likes the *thirtieth* verse of the sixteenth chapter of Ezekiel. And maybe somebody should try the *fifty-second* verse on for size. And before Carrie can lick that thumb and flip over the page, Eve is quoting it by heart:

  —Thou also, which hast judged thy sisters, bear thine own shame for thy sins that thou hast committed more abominable than they: they are more righteous than thou: yea, be thou confounded also, and bear thy shame, in that thou hast justified thy sisters.

Carrie's chest starts heaving and she's just licking that thumb and flicking those pages until they're a blur. She's heading towards Revelation. That book of the Bible is big on whores.

  —And somebody should try something else, Eve shouts, somebody should try Isaiah, the twelfth chapter . . .

I gotta jump in and stop Eve now. Cause Carrie is working herself up into a frenzy. The next thing, she'll be running over to the Temple to bring back reinforcements, and my nerves can't take all those tambourines and drums.

———

This same thing goes on time after time; Sister Carrie seems to forget that Eve was raised by a preacher. No, I think she *needs* to forget that Eve was raised by a preacher, cause that fact makes her own world a lot more uncertain. But I don't know, to me there are a lot of ways to be a Christian; the Bible is an awfully large book. And if you want to get technical about the matter, the whole thing was a gift to Christians from Jews. Sure, Eve is a strange cookie and that setup at her brownstone walks a real thin line, but Carrie will be hard pressed to condemn her with the Bible. Just look at what Eve did for Jesse. She went the distance and cured her—and I mean, cured her—in less than a month.

> *And when I passed by thee, and saw thee polluted in thine own blood, I said unto thee when thou wast in thy blood, Live; yea, I said unto thee when thou wast in thy blood, Live.*

Now Jesse's reading on how Eve helped her beat the habit is a whole lot different. She swears that Eve wouldn't have cared if she had died. The funny thing is that Jesse is probably right. *But I said unto thee when thou wast in thy own blood, Live.*

After Jesse finally found Eve, they came back in here for a cup of coffee and a very long talk. Jesse did most of the talking, and she also ordered the peach cobbler and heaped on spoonfuls of sugar. I didn't take it as a comment on my wife's specialty; she wasn't the first junkie we'd had in the place. Jesse ran on and on, swore up and down that she wanted to quit. She'd gotten on the junk because once it was the best thing she had in a bad situation, but the horse had started taking her as low as it had taken her high, and yes, she wanted to quit. She smoked like a chimney, drank cup after cup of syrupy coffee, and tried to figure out what the stone-faced woman across from her was thinking. She knew she'd probably heard it all before . . .

—Yes, Eve said, I have.

But this time it was coming on the square; she'd taken her last ride.

—How long ago? Eve asked her.

—Not since the early morning.

—How long ago? Eve asked her again.

—All right, more like four hours.

—You're too calm; it's more like three.

All right, so it was three, just before she'd knocked on her door. But it was the last ride and she was gonna quit.

Jesse didn't like the way Eve was looking at her. It's not that Eve was looking like she disbelieved her, or even looking at her with pity or disgust. Eve was only looking distracted, like she'd been waiting at a bus stop five minutes too long, and Jesse was the five minutes.

—There's something extremely important you need to know about me, Eve said. I never waste my time. Never. And if you don't come off the dope, then I've wasted over an hour listening to you claim that you will. Do you understand what that means, Jesse?

Jesse didn't quite know what it meant, but this weird mama-jama was beginning to really scare her.

—It means, Eve continued, that now you've put me into the position of ensuring that I have not wasted this hour.

Then Eve led her straight to the back of the cafe. She flung open the door and let her see all that black, empty space. Jesse dug her fingernails into the door frame like a cat, thinking that the crazy bitch was gonna shove her out into oblivion. A dead junkie was certainly not gonna be using anymore, and a dead junkie would save Eve her precious hour.

—What do you see? Eve asked.

Oh, Mother, get her out of here. She'd just try to take the cure at Lexington again. She'd go right back to Lexington and this time behave herself. No more stealing needles. No more cussing out the doctors and bribing the orderlies.

—You know I don't see a fucking thing.

—Then I know that you've been lying. You have no intentions of quitting.

—I *do* want to quit, goddamn you!

—So what do you see?

And there it was: the simple bedroom she'd had as a girl. The raw pine floor. The single window looking out at other tar-paper shacks on the waterfront. Her bed with the chenille spread. Her secondhand dresser. Her movie-star posters torn from *Modern Screen* and tacked on the mildewed wall: Bette Davis. Irene Dunn. Clark Gable. Joan Crawford. She could even hear Mother wrestling with that old wood stove in the kitchen, smell the frying butterfish and turnip greens. A lump formed in her throat. But it wasn't real; it couldn't be real. She was going around the bend and starting to hallucinate. God, how she needed a fix.

—The towels and extra linens are my own contribution, Eve said. That's when she saw the rosewood rocker and matching chest in the corner. She stepped off the back steps, just to touch it all, because it couldn't be real. But the latch on the chest felt solid in her hand, the top opening up to reveal neat stacks of thick cotton towels and beige sheets. A small door led into a bathroom: a claw-foot tub with gleaming faucets shaped like swans, cool blue tiles underfoot, scented French soap in porcelain trays, crystal jars of bath salts sparkling on the windowsill.

—I dreamed of a bathroom like this when I was a little girl.

—I did too, Eve said.

—None of this can be real. Where am I?

—Hell.

Jesse once tried to describe to me what it means to go cold turkey. Imagine, she said, that you're speeding along at, say like, seventy miles an hour. No car, no nothing, just your body, seventy miles an hour. And suddenly your whole body slams right into this big brick wall. But you don't go unconscious, so you can feel crushed pieces of your skull stabbing back into your brain, your lungs collapsing in, each bone snapping and crumbling, your insides busting open as your guts rip apart. That's how much it hurts. Now, imagine, she said, that your body gets slammed into that same wall again and again. Red-hot bricks one time. Blocks of ice the next. Imagine it going on for four straight days. And imagine, when it was over, that bitch put me through it all again.

The room looked like it had been hit by a hurricane. And Jesse looked like she had taken the front end of the storm. Eve had rode it out within the calmer region of the eye, but she was still drained and tired. Jesse had fought her and scratched her, she'd banged her own head against the wall, shattered the windowpane trying to throw herself through it. Eve had wrung out towels full of sweat, changed her soiled sheets, and shoved cardboard between her teeth to keep her from biting off her tongue. As Jesse fell into deep, fitful sleeps, Eve dozed in the rosewood rocker. She was napping that way when Jesse woke up, this time finally free.

—I can't believe I'm still alive.
Her voice was weak, her tongue swollen.
—It was touch and go for a while. Would you like a drink of water?
After giving her a sponge bath, Eve powdered her down and combed her hair. She kept telling Jesse not to thank her. Jesse thought she was just being gracious. She should have known better.
—I have a gift for you, Eve said.
She laid the velvet case beside her on the bed. It was lined in sky blue silk. The eyedropper was made of crystal, the teaspoon and syringe pure silver, the book of matches embossed.
—What's this? Some kinda joke?
But the woman sitting on the edge of the bed was definitely not laughing.
—You think I'd touch this crap after what I've just gone through?
—Yes, Eve said, I do. But the next time you shoot up, it's going to be with style.

———

She left Jesse and went into the bathroom to wash the dirty sheets and towels. Jesse picked up the case and shook her head. As soon as she was strong enough, she was getting out of here, wherever here was. She snapped open the case and looked at the neat compartments. She'd never seen works so fine. And to show you how square the broad was, she hadn't even put in the stuff. She checked under the matchbook and the syringe just to be sure. No, not even half a cap.

—It's in the bottom drawer of your dresser, Eve called from the bathroom.

—You can just go to hell, Jesse shouted as loud as she could. But her throat was sandpaper and the words hoarse. You can just go straight to hell.

On shaky knees Jesse made it over to the dresser and yanked open the bottom drawer.

—Straight to hell, she said as she rummaged through the sweaters and blouses.

She just wanted to see if the bitch could be that cruel. If she could be that goddamned cruel. The smooth white packets were wedged into the corners. Dear God, they were all quarter-ounce bags and there must be at least a dozen. Yeah, a dozen bags of powdered sugar. She wasn't gonna be fooled. She tore open one just to see. Flicked it with the tip of her tongue—just to be sure. The stuff was so pure, it split her head open. If she tried putting that in her veins, it would send her to Valhalla. No, you had to cut something like this. Out on the streets it woulda been easy. Any druggist could sell you milk sugar or a little quinine powder.

—Look in the top drawer, Eve called over the sound of running water.

—Didn't you hear me before, you sadistic . . . ? I said, Go to . . .

————

Jesse pulled open the top drawer to find a brand new box of milk sugar. A setup, that's what it was. Nothing but a setup. Eve didn't want to help her. Had never wanted to help her. She sagged against the open drawer, resting her head on top of the dresser. She could still hear her mother moving about in the kitchen, the scraping of pots against the iron stove. But Mother wasn't there anymore; if Mother were still alive she wouldn't have to go through this. They'd taken her mother, taken everything. Didn't that cold-blooded monster understand that? No, she didn't. Well, fuck her. Fuck them all. She stumbled back to the bed and the velvet case.

Jesse could see Eve standing in the doorway of the bathroom as she began that mellow climb, higher and higher. Eve's face was blurred, but was it possible she was smiling?

——You can just go to hell, Jesse mumbled through the sweet relief of it all.

——I think you've forgotten that's where we are.

Eve let her shoot up with the silver needle for another four days. She agreed it was all her fault. She agreed that life was one big stinking sewer. She agreed that there was just no way for any woman to get a fair shake. And then the world turned blood red when the dope suddenly disappeared. Jesse begged Eve not to put her through it all again. It was much too soon. It would probably kill her. And Eve agreed it probably would.

Jesse has never tried to describe for me what it was like that second time around. She says there are no words for the experience. I can only tell you this, Bailey, I sincerely prayed to die.

And it was something only half-living that Eve sponged and powdered at the end of the next four days. Clumps of Jesse's hair would fall out as Eve combed it. It took another four days for her to gain the strength to even sit up in bed. And there was yet another velvet case.

Resting a bruised and swollen hand on the velvet case beside her, Jesse turned her head to look around at the room that had no doors.

—The needle is gold this time, isn't it?

—It's gold, said Eve.

—And if I made it through, I suppose I'd get platinum. Would that be the end of the line?

—Remember where we are; that's only the beginning of what's available here.

Mary (Take Two)

You already know that my name is Nadine, and my husband's told
you that I don't like to talk. I've only agreed to set this one up
because there isn't a man in here who's willing to do it. Why am I being
so generous to those cowards? The truth is that, right now, there ain't
a man in this place at all. They all cleared out when they knew we were
coming around to the little Jew gal who just moved into Eve's. All of a
sudden that coffee grinder I've been trying to get fixed for months gets
pushed right up to the top of the maestro's list, and he's out of here as
fast as grease on ice, with everything else in pants following behind.
Maybe I'm being too hard. This isn't a story that any man can tell. And
the girl can't do it for herself; she's a little off in the head.

No man has ever touched me.

She's fourteen. She's pregnant. And yes, I believe her. Because I finally
saw Eve cry.

No man has ever touched me.

I was out in my garden clipping the final buds from the camellias. And I was thinking that it was a pity I had no boarder who wanted them. Camellias are easy to grow late into the fall. I looked up and she was standing there with Gabriel, of all people, who was pointing to me over the wall. She had a vacant look to her face; she didn't seem retarded at first, just stunned. And her clothes were filthy. I was more surprised to see him than the girl; he rarely leaves that shop.

No man has ever touched me.

THIS CAFE SITS ON a street between two other places. Eve has the board-inghouse and Gabe has the pawnshop. I bet you haven't heard my husband talk about him, cause he's always losing arguments with the old man. They've gone on for hours about politics, the war, and that bloodbath over in Europe. I tend to side with Gabe myself, since he had a front-row seat in that disaster. My husband didn't serve in that part of the world—and he isn't a Jew. But that doesn't stop him from thinking his view on the whole thing is right. I guess you've learned by now he has a lot of opinions. Unsolicited opinions. But his biggest bone of contention is that Gabe won't ever eat here, although on the weekends we can keep a kosher kitchen and have done it for those who ask. I've told him that man is nobody's fool; offering to go kosher still wouldn't improve his cooking. But Gabe says he's really too old and alone to have Shabbat in the back of the cafe. A proper Sabbath meal means family, and that would mean calling up ghosts; and it'd be too tempting just to stay back there forever. Then who would be on his end of our relay for broken dreams?

A lot of customers get directed here from his pawnshop if they're smart enough to understand the sign. One side of the cardboard hanging on his front door has a painted clock with movable hands. It reads, Back at——, and each hour he keeps moving the hands one hour forward.

And under the clock is a red-and-gold arrow pointing down the street to us. After two or three hours, if the person keeps coming back without getting the message, and he thinks they're still worth it, he'll flip the sign over to where it reads, Out of Business, with that same arrow pointing down the street to us. Gabe is never open—we never close.

No man has ever touched me.

I should have guessed there had to be something different about the girl, because Gabriel had broken the pattern. A certain kind of person he sends to the cafe; a certain kind of woman Bailey sends to me. It was clear she was a foreigner, but he told me she was also a Jew. One of us who keeps the old ways. And it was hard to imagine what he could mean by *old*. His birth is on his face. He carries every crevice and ridge of the Caucasus Mountains. A speck of a town hidden in the seam holding together two continents and two seas. His spine is bent from straddling so much of the world for so long and his eyes water constantly from the strain of all he's seen. And you must take her in, he said. I told Gabriel that I was the one who decided who stayed in my place and who didn't. He ran his business and I ran mine. And why had he gone against the system? If she couldn't find me on her own, she shouldn't be standing at my garden in the first place. Without a word he left the girl right there and turned away. Then she handed me the plum.

No man has ever touched me.

EVE WALKED IN HERE with that plum and placed it in the middle of the counter. I have a new boarder, she said. The fruit looked tender and soft. The reddish black skin was so thin you could already smell that the flesh would be sweet. Nadine, please, bring me a knife. I didn't want to move. I didn't want to be any part of what was about to go on. God knows, I didn't. And there wasn't a man in the place, not a man to be found. This was women's business. Nadine, please, bring me a knife.

No man has ever touched me.

She wasn't the first pregnant girl to show up at my doorstep. But she was the first to make such claims. There was no way for the girl to be lying, or the whole village would have heard her screams. Echoes carry well in the green hills of Ethiopia . . .

Elell, elell . . . nine shouts of joy from the hut kept far away from the settlement. A female child is born. Yes, the sound carries crisp and full through the eucalyptus as all stop to count. Twelve shouts for a male child. Nine for a female. Even down at the foothills of the plateau the oxen are stilled in the barley fields. *Elell, elell* . . . a new daughter. New life for the Beta Israel.

Hear O Israel, the Lord is our God, the Lord is One. And thou shalt love the Lord thy God with all thine heart, and with all thy soul, and with all thy might.

They're outcasts in their own nation and only allowed to be tenants on the land. All prayers turn toward Jerusalem as they spin linen, shape iron, and bake pottery outside their broken hovels. Keepers of the Commandments. Commandments given to ex-slaves. To the dispossessed. It is a poor man's faith, so it has thrived among them well. A faith built on what is always attainable for the poor: prayer, children, and memories. In a nation that time forgot, a nation ringed by mountains, they are hemmed in by huge stone churches but have clung to the God of Abraham and the Law of Moses. They believe they are the last Jews in the world. They are certainly the last to build sanctuaries and anoint a high priest.

And these words which I command thee this day, shall be in thine heart: And thou shalt teach them diligently unto thy children, and shalt talk of them when thou sittest in thine house, and when thou walkest by the way, when thou liest down and when thou risest up.

So each child is welcome. Each child means survival. But it is the girl child who will carry the special honor of keeping the home and bearing sons. *Elell, elell* . . . nine shouts of joy from the hut of blood.

I STOOD ROOTED to the floor as Eve took the plum from the counter and cradled it gently in one hand. Fruit that tender will bruise easily. With the tip of her fingernail she traced the faint seam that ran from the little round dent in the center that looked like a belly button. It was perfect and whole, with the seam dividing the front of the plum into two plump mounds. Without warning, she squeezed it quickly and the seam opened. I had been right: this fruit was very sweet. It was only a slight opening, but clear juices were already beading up from deep within the middle. And down within its fleshy walls was just the glimpse of a hard little nub. Eve held the split fruit between her fingertips and, this time, demanded the knife.

And God said unto Abraham, Thou shalt keep My covenant therefore, thou, and thy seed after thee in their generations. This is My covenant, which ye shall keep, between Me and you and thy seed after thee; Every man child among you shall be circumcised. And ye shall circumcise the flesh of your foreskin; and it shall be a token of the covenant betwixt Me and you.

It is hot and airless in the hut of blood. But the mother of the new girl child knows she must stay for fourteen days. From there she will move to the hut of woman-in-childbed, where she is still declared unclean until sunset of the sixty-sixth day. After bathing, washing her clothes, and shaving her head, finally she will be allowed to return to the village. There has been no need to enter this child into the Covenant of Abraham, or to redeem this firstborn from the duties of the priesthood. The jubilant gongs and drums of the sanctuary at the very heart of the village remain silent at the first sounding of her name. Quietly it comes to be known that she will be called Mariam.

EVE'S EYES NEVER LEFT mine as she held the open plum and squeezed again. The fleshy walls were spreading wider apart and its juices began to drip onto the counter. Inside, it was deep amber and red; veins swollen with sugar ran through the soft flesh. A firm tip was pushing up through its center, moist and fragile.

Her mother tells no one how hard she begged Adonai for the firstborn to be a girl. She knew she would remain unclean much longer than with a male child, and so there would be more time to heal before returning to her husband. Even in the hut of childbed there has been so much blood. And she secretly hopes that the second born will also be a girl. Two girl children before she bears the sons. She knows that the neighbors will not whisper about two as long as she remains fruitful and there are sons. But daughters will be there to take care of her husband while she is walled off in the hut of childbed. At five years old her girls will already know how to roast grain and bake the *injerra*. It gives her pleasure to think that they will go in her place to the sanctuary with the bread and beer for the Sabbath offerings. And unlike her, they will be allowed to cross the threshold. She will tell them, as her mother told her: While you are still young and unmarried, stand as close as possible to hear every utterance of the Torah. Listen well to the prayers and remember. Let your cries be loud and bend down low, low so your breasts touch this holy ground as you face east toward our beloved Jerusalem. You will be an old woman before you are allowed such a privilege again.

Yes, it gives her much pleasure to watch this girl child, her Mariam, grow. And she hopes to be forgiven for her lie as the greetings come: A fine daughter for the Beta Israel, but a son next time. Yes, she answers, a son next time. It worries her that the child seems to be slow. She must be kept from stumbling into the fire; after many warnings there is still no fear of the heat and she has burned her fingers often. When they journey into Tuesday Market to sell their pottery, she must attach a linen string to Mariam's waist or she will wander off and touch unbelievers. Then, with all else there is to do after such a long day, she must be cleansed before entering the village. While Mariam is kept at her side, the unbelievers know that the child is one of them and they will not pat her head or take her into their arms. The Beta Israel have a special place to sit in the market, and there is safety in their numbers. Some unbelievers will walk by and spit, *Buda*. Demon. But those who want to buy know to place the taler in the dust. If the child remains so open, how will she teach her to pass the clay pot without ever touching their hands?

But she gives her much pleasure, this daughter, her Mariam. She finds she must repeat often to the child—and speak very slowly. But with patience and many lessons she does learn to bake the *injerra* without burning her fingers, and to season the *wat* with the right amount of pepper. It is a cause for much laughter when Mariam's father cocks his head at the bowl of stew Mariam places in front of him. Can I eat this without burning my throat, little one? Yes, the mother thinks with pride, now he can. But for a while she was *very* worried. The child was almost into her sixth year and there had been no purification. Her own ceremony had taken place at three years old. She had begged the midwives for Mariam's ceremony but they said to wait. If there was some defect in the girl, no man would betroth his son to her anyway. She had rained curses on their heads. A defect in one so beautiful? Look at the brightness of her eyes. The strength in her legs. She will honor the home of any man fortunate enough to receive her. And when they come to her father for the agreement they will bring more than one lousy taler. A thousand talers could not seal the betrothal for one so precious. But she had railed against the old women in vain. For months she cried herself to sleep with the fear they would leave her firstborn, her joy, unfit to be a true daughter of Beta Israel. She remembers a girl from her own village, a girl who drooled and pulled at her own hair. And those ignorant midwives had doomed her. They had left her filthy and intact.

EVE'S FACE HAD BECOME like stone as she held the exposed fruit in her hands. You do understand, she whispered, that as a last resort, I will gouge it out with my fingernails. She didn't have to ask again. I brought her the knife. The sharp blade caught the overhead light and the glare made me turn my eyes away. I know my Bible well, I said, and this *isn't* in the Law of Moses. She was positioning the fruit, lining up the exposed head of the pit with the tip of the blade. No, she said, it's not. It's older than that. It's the law of the Blue Nile. And along those shores there is no woman in her right mind—Jew or Muslim—who will want her daughter to grow up a whore.

The preparation takes weeks. And the mother sings at her work as she spins new linen for the girl's robes and stores up extra wheat, jars of olives, and honey for the feast. She can hold up her head again because she's stilled the tongue of her mother-in-law. No, she would not bring her granddaughter to shame. She sends a message over the mountains for her own mother to come. And the message is returned: If I have to crawl, I will be there. The women of the village begin to bring presents for the child. They give so willingly of their little and call the mother blessed: fresh eggs, shiny tin cups, barley candy, and from the young wife of the high priest a new *samye* necklace with real amber. She tells her Mariam how fortunate she is to have found favor with such a learned woman. The high priest's wife came all the way from Addis Ababa, where they teach the Beta Israel girls to read and write. And all of these women will be there to dance and sing as the midwives squat the naked girl over the hole dug into the hut of blood.

We have a little sister, and she hath no breasts: what shall we do for our sister in the day when she shall be spoken for? If she be a wall, we will build upon her a turret of silver; and if she be a door, we will inclose her with boards of cedar.

EVE PLUNGED THE KNIFE quickly into the middle of the split fruit. With one twist of her wrist, she cut out the large pit. It carried ragged pieces of dark amber flesh with it as it fell to the counter.

It is a white-hot world of pain. A world filled with high-pitched screams, with the singing of women, with the gentle moans of her mother and grandmothers, with the press of soft breasts and soft arms against her heaving body. It is a world that will not end.

JUICE DRIPPED FROM the lightning blade, and bits of plum clung to Eve's wet fingers as she scraped away at the meaty sections left inside each half of the open fruit. She was so intent on being thorough and quick that she didn't notice the pieces on her bowed chin and the wet stains spreading down her blouse sleeves. Small chunks splattered as they kept falling rapidly to the counter. The plum was cleaned of everything but its delicate outer skin. She held what was left in her sticky palm and it was already beginning to curl inward like a petal.

The child's hanging skin is held together with acacia thorns and boiled thread. A clean straw is inserted to ensure there will be a small opening after the body has healed itself shut. She will need that opening, once she is able to pass her urine. Her mother will be there to comfort her because, at first, the feeling will be strange. The girl may cry when it is time to relieve herself. Drip by drip. But she will know this hut again. And she will know no other way to pass her blocked menstrual blood. Drip by drip.

The words of King Lemuel, the prophecy that his mother taught him. Who can find a virtuous woman? for her price is far above rubies. The heart of

her husband doth safely trust in her, so that he shall have no need of spoil.
She will do him good and not evil all the days of her life.

I WAS SO ANGRY I wanted to break something. Blame somebody. I told Eve to shut up. Please, just shut up. But she wasn't talking any longer; she was just staring at the plum petals folding over its own emptiness. And ever so softly she was crying. Her face was unchanged, her breathing so regular, I wondered how long she had been doing that. You do understand, Eve said, how much she loved her daughter. And she couldn't deny in her heart that the girl was always going to be slow-witted. Finding her a decent husband would be difficult with so many other virgins to choose from, and that is why she had the midwives close her up that tightly. It raises a woman's value.

So you see, if it had been rape, the whole village would have heard her screams. Even on the wedding night, the *ensaslaye*, with a willing bride and a cautious husband, the village will hear the screaming. Sometimes it will take months, and many trips to that hut of blood, before the wound he slowly makes allows him to penetrate her without pain. And sometimes she's not fully opened until her first child. Nadine, I don't want to get into a argument with you, or anyone else, about definitions, but depending upon how you look at it, it's not unusual along the shores of the Blue Nile for virgins to give birth. But I've bathed this girl and seen her body; no man has even tried.

IT HAD GOTTEN SO QUIET in the cafe I could hear the humming of the Frigidaire, the fluorescent tube overhead with its low whines and buzzing. So quiet I'd forgotten there were a few other customers—all women— who sat immobile on the counter stools and at the tables. Every face was turned toward Eve, and, I swear, as I looked into each of those faces, they all wanted to believe.

—So you're telling me, we've got ourselves a miracle?

—Well, Nadine, it won't be the first.

—Yeah, if we're talking the little girl in Galilee . . .

—She wasn't the first either.

—But you've gotta admit, she's gotten away with it longer.

—And I say, more power to her.

I WAS AFRAID that Eve was going to laugh. This had been a morning of enough firsts for me. My husband is always remarking on how Eve doesn't laugh. He should count himself lucky. I think he likes to forget who she really is, what she's seen. If this woman ever began laughing, unlike her tears, it couldn't stop. I asked where the girl had found Gabe's pawnshop.

On a back street in Addis Ababa. And the real miracle is how she'd made it that far south from the mountains. It's almost five hundred miles through steep canyons and gorges. After they expelled her from the village, the only town she knew was Tuesday Market, with only a short motor road leading out from there. The rest of the way is only the old caravan routes that wind across the high plateaus past the occasional village. It is the way most of the rural people travel with their pack mules and donkeys. And at night they can find a corner in someone's *tukal* hut to sleep protected from the bitter winds and the fearful *shifta* who rob and maim in the hills.

As a Beta Israel she won't have this protection. Most of the settlements south of her village belong to the unbelievers. She is from a devout home and trained to refuse their food; the animals they slaughter are not according to the Law. Unclean women are allowed to bake their bread. And once the villagers learn that the starving girl by the bamboula tree will only accept a handful of peas, she becomes a *Buda*. One of the demons who turn into hyenas at night and bring sickness to their children. One of those killers of Christ. In spite of the blisters on her feet, she must now run from that area quickly. To such a girl expulsion from her home village amounts to a death sentence and that is what her mother shrieks at the high priest.

Then let her confess to the father of the child. Let her bring the guilty man before the *kahĕn*s so they can do to him according to the Law. He has defiled a virgin and he must marry her and pay her father just restitution. The mother tries once again to get Mariam to understand: This man has done an evil thing. If she is too ashamed to utter his name then just lead her to the *tukal* where he lives and point. She will do the rest. But Mariam insists that no man has ever touched her. The girl's simple face is like a clear stream. It holds no fear, no cunning. Can it be that the light in her daughter's mind glows more dimly than she thought?

She lifts the girl's skirt and, taking two fingers, she pokes along the closed seam between her legs. Here, she says, who has been here? And here? here? The only opening down there is smaller than one of those fingertips. She pokes at it again and again. Here, I say, what man has touched you here? And the girl repeats that no man has ever touched her. But a child is growing in her belly and so some man must have; some man *must have*. She tells Mariam she has to stop this lying; the time for patience is long past. Confess the name of this beast and let them salvage what they can. And when the girl repeats her innocence once again, the woman raises her fist and strikes her. She beats her until she breaks free and runs from the *tukal*; she races behind Mariam, flinging dust at her back. The *kahĕn*s will expel her from the village! Does she know what that means?

There are no cooking fires lit on the eve of Atonement. That entire night and all of the next day will be spent in strict fasting and prayer. At sunset the settlement begins to gather at the sanctuary to receive the blessings of the priests. It is starless and chill as Mariam's mother approaches the holy place. Her three sons will follow her husband onto the sanctuary grounds to pray with the other men on the north side; the very young girls and old women pray on the south side. Tonight she does not maneuver for a space among the other married women to sit as close to the threshold as possible; she wraps her shawl around her and drops to the ground with her back against a juniper. There isn't the familiar stir of pride in watching her husband and sons step into the lighted courtyard. In knowing that they will be praying so near to the Holy of Holies. So near to the blessed Torah. She sits alone tonight. The one daughter is to leave after the fast of Atonement. And Adonai did not see fit to answer her prayer for the second daughter. And that was to ask for so very little.

The crisp air carries the smell of the incense and the voices of the priests as they begin the chant. Her own lips give the reply in wordless pantomime. The night allows her much time to think. The *kahĕn*s had waited as long as they could. If the girl had confessed up until the eve of Atonement, then the whole village would have had to join them in her forgiveness. She knew the hand of the high priest's wife was in this extended period of grace. A good woman. But is this not the night for *God* to forgive? She does not look forward to the moment when she must kiss these neighbors as all turn to the others—Forgive me, forgive me. Because in her heart she must truly pardon—the filthy whispers, the vicious lies—if she is to find the courage to enter the sanctuary and go before the Everlasting God.

She thinks of all the offerings she has brought to that threshold. Her portions of barley and wheat were full to the measure and always from the first threshing. Unlike some, she did not hide the best loaves, and when she poured her beer into the vessels for the priests, it was always from the first brewing. And when their goat bore twins, did she not insist that her husband take them both for the sacrifice? She knew many sitting right here who would have only given one—if any. No, she must stop this type of thinking. Adonai, forgive her the false pride. She was not going in there to bargain with God, to plead her goodness. She was going to demand pure and simple justice.

The congregation keeps the vigil through the night. And just before the first light of dawn, with many nodding and fighting sleep, she rises and weaves her way through the prone women littering the front of the sanctuary. Fear tightens inside her throat until it chokes up her breath as she stands with her toes inches away from the threshold. There is a prayer to be said at this time of day. *Kalhu.* It is spoken before dawn when the hens cry. And then there is a prayer at dawn itself: O Lord, I called. There are ten prayers alone just for the hours of the day. The Beta Israel bless the rain, lightning, and thunder, the sunshine, the olive harvest, the wheat. They bless each meal before and even after it is eaten. They bless new clothes, new lambs, new roads on which they travel. In this ancient faith there is a blessing for everything—except her body. She is the mother of four children and so has spent much of her life unclean.

The first foot she places down on the inside of the threshold burns like fire. But it is done. She has sinned. And, yes, there is a prayer for this:

> *God will help me, for He is great, God, my Lord. Put me not to shame, my Lord, God our judge, God our Lord, God, Lord of Israel, our King, because I transgressed the laws of sacrifice. There is none pure, none without blemish before Thee, O Lord, that seest the hidden things, that triest the heart and the reins. Mistreat me not, but remember the covenant of Abraham, Isaac, and Jacob, Thy servants.*

But I am also His servant, she whispers as she moves farther into the sacred ground toward the Holy of Holies. I am also His servant and He is my God too.

The air in the sanctuary is hazy from the sesame-oil lamps. In the predawn light they think it is a spirit moving between their kneeling bodies. The hem of her dress touches a praying girl's shoulder, and when the girl looks up to discover that it is Mariam's mother violating the sanctuary, she shrieks. It gets echoed over and over. Chaos breaks out. The woman begins to run in circles. She knows that the Holy of Holies must be somewhere toward the center, but there are so many people shouting now, hands reaching out to strike her as she's shoved against walls and spat upon.

She tries not to fight back; she must keep forgiving them if she is to ask God to spare Mariam. In the crush of bodies she is shoved out into the eastern section of the courtyard. The crowd becomes dead still. No one—man or woman—dares to follow. The Law is clear. That inner threshold is the point of no return. The backs of her legs hit the sharp edges of the sacrificial altar and she loses her balance. Her hand knocks over a clay vessel for catching blood. It shatters as it hits the ground. Stumbling back to her feet, she sees the double-edged knives hanging at the side of the altar. There is only one type of prayer to be said in here. She turns to stone. And before the world goes blank, she hears the wailing of her youngest boy as the silent crowd begins to part for the high priest.

SOMEWHERE ALONG THE LINE I had forgotten to breathe. And when my words came out they sounded choked and strange. But this is 1948. They couldn't have . . . Eve gave me a look that shut me right up. It's also Ethiopia, she said. The hills of Ethiopia.

Mariam's long trip through those mountains is also to become a journey through time. The high priest's wife hides herself and waits for the girl at the edge of the village. She places an amulet around her neck with a note pinned on it to be given to one of her old friends in Addis Ababa. Walk toward the rising sun, she tells Mariam. And if God be with you, so that you reach the town that looks and smells like Tuesday Market, follow the motor road south until you see the place where the people build their houses on rock ledges like the pigeons. Show someone this note; they will then tell you where you go. She repeats it several times until she believes the girl understands: Walk toward the rising sun.

But the Addis Ababa this woman knew was gone. She was one of the few Beta Israel who had met other Jews from the outside world. Years ago there had been a Frenchman who came to tell them that they had wealthy brothers and sisters in his land and many others. There were new and wonderful things to teach them, and their suffering would soon end. When these brothers and sisters did not appear, her father told her that the Frenchman was lying. He was alone out there beyond those mountains. But she was hoping to send Mariam to a cousin who taught in a boy's boarding school set up by this man. He could take her to women who would help her. But Mussolini had been through Addis Ababa since she'd left. All of the Jewish schools that the Fascists didn't close, they burned to the ground. And when the rightful government came back into power, they decided to leave matters just that way. The Jewish boarding school she sought was a heap of rubble. And the names she had written on her note were the names of dead men.

Mariam is terrified of the heavy traffic, the loud noises, the people who shove and push. Bird monsters fly overhead with the sound of a thousand wasps. She runs into doorways and covers her head when she sees them in the sky, to keep from being swept up and eaten. And the high priest's wife was wrong. There is no one who will show her where to go. They read her note and look at her as something despised. They must know that she has touched the lepers, because they are everywhere in the streets, all talking in strange, strange tongues. But she knows she is unclean, and if they will just direct her, she can find her people, who will show her where to wash. It is another bird monster that sends her running to crouch in a doorway on a back street. And she sees another leper staring at her through the shop window. Why would the high priest's wife do this? Why would she send her into such a world?

Mariam curls herself into a tight ball when Gabriel opens the door. She is too tired to run anymore. She cannot believe that the old man is beginning to speak to her in her own tongue. He tells her that she shouldn't be afraid; he is not diseased. It is only the color of his skin. He extends his wrinkled hands and turns them for her to see. I am in exile like you, he says; I am a white Falasha. And I will lead you to a place where you can rest.

EVE TOOK A PAPER NAPKIN and cleared away the mess on the counter. I was relieved when she did, because I had no intentions of touching it. I picked up the sticky knife between my fingertips and threw it into the garbage.

    —Whatever happened to that girl, Eve said, she is pregnant. And I have an entirely new situation on my hands. My place is a way station, just like yours. And there is no world for this girl to return to.

But I'd heard my husband and Gabe talking about the Jews finally getting a land of their own so they wouldn't have to be treated like garbage anymore. Maybe she could find a home there. But Eve wasn't too hopeful:

    —They've barely begun to set up that new government in Israel. And even if they're willing to accept her as one of their own, making the arrangements will take time. Like it or not, she's ours for now. And my guess is that her baby will be due by next summer. I don't mind admitting that worries me, Nadine.

I knew what she meant. A child has never been born on this street. And the closest thing we have to what you might call a youngster at all is Carrie's daughter. But Angel is an odd thirteen, with those long skirts and stooped shoulders. Her distrust of anything natural and free. Her spirit was aged a long time ago. And it's a shame that Carrie doesn't realize she's pushing that girl to the edge. Hasn't she ever wondered how Angel can even follow her into this cafe? No point in trying to cue her in, though; you can't tell Carrie nothing. Once Eve just remarked in passing that *Angel* was a strange name for the girl. And Carrie really flew off the handle, talking about how sweet and innocent she is, and missing Eve's whole point: all the angels in the Bible are men.

I hope little Mariam will find a place to go before it's time for the baby. A child isn't *supposed* to be born on this street. I don't care what kind of worlds we all came in from; there isn't much of a prayer for life itself if a baby has to be born here. But maybe it's meant for this baby to bring in a whole new era. Maybe when it gets here, it'll be like an explosion of new hope or something, and we'll just fade away. And maybe I should just stop talking and wait to see.

Miss Maple's Blues

I want you to know right off that Nadine lied on me. I did not run out of here because I knew she and Eve were gonna move into that duet. If you had seen the dirty looks she gave me just before—like I had something to do with what happened to that little girl. Like it was somehow my fault for just being a male. And I only used fixing the coffee grinder as an excuse to cover up the fact that I was sneaking out to buy her a Christmas present. It'll be the first time since we've been married. Each year she tells me not to bother, so I don't. But I found myself with the urge to do something nice for my wife. To let her know that she was appreciated. And underneath it all, I hoped that she would know I was saying that Mariam's story hurt me too.

We don't put up decorations here for the holidays. There are too many different kinds of people in and out, and to make it festive for one's tradition is to give slight to the other's. Everybody in the world isn't a Christian. The truth is, most people in the world aren't Christians. Nadine says I have the utmost authority to speak about that club since I joined it a long time ago. But I'm not about to let her spoil my goodwill this season.

Even me and Gabe make up around the holidays. You haven't heard me mention him before because he gets on my nerves. When I've got him backed into a corner on some of his more farfetched arguments, he'll always try to win by pulling rank with his age.

I am an old dog, Gabe says, and do not have patience for the whining of a puppy. He thinks he knows everything. It's true, he's old enough to have just about *seen* everything, but one don't necessarily follow the other. Now, it was coming up to his Hanukkah, mind you, and I made him latkes. And he's gonna take one hard look at them heaped up on the platter: My puppy, surely you do not want this to be my last Hanukkah? A fella can't win for losing. I woulda told him just how much I resented those comments after all the trouble I went through, but then that woulda meant he woulda told me that he could care less, which means we're off and running to a big blowout then and with it coming up to my Christmas Eve I didn't want to risk his not dropping off my usual gift. A quart of Russian vodka so smooth it goes down like silk. Between his new year and mine, we try to keep our truce: no discussion of politics, religion—or food.

This season always gets to me. It's bad enough we have to stay open. A vacation would be nice—winter or summer—but it's one of the occupational hazards of running a business like this. Another is the suicides. We get more than our share this time of year, people who come in through the front door and head straight on to the rear of the cafe—and don't come back. I try to mind my grill and stay put, although sometimes you'll hear the most beautiful music. A chorus of Christmas carols. The blowing of a shofar. Ghantā bells. Jade gongs. Gong chimes. Or the silver sounds of Tunisian finger cymbals. I might peek through the rear door then, and there'll be small parties or huge parties going on. Sometimes there's mellow candlelight spread over dining-room tables or crystal chandeliers sparkling down on dancing crowds of people with children running among their feet. There's not always a Christmas tree, but there is always laughter. I can tell if it's gonna be a suicide when the whole thing starts to glow so brightly it hurts your eyes, and the beautiful music gets so dim it hurts your head to strain to hear it. I'll turn away and come back inside, but I know what that particular customer has planned: they're going to stay out back until a certain memory becomes just too much to bear.

In that way the sparseness of this place during the holidays can be a relief. It reminds no one of anything but the last time they had indigestion or the last time Nadine may have insulted them for expecting her to leave the cash register to wait a table. Business as usual at the cafe. Sugar Man is telling me that, tonight of all nights, I should keep Miss Maple out: It's bad luck to ring in the new year with a faggot near a salt shaker. Now, I don't think he pulled that superstition out of anything but his own mind. And it does no good to tell him for the thousandth time that Miss Maple isn't a homosexual. Sugar Man has had to cling onto that or he would just about lose his senses when Miss Maple is around.

Miss Maple wears dresses. Light percale housedresses most of the time, because he's Eve's housekeeper. But in the summer, when he takes a day off he might show up in here with a backless sundress or a little cotton romper. We're talking no wigs. We're talking no makeup. No padded falsies. No switching. And if it's near the evening, we're talking a five o'clock shadow that he runs his hands over like any tired man after a day of hard work. In fact, it's impossible to look at the way Miss Maple walks in here and not see a rather tall, rather thin, reddish brown man in a light percale housedress. And that's about it, with the exception of a pair of flat canvas sandals to round off the outfit. He'll straddle the counter stool like a man, order in a deep voice, and eat his meal in a no-nonsense fashion. And if you want a conversation—although most folks don't—he'll hold one with you in a very sane manner.

I'll admit at first I thought it a little different—if not downright strange. But Sugar Man can't bear it, just can't bear it. He'll start vibrating like one of those jackhammers, his eyes blinking fifty thousand miles a minute, and *faggot* has been the kindest thing he's called Miss Maple. But he better not call him anything nasty within hearing distance; once was enough to make that mistake. He found out why Miss Maple doubles at night as Eve's bouncer. When Miss Maple tells the gentleman callers it's time to go home, print dress or not, they go. But as soon as he opens his mouth, you can tell he's not from the rough side of town. If anything, it's a cultured voice and it's clear he's had a lot of schooling. Still, those lean arms are muscled and those fists pretty large, and if he's pressed, he'll use 'em.

It doesn't bother him to answer to *Miss Maple,* though, because I think it was Eve who started calling him that. Yeah, it must have been Eve, because she was the first person he met in here. Sugar Man swears he was wearing a crinoline skirt and high heels when he first walked in and announced out loud that his name was Miss Maple; had Sugar Man so upset he almost threw up his food. That is an out-and-out lie. To begin with, the man doesn't own a pair of high heels or a crinoline skirt. And second, I was right where I'm standing now when he first came in. Dressed like a Wall Street banker. The only thing odd about his clothes then was that he had his shirt unbuttoned and he was carrying the jacket to his gray flannel suit. I didn't have time to strike up a conversation with him; it was busy as the dickens that day. But I don't think Sugar Man was even in here. And if he was, he wouldn't have been anywhere near Eve. And it was Eve who first used that name. Had to be Eve, because I remember her calling me over from the grill. Well, I've finally found the right housekeeper. Bailey, meet Miss Maple. And Eve isn't one to make light—of nothing. So in that long talk they were having at the end of the counter, he must have told her that was his name. Or decided to let people use it as his name. Or whatever.

I can get inside a lot of heads around here if I've got the time or inclination. But how Miss Maple first got tagged with that name isn't high on my list of priorities. And he hasn't a bit of trouble speaking for himself; if he wanted to explain it to folks, I'm sure he would. What's *real* interesting to me is that he came in here two years ago with a worn briefcase and a wrinkled gray flannel suit, and set on using the last money he had in his pocket to buy a pawnshop revolver—and just one bullet—while now he's about to ring in the new year worth close to fifty thousand and counting. Not bad for a housekeeper.

My name is Stanley. My middle names are Beckwourth Booker T. Washington Carver. The *T* is for Taliaferro. Most people don't know that's what the initial stands for in Booker T. Washington's name, and they don't know that James P. Beckwourth was a scout who discovered the lowest point for wagon trains to cross the Sierras, getting the Beckwourth Pass and the town of Beckwourth, California, all thrown in for the effort. Someone like Sugar Man, who thinks he has the right to ridicule me for my choice of clothes, doesn't even know where the Sierras are, or that colored pioneers like Beckwourth existed, or that George Washington Carver did a lot more for the world than refine peanut butter. Whenever he licks a postage stamp this season to send out those misspelled Christmas cards to whoever has the misfortune of his knowing their address, he gives no thanks to Carver for it not falling off the envelope. That's because he's only been taught what we call American history.

Papa named me after great men because he expected the same from me. I like to think I didn't disappoint him. But I sure wish he'd had more than one son so I wouldn't have to carry all these names. Since there never was enough space on job applications, I'd just abbreviate it to Stanley B. B. T. W. C. and then my surname. Sure, I could have left out the B. B. T. W. C., but that gave me a chance to give a miniature and, I hope, memorable history lesson to whatever miseducated individual was sitting behind a desk deciding whether I could make a decent living or not. Thinking back, I'm sure they probably thought I was lying, the rest of my application being outside the scope of their miseducation as well.

Colored people weren't born in California—second generation no less. And colored men didn't have Ph.D.'s. A few grew more comfortable with the fact that I claimed it was *southern* California, and we did grow cotton on the farm. I guess that, along with the expensive cut of my suit and vest, made them comfortable enough to risk offering me the job of head custodian at a firm where I'd applied for the position of statistical analyst. B. B. T. W. C. The history lesson would have to be repeated a bit more tersely, condensed into language that even they could understand: My training had been in the application *not* of mops and brooms, but of variance, square roots, and bell curves. Well, there was no need to get huffy—the offer was *head* custodian. Ah, so now it was much clearer: the job brought along the responsibility of *counting* the mops and brooms. And this was in Los Angeles. San Francisco. Sacramento.

And later, as I rode the bus east along the paved highway that now ran through Beckwourth Pass, it was Denver, Kansas City, Chicago, Philadelphia. I didn't travel below the Mason-Dixon for what I thought then were obvious reasons. A victim of my own stupidity—anywhere that bus could have taken me in the forty-eight states was all *south* of the Canadian border. The offers accumulated: bellboy, mailroom clerk, sleeping-car porter, elevator operator. And after all, who was I to turn down an honest living? There were other Negroes with Ph.D.'s doing this work. Who was I indeed?

Well, my grandfather made it to California in 1849 through the Arizona desert. And where he came from before then is sort of hazy. I know he wasn't a slave, because that's how Aunt Hazel used to phrase it: My daddy wasn't a slave. There were only two types of Negroes then, she would say, those who were slaves and those who weren't slaves. She knew enough never to call him free. And from what I gather, he wasn't real smart. There were thousands on that same trail with him, heading for Box Canyon on their way to either disappointment or untold riches up near Sutter's Mill, but after making it through the most hellish part of the trip, he called it quits near the junction of the Gila and Colorado rivers. He struck gold anyway when he met my grandmother. At the time he didn't know it, figuring he'd come into the clutches of some crazy Yuma squaw.

Papa ended up inheriting 3,000 acres of what was to be some of the richest land in Imperial Valley because his father had been afraid of his wife. *Seen-yae-n'ye-handc*, the marriage broker said, pointing to my grandmother; and indeed she was: a handsome girl, with her oiled mahogany skin and jet black hair, and dressed only in a girdle of bark fringed at the thighs. But it was probably her incredible breasts with nipples the size of silver dollars that sealed the bargain. My grandfather would have been just as happy to stay where he was, even though he found out he'd been cheated in the dealings for my grandmother. Although she was a shaman's daughter, that same string of pook shells could have gotten him a mule to help plow the fields for his corn and melons. And a mule wouldn't have talked back. My grandmother spoke some Spanish and her native tongue, Cuchan. My grandfather set about teaching her the most important phrases in English: *I am the man. You—woman*. But he found himself learning her language a whole lot quicker: *co-barque*. That meant *no*, and he was to hear it often.

Even after she had learned English, she resorted to Cuchan when she had a point to make. And she made the point over and over that she wanted them to head farther west. And here I'll have to side with my grandfather. There was nothing on the other side of the Yuma settlement but mountains and desert. But just before their wedding, my grandmother had done the dream dance: She saw the meeting of the red river and the black river, the waters swirling and forming straight as an arrow to leap through the hills and spring up, flooding the desert. And she saw her sons, dark as the night, proud as the eagles, picking white gold from the ground. Translation: I could have had one of my own kind. But now that I've married you, Negro, take me west.

She gave him no peace, as she insisted she was going to California: *N'ya-hap me-ye-moom*. No help with the crops: *N'ya-hap me-ye-moom*. No cooked meals: *N'ya-hap me-ye-moom*. And finally, no sex. But you're already *in* California, you damn fool, my grandfather would hold his aching balls at night and rage. But he knew what she meant and he also knew better than to try beating her into submission. That was how he'd learned the Cuchan words for his nose—*e hotche*—because she'd broken it.

They went into the desert to live on mesquite beans, the roots of the wild maguey, and my grandmother's dream. The adobe hut they built kept them shaded when the midday temperatures tipped over 110 degrees, and provided shelter from the night winds that were cold enough to make their teeth chatter. My grandfather cursed his fate as he hauled enough water from a nearby stream to irrigate a small garden; my grandmother drew a circle on the ground, sat through the bitter night as meteors lit up the southwestern sky, and arose at dawn to say: We must claim this land. If there had been a way to do that, they certainly wouldn't have had much competition. But the problem was that the Mexicans had recently lost it in war to the United States, and neither of my grandparents was an American.

That didn't stop their first child from being born. By the time the second one came along, all of those Negroes who supposedly weren't living in

California had held a state convention in 1855 and raised enough money to kick up enough dust in state courts to give my grandfather the right to buy that patch of desert—if somebody had owned it. But nobody did, which put it in the public domain. And while he was now allowed to buy all the *private* property in California that anybody wanted to sell him, public property belonged to all of the united states in America, and it would take him another war, another thirteen years, and two more children to become a paper American. That's how Aunt Hazel used to phrase it: In 1868 my daddy became a real American—on paper. My grandmother was to live and die an alien. So anything to be done with that land had to be done through him. Not that the two of them were affected by all of the anguish going on in the cedar halls of Sacramento or the marble halls of Washington, D.C., to decide who and what they were. They knew what they were: a man and a woman with four children to feed and another one deciding to be born in the middle of a sandstorm. My grandfather caught that one daughter with his own hands, my grandmother unable to go off as usual and squat by the creek.

I've just brought all this up to say that when they finally took the long trip to San Diego to register the first 160 acres, the Homestead Act was not another boulder standing in their way. Marking off the boundaries on the map, the federal clerk asked my grandfather if he was crazy. He said no, but that his wife was. After work, the clerk had a drink in the saloon with his buddies and a good laugh over the stupid dust ball who'd let his squaw henpeck him into staking a claim in the middle of the desert cause she'd dreamed about white gold. The saloonkeeper heard them out of one ear and repeated the story to a group at the other end of the bar. It got repeated later at the blackjack table, the next evening at the local whorehouse, and then at the Methodist Sunday service. By noon Monday morning, the claims office was mobbed.

They came with pickaxes, shovels, and dynamite. They came by the wagonloads, by the buggyfuls; they came walking. Their horses muddied the creek my grandparents used for drinking; their children stole melons from the garden. And the fifth baby would scream throughout the day as explosions rocked the earth around them. Most gave up in a few weeks; the hardiest lasted a year. The longer they'd stayed, the cheaper it was for my grandfather to buy off their claims. It ain't worth ten cents an acre, one disgusted prospector spat out; just stay here until you drop and call it a gift from heaven. But my grandmother insisted on my grandfather paying them something, if only a penny a parcel, to make the sale papers legal. The Yumas had already learned what the white man could do when your land was given by God.

So they ended up with a little over 3,000 acres of cacti, dwarf cedars, and wild sage. But my grandmother was to realize her vision of water flooding the desert, because the Imperial Canal was completed just before she died. And she had given my grandfather those dark sons—eight of them—and two daughters. The white gold was to come later. Cotton wasn't only king in the South; we grew a lot of it in California. And we were able to produce the finest staples of it on our farm, the long-fibered pima cotton, because my father's older brothers had been trained in agricultural science. They wouldn't have been welcome at the nearest county school; a Negro is a Negro. So, keeping her husband far in the background, my grandmother had enrolled them in the missionary school set up on the Yuma reservation. And since an Indian is an Indian, their mother was able to get them an education while their father had gotten them the land.

Papa was their last child and never really suited to be a farmer. In another time and place, my father would have been a philosopher or perhaps a poet. His brothers just thought him spoiled and lazy. And sadly, I thought him a coward. He'd had engraved on my mother's tombstone: Flower of the Desert. Daughter of the Wind. Wife of My Heart. Mother of Our Future. I guess he would have kept going on, but he ran out of space, needing something leftover for her name and the date. She was murdered young. My mother was the youngest child of a fugitive Texan slave and a Mexican ranchero. I don't remember her, but they told me she spoke only Spanish, and she was fiery and beautiful and as dark as the midnight air she liked riding bareback in. Her father never forgave her for marrying mine, especially after he wouldn't help them lynch the itinerant drifter who had raped her and left her to die in a ravine. My father just had no stomach for castrating a man and then roasting him alive on an open spit. Aunt Hazel did; she kept them supplied with the wood because my mother was one of her favorite sisters-in-law.

But Papa loved my mother; he was the only one of his brothers who had actually married for love. The others knew that something like that was risky at best. Wives were to be chosen who were suited for the life my uncles had to offer in Imperial Valley. And I had aunts of all assortments: pure-blooded Yumas; full-blooded Negroes; full-blooded Mexicans; Yuma-Mexicans; Mexican-Irish; Negro-Mexicans; and even one pure-blooded African who still knew some phrases in Ashanti: all hearty and strong. Women who could straddle a row of cotton all day and still straddle a man at night. Because there had to be a lot of babies; we had a lot of land.

Growing up, I never gave much thought to what my cousins and I were; you could get a little dizzy tracing all of those lines. The Americans had no problems with our identities, though; they imported one six-letter word to cut through all that Yuma-Irish-Mexican-African tangle in our heritage. And after the valley was flooded with water, we watched them pour in across the eastern border. Brawley, Holtville, and Westmorland became thriving towns, and El Centro an actual city. The American flag was hoisted in front of the new post offices and on the tops of city halls. Our profits almost doubled because shipping costs were cut in half with the new cotton exchange set up in El Centro; the American flag flew over that too. And in the valley we learned the new language of progress: *Hoover Dam. Electricity. Highway.* My uncles' wives left the fields, to be replaced by migrant workers and sharecroppers. My cousins went off to private academies. Papa couldn't bear to part with me, and he said he didn't trust what I'd be taught in any of their schools, so he hired a special tutor. All of this in the middle of a depression, because even with the times so hard, Princeton and Harvard certainly didn't close down, and nightclubs flourished; we were growing the pima cotton for those dress shirts.

We were pretty much ignored by the Americans until they found out we actually owned all of the land we were farming, and the barns and the reapers and the trucks and the gin mills. They'd stand speechless at the edge of our fields, which stretched farther than they could see over any horizon; progress had given them no vocabulary to reconcile the land and us. They already knew what we were and any fool could see what the land was worth. But how do you put the two together? And having no words for what was in front of them, they believed it had no right to exist. The real Americans didn't know that this is what they actually believed because, you see, what they'd been taught in school is that they believed every man—whatever race of man—had a right to anything he was willing to work and sacrifice for. But somehow, somehow, the sight of Papa pulling up in front of the Holtville bank in his La Salle convertible would set their teeth on edge. He'd come back out of the bank to find all of his whitewalls flat and that six-letter word scrawled in mud over his windshield. Hoodlum pranks, the sheriff would tell him. And yes, he'd tried to find witnesses from even the last time, but it was funny how nobody claimed to see a thing. Papa would make his job a whole lot easier if he'd just stop asking for trouble and not bring that automobile into town.

But he couldn't go into town without any clothes on. And besides good motor cars, my father liked tailored suits. The weather made us dress differently in southern California; short-sleeved shirts with open vests and cotton slacks were just common sense, as well as the huaraches and moccasins. Top that off with either a straw panama or a sailcloth cap, and you had what we called Holtville casual. Papa tended more toward *Esquire* casual (dandy clothes, my uncles sneered) and stayed about as comfortable as we did, but there was no mistaking that his hunter jackets and foulard scarves were straight out of Palm Springs. And if he didn't like huaraches, he didn't like huaraches. Your toes don't burn; mine don't either, Papa would say. And he'd wear those linen loafers with the calf trim, even though they always managed to get stepped on in town.

I understand a lot now that I didn't then. I thought my father was pathetic for never fighting back. He had to know it wasn't accidental that a wad of tobacco spit would splatter right in front of us, staining the cuffs of his slacks. No storekeeper was so nearsighted that he waited on everyone else at the counter before he finally saw us. Holtville wasn't so crowded that we had to be bumped and shoved aside while trying to cross the street. My uncles wouldn't have stood for it. And none of that, certainly, happened when Aunt Hazel was with us. Witch Hazel, they whispered behind her back in town. And she took it as a compliment. Aunt Hazel was the only mother I knew, she having raised me and taken care of our home after my real mother was killed. Everything I'd learned about my grandparents, she'd passed on to me. And she said that one day I would understand that my father was also teaching me something very special: how to be my own man.

But I didn't see him as a man at all. I was the only one of the boys who didn't get a cowboy suit and a pair of cap pistols for Christmas—I got books. And I was the only one who couldn't go to the pictures when a Tom Mix feature was showing. We don't applaud genocide in this house, he'd say. But kids are still going to play cowboys-and-Indians, and with me never having a holster and pistols, I was tagged for the Indian. Even my cousin Tomaso, whose mother was a full-blooded Yuma and had named him after a famous chief, even *he* got a cowboy suit. But there I was, the one always having to climb up into the cottonwoods and give a blood-curdling cry before I was shot down and made to eat dust. A loser. And the son of a loser, the way my uncles told it. The older ones still had memories of what it had been like to survive in a desert and they were hard, dry men who saw Papa as soft. They called my father *butter britches*. They'd never tell me what it meant. I wanted to believe the nickname grew from his being the baby brother and the only one my grandmother had the time and leisure to coddle. But knowing that they considered my father strange in waiting so long to marry and in not remarrying after my mother died, and knowing how my uncles' minds turned, *butter britches* had to mean something much, much nastier.

They thought his library was a waste of good money—not that they were against books, but his books were bound in Moroccan leather and gold-leafed, and not one of the damn things could help you fight a boll weevil—or anything else. Sure, their sons were off in school, studying, but even though it worried the hell out of them for the boys to be taking up an old maid's language like Latin, at least it was by reading *The Wars of Caesar*; while that little pansy he was raising had to learn it through Plutarch's *Lives*. Aesop. Aristotle. Aurelius. He kept them in alphabetical order. He read almost everything but only chose to bind certain ones. Dante. Donne. Du Bois. Dunbar. I'm leaving you a legacy, he'd say, a *carefully* chosen legacy. Personally, I wasn't very interested in either James, C. L. R. or Henry, Sr. Philosophy hadn't saved my father from the contempt we met in town. Philosophy didn't give him guts. I hated being ashamed of my father and when I finally told him so, there were tears in his eyes. And I was ashamed of him for that.

Funny, I had almost decided not to follow him into Holtville that day. I had three more weeks before I left for the university, and I was counting. He was really excited because my graduation gift had been freighted in, but who wanted it? I hadn't gone to a real school, like my cousins, so what was I graduating from? And I didn't call a complete set of Shakespeare a real gift—cream vellum or not, from England or wherever. And the prevailing theory was that the old Bard had had some real dilemmas over his manhood. Manhood is a pervasive preoccupation when you're an adolescent boy, and you tend to see a fairy under every bush. I definitely saw one lurking under Iago, Brutus, that whining Hamlet. And here Papa was, expecting me to haul that crap all the way to Stanford. Stanford, mind you, while my cousin Tomaso, who was so dumb he could hardly tie his shoelaces and barely eked into one of the state colleges where they had to take anyone—even us—had gotten a box of French rubbers from his father. And my uncle had patted him on the back and said, Make sure to use 'em all in one place. Now, that was a *real* gift. A man's gift. So, thank you but no, Papa, I don't feel like riding into Holtville.

But my father was so proud over what I'd managed to accomplish, he wasn't even going to let me stand in the way. He waxed the La Salle and then got himself really spiffy that afternoon: double-breasted blazer, madras silk for the foulard scarf and matching pocket handkerchief, a coconut straw for the sun, and yes, those linen loafers with the calf trim. After he was dressed, he leaned against the convertible and played his trump card. The bank wouldn't honor any drafts I drew while away at school unless they had my signature on file, and I might consider it a useful bit of information to know that today was one of the precious few that, in spite of my attitude, he felt moved enough to vouch for my identity as his son. Translation: Get into the car or else, you ungrateful little snot. But he did let me pretend I still had to think the whole thing over. He even waited patiently while I took my dear, sweet time changing into my own clothes: a beat-up pair of dungarees and a plaid cotton shirt. I sauntered back out of the house and announced with all the arrogance that only an eighteen-year-old who someone else is supporting can summon up, I'm not going if we don't take the truck. I'm sick of changing flat tires.

We took the truck. But it still didn't matter—he was fair game by then. And while the Gatlin boys would probably have shared my opinion of

Shakespeare if they hadn't been illiterate buffoons and had had the slightest inkling of who he was, they knew that whatever was in those crates being loaded into the back of our truck was bought with money they didn't have, from a farm where they'd been considered too shiftless even to be taken on as sharecroppers. Real Americans, like them, turned down from working, mind you, by the likes of us. This country wasn't shit. This country was going to the frigging dogs. When the four of them weren't warming the bench in front of the freighting office, they were getting drunk and beating each other up at the local barroom; and when they'd gotten thrown out of there, if it was late enough in the day, they could make it to their Klan meetings.

The Ku Klux Klan got imported into California not too long after the American flag; created in the heartland of the country, it radiated out from Indiana until there were chapters in almost every state. But it had a hard time catching on in our area, although, like the Communist party, it started gaining strength during the depression. The displaced Okies, running from starvation, had a problem with our being so close to the Mexican border; they soon discovered that the other migrant workers weren't just niggers who spoke Spanish but a bunch of sneaky lunatics who spoke Spanish, and when you mauled one of their women, they'd more than likely follow you back home at night and slit your throat. And actually, rowdy members like the Gatlins were an embarrassment to the local Klan and discouraged from joining. Our Klan was a quiet social club of businessmen and wealthy landowners. They met to reaffirm their right to be and ours to not, while working through the chamber of commerce and Grange to keep it that way. They hid the good brandy whenever the Gatlins showed up, and they were forced to sit in pained silence as they were denounced as a bunch of dickless wonders.

As a matter of fact, the head clerk at the freighting office was a Klan member. Peters was a nearsighted, hunchbacked little fellow who was never without a worn copy of *Collier's* or a penny dreadful. He told us to open the crates in front him because he wasn't honoring any claims for damage once those boxes left the place. But Papa already knew that's how he conducted business with us and had come prepared with his own crowbar. Peters never seemed to have one that he could spare for our use. I turned my back on the whole operation and stared out the office window. He could make me tag along, but I saw no reason to help. The streets were getting busy again, people slowly venturing out, with the hottest part of the day almost over. The Gatlins were still out there in their regular spot, and I remember thinking how strange it was that they hadn't said too much as we walked in. One of them had given a halfhearted attempt at making monkey noises, but that was pretty light. The weather had probably slowed them down.

I could hear Papa grunting as he worked with the crowbar to remove the lid. The crate was packed with straw, and nested inside were oilcloth envelopes. Each envelope closed with a hook and eye, and inside was a bundle wrapped with brown paper and taped firmly. After the brown paper was removed, there was still a wrapping of royal blue felt to be undone before you got to the single volume. As Papa finally uncovered the first volume, Peters emitted a slow whistle. It was a work of art.

—How many of 'em you got there? Peters whispered.

—There should be thirty-eight, Papa said.

Neither man's eyes left the finely stitched binding and jet silk cover as Papa turned it over and over in his hands.

—But Shakespeare only wrote thirty-seven plays, Peters said.

And then each looked into the other's eyes, knowing what they were doing while knowing they couldn't stop.

—There's a separate volume for the poems and sonnets, Papa answered.

Peters nodded, and Papa handed him the book. Peters opened the cover like a man making love and wiped his sweaty hands on his trousers before daring to touch the tissue overleaf.

—I ain't never seen nothing like this.

The title page was wood cut, the edges hand sheared.

—You musta mortgaged the back forty.

—He's my only son, Papa said.

And Peters nodded again. The spell was broken as the bell over the front door clanged and the postman came in to drop off the afternoon mail. Peters gave the volume brusquely back to Papa and said, No point in trying to check each one, you'd be here until doomsday. Just take 'em on home and if anything's wrong, bring 'em back for reshipment. It was the first time he'd ever said that and also the first time he offered to carry anything out to the truck.

The Gatlins were stunned when Peters came out with the first crate. And by the time he'd loaded all three crates, they'd worked themselves into a silent fury. Next thing you know, that spineless turd will be eating dinner with 'em. Next thing you know, he'll be asking them to join the Klan. Papa was getting ready to sign the release forms when they came in. They entered one at a time, the bell clanging, the door slamming behind each one, until all four stood blocking the entrance. A slight tremor started around Peters's mouth, and he swallowed real hard. Papa ignored them. He was on his second reading of the release forms, always checking everything twice before he signed it. He told Peters that the delivery date was wrong and needed to be changed; today was August 12th. Peters snapped, Change it yourself, and then gave the Gatlins a nervous smile. But it was too little and too late.

The fat Gatlin reached back and pulled the bolt on the door. The greasy Gatlin drew the shades on the windows. Peters was shaking visibly: Please, boys, I don't want no trouble. I had started inching toward the crowbar on the counter when the bald Gatlin beat me to it. He handed it to the cross-eyed Gatlin, who took it and jabbed Papa in the middle of the chest: We came in here to ask you a question.

—So ask it, Papa said.

Animals like them can smell fear, but the only ones sweating in that room were me and Peters. My father folded up the release forms and put them in his jacket pocket and stood there waiting. He had the expression on his face of a man who was becoming extremely bored. The cross-eyed Gatlin was at a loss; he looked at the greasy Gatlin, who looked at the bald Gatlin, but it was the fat Gatlin who finally stepped forward: Well, my brothers and me was out there asking ourselves how it is that a low-down, scum-bag, filthy piece of shit like you—ya know, something that looks like it swung in from a jungle—how it is that he thinks he can parade all up and down town wearing them clothes? And then he grinned as he braced himself with his fists balled at his side as the other Gatlins started to close in. Papa looked the fat Gatlin straight in the eye.

—That's not a difficult question. I wear these clothes because I can.

Then he started walking away from the counter and motioned for me to follow him to the door. I stood still because I knew they weren't letting us out of there that easily and I was furious at my father. If I'd been there with one of my uncles, he would have told these bastards about jungles. My uncle Leon would have pulled out his pistol and shot that tub of lard right in his bulging gut. He's talking about shit, there'd have been more shit all over this place than anybody could use. My uncle Leon once beat a man to a pulp just for calling him black. And even Aunt Hazel, dear Jesus, Aunt Hazel carried a stiletto in her garter. *I wear these clothes because I can.* But that Gatlin had seen something in my father's eyes that I didn't—he'd seen he was being dismissed.

He gave a wounded howl—No, you *can't* wear those clothes. Hear me? You *can't*—and knocked the straw hat off of Papa's head. As Papa bent over to retrieve it, the fat Gatlin grabbed him by the back of the belt, pulled out a Bowie, and slit his trousers straight down the rear seam before shoving him over on his knees. The blade also ripped through his boxer shorts and at the sight of one of his testicles hanging beneath the torn cloth, I felt something heavy and sick lodge in my throat. The next wounded howl came from me—I sprang onto the back of the fat Gatlin.

The huge man shook me off as if I were a fly. But that's all the others were waiting for, and the fun was on.

I don't remember everything that happened before they locked us in the storeroom, but I can remember the speed of their knives and the absolute joy in their voices as they pinned us down and ripped off every stitch of our clothing. What they couldn't tear apart, they stomped—My God, look, it ain't got a tail after all—what they couldn't crush under their feet, they spat on—And it ain't got a big wanger neither. After being flung naked into the storeroom, I fell on my elbow and the pain made my eyes sting. I sat on the dirt floor rocking and holding the bruised arm. I won't cry, I kept thinking over and over; I'll kill myself before I cry.

　　—Did they hurt you, son?
Papa reached out to me in the darkness and I jerked my shoulder away from his hands. Don't you touch me. My teeth were clenched. Just don't touch me. My eyes were adjusting to the dark and I could make out the shadowy silhouettes of packing crates and of his bare feet as he stood beside me. The air was close and stale; a trickle of sweat ran down the side of my nose and pooled in the crevice on my upper lip.

　　—Don't worry, Stanley, I'm pressing charges for this outrage. They've gone much too far this time.
The throbbing in my elbow kept time with the throbbing in my temples. Pressing charges? So he was going to press charges? If it hadn't hurt just to breathe, I would have laughed.

But we could hear the Gatlins laughing on the other side of the door. The thuds of their heavy shoes. Peters's high-pitched voice. All right, boys, let 'em out, the joke's over. The joke's over, I got a business to run. The heavy footsteps moved toward the storeroom and a fist banged on the plywood door. I could see the tips of his shoes in the wide space between the bottom rail and the threshold. Hey, you in there. It was the bald Gatlin. Hey, we figured you might be hungry. He kicked a banana peel under the door. It lay there twisted and rank. A fist pounded on the door again. And we was thinking, ya know?—it was the cross-eyed Gatlin. We was thinking of a way to make some money out of all of this, times being so hard. We was thinking of turning this place into a zoo and selling tickets. Think you worth a dime a look? They were having a great time, and I could hear my father's breath deepening beside me. Naw, they ain't worth a dime. It was the fat Gatlin. Folks'll want their money back after seeing them little wangers. And I could hear the greasy Gatlin through their laughter. Just shut up, Peters, you . . . But surely they couldn't go on forever with nothing feeding them but their hate, because we were silent in that close and stale room, so very very silent. Peters won't let me use the phone—it was the greasy Gatlin. What you mean, Peters won't let you use the phone? The fist banged on the door again to be sure we were catching the act. See, I was gonna put me in a collect call to Louie B. Mayer—up in Hollywood. And tell him he could buy a coupla apes real cheap for his new Tarzan movie. Aw, don't worry, it wouldna happened; I don't know any Jew who'll take a collect call. Surely it couldn't go on forever. But our silence seemed to goad them on and on . . .

I wouldn't be able to breathe in that room much longer. The air was pressing in on me. My chest was tightening, my head was throbbing, and I knew I was going to explode. There would be pieces of me all over the packing crates, smeared on the sides of these old boxes, flung into the corners among the dried mouse droppings.

—As God is my judge, Stanley, I'll make them pay for this.
And to my horror it began to happen: There is no God, Papa. I was on my feet, the words hissing through my teeth as my lungs did explode, and my head started spinning, spinning toward the cobwebs on the ceiling. There is no God, or He would have struck you dead a long time ago. You're worthless. You'll make them pay? How can you make them pay? You don't even amount to the ape they called you—you're nothing. And you've always been *nothing*. Nothing . . . nothing . . . noth . . . My whole

body started vibrating, my teeth chattering, my hands and leg muscles moving with a will of their own. He caught me in his arms before I fell to the floor. And then he placed me down gently to hold me as I cried like the child I was.

My flesh against his flesh: his chest was lean and hard, the arms around me strong and firm. His hand rested on the back of my head as I buried my weeping face deep into his shoulders. All of these years, he said, I kept hoping you'd understand. I should have just come out and explained why I've lived the way I have. It hasn't been easy, Stanley, but I did it for you. From the day you were born I've been speaking to you in a language that I wanted you to master, knowing that once you did, there was nothing that could be done to make you feel less than what you are, and I knew that they would stop at nothing to break you—because you are *mine*. And I wanted their words to be babble, whatever they printed, whatever they sent over the radio. Babble—as you learned your own language, set your own standards, began to identify yourself as a man. You see, to accept even a single image in their language as your truth is to be led into accepting them all. Do you think that I'm afraid of the Gatlins? Do you think that what they say *means* anything to me? I don't hear them, Stanley. Most of the time, I don't even see them. But in my self-absorption, I'd forgotten that it wasn't the same with you. I lost sight of how much you still have to learn. Forgive me for pressing you so hard and so quickly to become a man; I shudder to think of how close I've almost come to losing you as my child.

Then he told me to get up and clear the snot from my nose. He was fed up with this whole mess and it was time we got out of there. The Gatlins hadn't tired of coming back and forth to taunt us as they banged and kicked on the door. If anything, the attacks were getting uglier, their voices close to snarls. Whatever reaction they'd been hoping for, they hadn't gotten. Begging might have satisfied them before, but soon they would need blood. And there we were without even a pair of shoes between us. The door wouldn't be a problem, Papa said; it's nothing but plywood and this frame is so dry-rotted that the latch won't hold. But we'd have to confront them again, and I'd prefer for us to slip out quietly. There was a small casement window near the ceiling, and he thought that if we stacked up enough crates we'd be able to pull it off its hinges and squeeze through there. This man was amazing; he was standing there talking as if we weren't as naked as jaybirds.

—I think it best if we could leave without someone getting hurt. God forbid it be us, because you know what your uncles would do then. My way is to take care of them in court.

Talking as if those animals deserved anything but what I, indeed, knew my uncles would do. He was making no sense and I told him so.

—They aren't animals, Stanley. They're pathetic, but they aren't animals.

They were animals. Still, my father's plan seemed to be working; we had almost stacked up enough wooden crates to reach the window when we heard Peters cry out. It was muted, and cut off as suddenly as it began, but for some reason it was chilling. Heavy footsteps approached the door. It might have been one or all of them; they didn't say a word this time. A thud as something was kicked under the door. We smelled it before we saw it. They had gotten to the books. The silk cover was gouged with holes, the spine busted and bent over double. They'd torn out handfuls of pages, crushed what was left between their fists, and then urinated on the whole thing. The stench of *The Tempest* was quickly filling that close room.

I can't really say that my father was angry. Anger had to be a part of what he was feeling, and revulsion as well. But when he finally spoke it was only with a deep sadness.

—I see they are determined to leave me no choice. Now I'll have to go back out there and speak to them.

I didn't want to go anywhere but out that window, as quickly as we could. And anyone who'd seen the message they sent in through that book would wholeheartedly agree with me.

—They don't speak your language, Papa.

—I'm aware of that, he said.

There were cardboard boxes among the nailed crates. Things that had been shipped and never claimed. Most of it was useless to us as we sought something to cover ourselves: reams of yellowing typing paper, notation pads, inkwells. Candles, doilies, knitting yarn. Porcelain dolls, stuffed bears, wooden soldiers. We finally unearthed a steamer trunk marked, Lulu and the Little Ladies. The little ladies turned out to be dancing poodles; there were rhinestone collars, silver leashes, and tiny voile tutus. But Lulu's costume was in there as well, and it seemed she was hardly little. My father took the dress and forced me to take the corset: Don't be foolish; things might turn ugly out there, and you can see that they're the type who go straight for the balls.

He was right about the door. We used our shoulders, and with two good whacks the frame gave way. And yes, the Gatlins had heard the splintering wood. They were coming toward the back when we appeared in the office doorway. My father's dress was red taffeta with spaghetti straps and a huge circular skirt puffed out with yards of lace crinoline. And I'd had to tie knitting yarn around my waist to keep Lulu's corset up. Of course, they laughed. They laughed so hard their knees got weak. But Papa waited until the noise had died down some, making sure he would have their undivided attention.

He headed straight for the big one and spoke to him first. Grabbing him by the collar, he slammed his face down on the counter and dragged his unconscious body along the whole length of it, the fat Gatlin picking up splinters in his broken nose and leaving behind a trail of blood and chipped teeth:

My friends, I'll try to be brief: I am a man. And the founding fathers of this democracy passed on to you who call yourselves real Americans a monumental lie. All of us are not created equal. Some of us are more intelligent and physically fit than others. Some of us have the iron will to hold on to a dream. My parents were such people. Some of us are more shrewd and ruthless than others. Some of us wealthier by being more determined to step on whoever gets in their way. My brothers are such people. So for better and for worse, you are not my equal. I want that to be perfectly clear, and to avoid any further misunderstanding on your part, I'm now going to proceed to kick your ass.

Papa's skirt whirled as he aimed the fat Gatlin's body like a rocket into the chest of the bald Gatlin at the other end of the counter. The bald Gatlin was knocked to the floor and as he tried to push off the fat man, he looked up into nothing but a sea of lace crinoline. Papa smashed his bare heel down on his Adam's apple:

I am a man of peace. I am a sensitive man. I can spend hours with Proust and have been known to weep at a sunset. Those are the qualities I wanted to pass on to my son. I believe he has the capacity to be a great leader. And I've tried to teach him that a man rules best when he rules with compassion.

The other two Gatlins had recovered their senses by now. I swung at the greasy one with the crowbar while the cross-eyed one lunged at Papa's back with his Bowie. I yelled out to warn him. It was an old Yuma war tactic: if he's started the upswing to stab you in the back, there's no time to look around. Drop like lightning to your stomach and the enemy's knife will cut through empty air. It also helped that this Gatlin was cross-eyed. He missed Papa by a mile and wasn't given a second chance. Papa rolled over on the floor, the Gatlin's feet tangling all up in his taffeta ruffles. As the Gatlin started slipping, Papa raised up and slammed an uppercut right into his kidneys before finishing him off with a broken rib:

There is no greater strength than what is found within. There is no greater love than reaching beyond boundaries to other men. There is no greater wealth than possessing true peace of mind. When my son left me to go out on his own, I wanted to give him the vision of such a brave new world. You pissed on that gift.

The greasy Gatlin kept dodging my swinging crowbar—and he did try to kick me in the balls. But his toe only kept making contact with the whalebone in front of my corset. By then my father was ready for him. Papa made me drop the crowbar. The greasy Gatlin stood alone against the two of us—or more like, one and a half of us—but it was enough for him to lose his nerve. He tried to make it out the front door and Papa blocked the entrance. One of Papa's spaghetti straps had slipped off his shoulder, and he pushed it back up and stood there with his hands on his hips. He was breathing heavily, perspiration soaking through the bodice of his dress. Well, it's come down to you and me, Papa said; man to man. The greasy Gatlin begged Peters to call the sheriff. Peters, who had eavesdropped on the entire conversation while hiding behind his desk, was silent. The Gatlin at the door was close to tears and started whining, Them others made me do it—I ain't wanted to. And I got a bad heart. Peters can tell you I got a heart condition. Will you tell 'em, Peters? *Peters.* Yes, it was pathetic. Papa had already made his point; he could have let him go. While my father was exceptional, he wasn't a saint. He dropped him as hard as the others.

A sizable crowd had gathered outside, drawn by all the noise inside the locked freighting office. And when we came through the door and walked out to our truck, they parted before us like the Red Sea. I don't know what was in their faces; I didn't see them. My father filled my world at that moment. He said we were going straight to the sheriff's—just as we were—and I would have followed him, dressed like anything, bound for anywhere.

———

Stanford wasn't easy. And I ended up taking a major in something as difficult as mathematics because it was becoming increasingly clear to me that unless I could sit for exams where my use of a given language wasn't open to question, I wouldn't get decent grades. In statistics, while $F(x) = P(X \leqslant x)$, $-\infty < x < +\infty$ may look like Greek and, in fact, is Greek, the F is *defined,* and so if you're told to find the value of x at the pth quantile and you find it, they have to give you the grade you deserve. But my English-literature and philosophy papers were always open as to interpretation, execution of style, compelling ideas; and my professors never seemed to find the same degree of depth, the same innate under-standing, in my treatments of *Beowulf* as they did in my peers'. They'd look me straight in the face and say there was something they just couldn't put their finger on—something crude, something lacking in my essays. With those cultured voices, the pained and gentle air with which they returned the D's and C's, I was tempted to think the fault lay within me, that I couldn't make the snuff. But there were forty other under-graduates of the dark persuasion on campus and when over thirty of us got together and formed the Ethiope League, it was awfully strange how none of them were making the snuff either. Single paranoia? Mass par-anoia? Perhaps.

We decided on a little experiment and I volunteered as the test subject. I had a paper due in my theory class, and a group of us sat up all weekend reworking Kant's *Critique of Pure Reason* into contemporary English. We literally stole every one of his concepts and put my name on top of the page. I knew I was risking expulsion, but I took the gamble. I shouldn't have worried; it was the same D. The professor even took me aside after class to suggest that I attempt another major; please, don't misunderstand; he had agonized greatly over this inevitable conversation, but I just didn't have the necessary equipment for tackling erudite thought. I thanked him for his concern. Against all advice I switched to mathematics; would have come out with an A average, but those freshmen-year courses had pulled it down to an A−. It was still enough to earn me a scholarship for the graduate program, but hardly enough to keep me out of the draft.

Father Flanagan wouldn't have avoided the draft if he'd been colored. By 1942 the armed services found themselves so in love with Negro soldiers that all of those mentally deficient volunteers who had been turned away by the thousands when the war first broke out were now considered more than able to figure out one end of a rifle from another. Love is blind, isn't it? And if I sound bitter, it's because I am. There was a massive blood drive going on at school and, like the rest, I went down to the Red Cross to contribute. I found out that they weren't taking Negro blood at the banks. And there I was with a draft notice in my wallet.

The hypocrisy of it sickened me, and I thought the three hundred thousand colored men who finally went into the armed forces were fools. The handful of white Stanford students—and it was only a handful—who went into the service were commissioned as officers. They needed those brains to direct the war effort. They told me I was fit only to die. Most of my friends in the Ethiope League had already been drafted—into the infantry, of course, some of them actually believing that they were making the world safe for democracy. I was all for the world embracing democracy; I just didn't see any way for the Americans to bring it to them.

They finally notified me to report to the local induction center and I called Papa to ask what I should do. True to form, he gave me a long-winded speech that had something to do with Pushkin being thrown out of Saint Petersburg and running around in parts of Russia with unpronounceable names while coming out of the whole mess with some poems and a play. He got pretty upset that I kept referring to *Boris Gudunov* as only a play, but if it's divided up into acts, what else is it? And what in God's name did all that have to do with my predicament? Which only got us off the track and into how much my education had cost him with this kind of ignorance as the end result. In all this time, if I wasn't prepared to make a persuasive argument for my beliefs in front of the draft board, I deserved to be in jail.

Aunt Hazel wasn't any more consoling, though a bit more down-to-earth. She heard me out and agreed with everything I said. Yes, it was unforgivable that we lived as second-class citizens in a segregated society and I was being asked to defend it all in a segregated army, but I should remember that refusal to go also meant a segregated jail. She left me with the words of Joe Louis: There's a lot wrong with this country. But Hitler can't fix it.

After hanging up from them, I knew there was absolutely no point in calling any of my uncles. If anybody could have pulled some strings for me, it would have been one of them. But three of them were veterans from the last world war, and all of them would have thought I was just too yellow to fight. A good dose of the slammer would be about what I needed to straighten me out.

Jail came up a lot in the conversations with my family, and it was just where I ended up. Three years in the federal penitentiary in Tucson. Papa told me I would have gotten more time if he hadn't relented and written that letter to the draft board on my behalf; I truly don't think so. My argument was to have been a simple one and unanswerable: If my blood wasn't good enough for the Red Cross, why was it good enough to be spilled on the battlefield? But I walked into that hearing with them holding a copy of his letter, which had me talking to the exiled spirit of Pushkin about my belief in a people's revolution to rid the human race of universal tyranny, where one part enslaved left all parts enslaved. It seems that I'd been mumbling this stuff in my sleep since I was twelve years old and rising out of my dreams to yell, *Dnepropetrovsk!* and

Mkihaylovskoye! That went over really big with the draft board. And believe me, I thanked them for the three years.

And, yes, the federal prison at Tucson was segregated. The cell blocks. The showers. The dining room. There was a Southwestern flavor to it, though: Mexicans, Yumas, Hopis, and Chinese were all honorary Negroes and in our group, while the various strains of Europeans, designated as white, went in the other group. But there was no distinction made with the slop we had to eat, or with the treatment from the guards. We were all worthless scum to them, even though, like myself, most of the other COs were educated and from good families.

My second year, the admission of three new conscientious objectors, who were of Japanese ancestry, threw them into a tizzy for a while. They'd had no experience with this type before. Since they were evidently not Chinese, would that make them honorary Negroes or honorary whites? Third-generation Californians, they all held law degrees, which might have helped to elevate them above the Chinese narcotics dealers in there. But then again, they had to be shipped from that Japanese concentration camp in Wyoming because they were guilty of being even more anti-American by refusing to join the armed services. Irony isn't a strong point in penal administration, but there must have been a pang of conscience somewhere, because they kept those three men in a holding area for a week until they decided. The warden finally made them honorary Negroes. After all, he told them, there are other good Japs out there fighting for this country over in Europe, and you agitators could have too.

Regardless of what cell block you ended up in, the day began at dawn with the clanging of a huge bell that startled you from sleep with your heart pounding. If you weren't out of the cot and at the cell door to be counted by the time the guard came down your row, that deafening bell would clang again and again until the count tallied up. It didn't matter if that creep saw a man struggling to make it up to the bars, he had to be right *at* the door or he wasn't counted. Line up for the cold shower. Line up for your breakfast of corn mush, coffee, and toast. Line up to go out on your work detail. I thought southern California was hot until I ended up with a pick and shovel in Arizona. They had to supply us with caps or they would have lost a lot of manpower from heat strokes. The caps didn't help me; I would break out in rashes, even on the palms of my hands, that blistered and ran. Getting a pass to the infirmary was almost impossible if you were a CO. They'd already branded us as traitors or cowards and thought that any physical complaint was an excuse to get out of work.

There were only a handful of COs in the entire population, and while all of us were there for different reasons—religious or political—we were all quite vocal and a general pain to the prison administration. We were paying a high price for our principles and so we certainly weren't going to be quiet about them now. The COs formed a committee and told the warden that we wanted to eat together in the dining hall. He told us that it wouldn't be possible because coloreds and whites weren't allowed to do that. We told him to show us the law in the penal code stating that was the case. He told us there'd be no point because the light bulbs would be too dim in solitary confinement for us to read it anyway.

We ignored his threat and organized a hunger strike. It went a lot better than I thought it would. Not that many of the convicted felons around us cared about our cause one way or the other, but it gave them a chance to be doing something that really put it to the screws. I learned that was what they called the guards, and I picked up other words in their language as well. To hear them tell it, there wasn't a man in there who had done anything wrong. All the armed robbers, murderers, dope peddlers, forgers, and Mann Act violators were up on a bum rap. But since I was only doing soft time, I'd better peel 'em or one of the screws might make sure I took a box parole. Translation: Since I couldn't be bullied with only a short-term sentence over my head, I had to be watchful about causing too much trouble or the prison authorities might decide to send me out of there in a pine box.

To be honest, I was more afraid of my fellow inmates than of the warden. I understood bureaucrats, and without a rule book, they are totally lost. Our dissent was organized, nonviolent, and within our personal rights. We had to be in prison. We had to get up when that bell clanged. We had to be in the dining hall at specified times. But nowhere did it say we had to eat. It was exhilarating to watch them crumble as our hunger strike went into its fifteenth day. Men were fainting on work detail and overcrowding the infirmary. The medical staff was going into overtime and triple time. They were running out of IVs. Things were simply getting out of hand. Rumors spread that there might be an official investigation. Bureaucrats have nightmares about investigations. Rumors spread that there might be an official inventory of the food supplies and budget. And bureaucrats have nightmares about inventories. The warden was losing more sleep than we were losing weight. He finally called the committee into his office and announced that his facility would no longer enforce segregated tables, although it would surprise him greatly if any inmate —of any race—could swallow his food sitting next to a bunch of yellow-bellied Commie agitators. But his attitude hardly dampened our spirits.

We COs marched into the dining hall victorious. Our country was born in dissent, built on dissent; and here was proof positive that there was hope in the American way. There were some diehards, colored and white, who still insisted on staying to themselves, but they didn't dampen our spirits either. The COs would grin and give each other Victory signs up and down the tables. I found myself rubbing elbows at my first integrated meal between one man who'd scalped his mother-in-law, hoping to pin it on their Indian gardener, and another who'd run a mail order specializing in postcards of donkeys with naked redheads. Is this democracy or what?

———

In spite of my tone, it is not my intention to make light of what we accomplished. COs don't need another bum rap from me; they were all brave men who were willing to sacrifice their personal freedom for their ideals. I'll dare anyone to spend just a single week in one of those prisons then return and tell me we chose the easy way out of the war. Winning that concession from the warden didn't stop that damn bell from clanging each morning, the head count like cattle, the endless lines. And I haven't spoken about the smell. I suppose because I want to forget it. The place reeked of fear. My own and everyone else's. No one trusted anyone else, and for good reason. Caged up there together, a guard held your life in his hands, and you held his in yours. There was one inmate given a boot party and three guards knifed that I heard about while I was there—and you hear everything through the grapevine—and yes, one box parole. A Mexican kid who made the mistake of being too pretty and too unwilling.

I was never raped, because I never resisted. And I bet you're thinking, So *that* explains it. Well, you're as wrong as Jesse. I'm not a homosexual, but I'm not stupid either. He was six-feet-two, as broad as he was tall, as ugly as he was mean, a repeat offender serving for three counts of murder with nothing left to lose. And he wasn't a homosexual either. He wasn't anything but something that could only gauge it was alive by watching other things die. They assigned me to his cell as a reprisal for helping to organize the hunger strike. The extra bunk had been left vacant by that Mexican kid. For weeks he never did anything but watch me as I read, as I wrote letters home, as I rediscovered my lost Catholicism. His oily tan face following me around that cramped cell. His hazel eyes burnt empty. And then for weeks I had to hear each night after the lights were out, I'm gonna fuck you or kill you. He never made a move. It was nothing more than that: I'm gonna fuck you or kill you. It does wonders for your sleep. I lost more weight than I had during the hunger strike.

I broke out in hives, even without the sun, and spent a lot of time in the infirmary. But eventually I had to be returned to my cell, and eventually they had to call lights-out. I'm gonna fuck you or kill you. I wept for that Mexican kid. He had only been in for passing forged checks. And he'd only been eighteen. And I'm sure he'd read that choice as no choice at all. But I knew better.

I received my walking papers fourteen months later and the Department of Corrections would have been happy to know that I was, indeed, a changed man. It was spring and the cotton stalks bloomed with creamy white flowers. The full sunlight made the tight petals glow, and to look out over the endless rows of them hurt my eyes. I blinked a lot when I returned home. I'd leave my bed and go no farther than the front porch, but there was nowhere to turn without meeting the brightness of it all, the space. It felt good to have the solidness of the house behind my back. I'd lean my chair against it, watching intently as the blooms began to slowly bleed into a deep pink. I only spoke when spoken to, but no one bothered me. Even my uncles knew better than to ask me any questions or to come by and lecture. Unlike my father, they weren't the type of men to read my eyes, but they saw that my hair was now streaked with gray.

I used all of that silence to think. V-E Day came that same season and I was glad that the war would be winding down. I had lost my cousin Tomaso and hoped I wouldn't be losing any more. So endless, those rows. They had shed the pink petals and were green now. And those small green pods would grow fuller and fuller until they burst open, once again, into my grandmother's dream. I thought a lot about my grandparents and what they might think of us now. Imperial Valley Enterprises. Was it about that for her? The sons and grandsons of her sons were already planning to diversify. The future was not in cotton. Yes, there would always be some of that, but the land itself was becoming more valuable than anything we could grow upon it. And we had so much land. I could spend the rest of my life right there, on my little piece of America, and lack for nothing.

And I thought long and hard about doing just that. I had another year left before earning my doctorate, but I didn't need to go back. I was more than equipped to take over our bookkeeping; my training in statistics could remain a hobby, something to amuse my children with. We could move from the toss of a coin to specifics about the crops. What are the odds that that far row of cotton bolls will burst open before the one in front of it? What are the chances that they'll do it simultaneously? How much do you factor in the hours of sunlight for each? How much the amount of irrigation? Because I will have to train my children about this land. I will have to breed it into them that this was their great-grandmother's dream. *And I saw my sons, dark as the night, proud as the eagles, picking white gold from the land.* And I must, above all, teach them that our dictionaries are totally useless when it comes to the definition of this dream. Look out there, I will tell them, and what you see is . . .

Ha lúp. It was the first expression in Cuchan that Aunt Hazel taught me. Because, she said, it was the first one her mother had taught them all. Obviously, she thought it more important than their learning *Mama* or *Papa* or *hungry* or *thirsty*, this word for something that they, as children, would never see. And that her own mother had never seen, or the mother before her. *Ha lúp.* They were an ancient people of deserts and dry ravines, with heaven for them a land where the Great Spirit would lead you to rest, where the shade was good and the cacti sweet; so what possible need for the word *snow?* I know how I used it in prison. After they called lights-out and the pain soared beyond the reach of my Christian prayers, it became a mantra to replace all of the discarded reasons for my having chosen not to die.

A lot of silence. A lot of time to think. The cotton bolls burst open a hundredfold and heavy, making it seem a small miracle for those slender stalks to hold so much. Horizon to horizon, the earth offered nothing that wasn't soft and thick and full. The farm was always its most beautiful to me then. As a child I used to ask, Papa, when did God have time to get everything so clean? I started rising at dawn to go out with the field hands. I lived with a hoe, chopping weeds until the calluses on my palms opened and bled afresh. And when it became the season to harvest, I picked cotton, dragging those heavy burlap sacks between the endless rows, working until my legs stiffened and my back ached. Sweat stung my eyes and I refused to wipe it away. And still my family left me alone. I began to remember why I loved them. With the crop brought in, I told Papa I was ready to finish my degree at Stanford. And after that? he asked. Well, after that I would just have to see.

I knew I wasn't returning to the valley. My grandparents had taken us as far as they could in that direction. Yes, I would always hold their land, but east of the Colorado was my land too. I had paid dearly for the right to be an American, and so without malice, without fanfare, I was going out to claim what I had bought. When you keep things at their basic, life becomes so easy. My goal was to open my own marketing firm. The first step was earning my own money. And you earn money by seeking employment that you're qualified to perform. It was that simple. From Los Angeles to Philadelphia, I applied at firms and industrial corporations that advertised for marketing analysts—no experience needed—and presented my credentials.

I began this whole saga with the result of those interviews, but the issue here is the process. It was a growing field; qualified candidates were few; an advertisement would stay in the papers for weeks. And I kept returning. I researched the firm's history in trade journals; the products, the customer demographics. But hadn't they just told me . . . Yes, I know what they had told me, but the job I was most qualified to do was still available. They began to know my entire name by heart. That was important. I returned again with sales forecasts, impeccably drawn charts. I exhausted every possible avenue for their reservations—and mine—over their giving me the position. That was important. Whether they ended up calling the police or hiring someone else, I wanted to be remembered.

I'm sure I was, in more ways than one, if this whole process took place over the course of the summer. And, yes, this is where we finally arrive at the reason for my present wardrobe. It wasn't a gimmick, and I was out to embarrass no one, least of all myself. In fact, it was liberating to be rid of the bitterness I had carried with me. Each new opening in my field was an opportunity to prove that I could handle the job, and putting in the extra effort made me quite proud of myself. It had the opposite effect on the people who kept turning me down, and I was even able to feel pity for them as they avoided my eyes and wilted a little with each page of my impeccable sales charts. I could feel the desperation in the way they kept reading and rereading my college transcripts, flipping through the charts—God, how they could use someone like this, *needed* someone like this—and then the shattered hopes when they finally looked back up at me and a different man hadn't materialized in front of them. Someday, one of the more tortured and honest VPs mumbled, we'll bring ourselves to hire a Negro. You'll be doing your company a better favor, I said, when you can bring yourself to hire the most qualified man.

The scenario repeated itself (with slight variations) in six major cities a total of thirty-five times and still counting, when a massive heat wave hit the northern section of the country. By this time I was as far as Chicago and had accumulated enough experience to venture a few projections about my personal circumstances. My conclusions were grounded solely in my professional training, although they didn't call for anything beyond the most elementary principles of statistics. I sat on the cramped bed of yet another rooming house in my boxer shorts with my feet in a basin of cool water; a slide rule, sheets of graphing paper, and pencils spread around me. Just walking to the general post office had made my flannel suit unbearable and it hung on a small hook next to a

sweat-stained cotton shirt. But the trip had netted me four more enthu-
siastic replies to my query letters to breakfast-food companies in Grand
Rapids and Detroit. If I met with no success in Chicago, I'd be moving
on to Michigan, then Indiana, Ohio, and Pennsylvania. By this time I had
also started targeting firms that could benefit from creating the position
of a marketing analyst and sending them tailor-made proposals that dem-
onstrated why. If the response was positive, I next telephoned and set
up a meeting based on my arrival time for that city. I stopped disrupting
my schedule for the excited Drop-everything-and-run appeals from company officials, because that had only meant backtracking and picking up
where I left off.

Besides my mail, I had brought in the afternoon papers and saw that two
of the firms I'd initially approached in Chicago were now due for return
visits; the positions were still being advertised. I knew these were renewed
advertisements because the third company had taken additional space to
print, Only White Need Apply. You saw such notifications often at the
lowest levels of employment, but it seemed that my presence had helped
to broaden some minds. Of course, I wouldn't be returning to that
company anymore. They had made their specifications for the job more
than clear. And I wasn't about to use my energy for crusading, especially
in all that heat. I was only returning to where they'd stated that they
wanted any qualified candidate for the position. But I was dreading the
thought of getting back into that suit and vest, and to delay it I began
to work on some projections for the probability of my future success. I
know some of you are already thinking that you don't need graphing
paper and a Ph.D. to tell me what that probability was. But you have
to understand exactly how much I was dreading getting back into that
suit.

The welts ran across my back in diagonal lines; they ringed my neck and
wrists where the collar band and shirt cuffs fastened. They were red and

puffy, and if I didn't keep my body temperature down, they kept swelling until they burst. I had resorted to a pocket watch at the beginning of the heat wave because it wasn't possible to tell when the blisters from the wristwatch would break and the drainage become visible. I could cover the other blisters on my body with a fresh shirt between appointments, or if there was enough time, cool baths in the middle of the day held them down to a fine rash. I couldn't afford to sit out the entire summer waiting for the weather to change; I needed to know if I could factor in another type of wardrobe without disrupting my future search for employment. And this is where the concept of statistical independence comes in.

I had already accumulated enough data from my previous interviews to use the law of large numbers with reasonable accuracy. I divided the number of times I had been rejected for a job by the number of places where I had applied, which brought me *toward* a probability estimate of total failure. Now, I could not say for *certain* that I would be rejected each time I kept applying for this job in the future, but the more rejections I accumulated, the more such an outcome looked like a possibility. You see, the closer you move the number of experiments to infinity, the closer you move the probability to certainty. Okay, so now I was at thirty-five and counting, with the reasonable conclusion that the probability assignment for my circumstances was very low, tending to zero, total failure in finding a company that actually wanted what they'd advertised that they wanted. But now we start applying some of the basic principles in my field: The outcome of one interview does not imply anything about the outcome of another interview. My past experiences should have no bearing on the next experience to come; someone, somewhere, is advertising for a qualified man as a marketing analyst and they actually want just what they print in the newspapers and tell me over the telephone, a qualified man. If it turns out to be false, the next time it might be true. False again, but the next time it might be true. Statisticians call this the independence of events. And it certainly helped me to stay free of bitterness or frustration. I would keep researching each company, preparing proposals, and trying in the next place and the next. All right, move on to the next city and the next. The independence of events.

Okay, so far I haven't done anything but take you through a little fancier version of the coin-toss math that you learned in middle school. Now we get to another one of the basic principles in my field, which was even more liberating for me in that miserable and hot room. I had been taught laws that allowed me to extend the definition of independence so that I could calculate how little the occurrence of one event changes the probability of occurrence of another event. If I now freed myself from that gray flannel suit and dressed in something else, how much would that change what was happening to me at these interviews? And you know, with the probability of success already established as low as it was, the answer was, not very much. A gray flannel suit made no more measurable difference than a brown tweed, a brown tweed than a pinstriped. Cuffed trousers, straight trousers. I kept plugging in the new factors with the differences between them coming out as minuscule.

You see, a two-piece sports ensemble with a V-neck and short-sleeve shirt would relieve me from torture. And John David had a line of them in terry cloth that would have been ideal. A white sailcloth hat and white leather moccasins would finish it all off quite smartly. I didn't jump up and buy an outfit right away. I returned to those two companies slated for another round and got rejected again. Then I went browsing in Marshall Field's. The men's department and haberdashery were loaded with the proper fabrics for enduring the heat: terry cloths, monk cloths, worsted gabardines—but all in a *sports* cut. And there was no use kidding myself; plugging the factors of a leisure suit into a business paradigm threw the numbers all out of whack. It was the equivalent of comparing apples and oranges while I needed apples and apples. You simply don't go looking for a job in a cosmopolitan city dressed like you're going to the beach.

I found a park bench under a decent shade tree, taking off my jacket and loosening my necktie and collar. I was able to splash water on my face from a nearby fountain and wet my handkerchief to cool the welts around my neck. I watched the people strolling past, allowing myself a moment of envy for the tiny tots in their sundresses and short pants. The bohemians certainly looked comfortable as well, women in their peasant blouses and flowered skirts, shirtless men in overalls and thonged sandals. I started thinking of other cultures where proper business attire was geared to tropical weather: the flowing Arabian djellaba, the light gauze Bombay dhoti. Or just to be an African with silk and gold worked into the loose folds of a ceremonial robe. Any of them would be taken as seriously as I wanted to be with this briefcase of proposals by my side. And the thing is, I could have passed for a real African or Arab, even an East Indian. And how far from the truth when there was some African blood in my lineage? The masquerade was tempting, believe me. Foreign attire wouldn't change the probability of rejections to any measurable degree, so why not?

Unable to sleep that night with the mercury staying above 80 degrees, I wrestled with the inevitable. The only business clothes that could keep me going through that summer were ones designed for the American female. The sleeves were short, the skirts loose and airy. I wasn't an Arab, and I wasn't a Ghanian, and I wasn't a native of Calcutta. And I was alone in the Midwest at thirty-five down and still counting because I couldn't afford to give up. If I got sick with heat prostration and lost my momentum, there'd be too much time to think. I might start believing that thirty-five down and counting was more than enough to speak for a finite truth. I might start believing that the right to call myself an American Negro had bought me just another jail. Nothing could save me then. *I'm gonna fuck you or kill you.* No, not this time. Thirty-five down and counting had, at least, earned me a pawnshop revolver to jam up into my own anus.

The calculations I did the next morning only confirmed what I had thought. Keeping it within the realm of business attire, an extremely conservative dress would make no measurable difference in my probability of success than a gray flannel suit. But I was still relieved when the heat wave lifted and I could finish my business in Chicago without having to resort to one. I wasn't that lucky in Michigan. I finished Grand Rapids in bearable weather, with the rejections up to forty-six and counting, to settle down for a reasonably long stay in Detroit. My mailed proposals had garnered me half a dozen interviews. And with postwar production in full swing, the automobile companies alone would take me several weeks. My first week there, the heat was tolerable enough to allow me to get by with my gray flannel suit. Even after all this time, I was still mystified by the shock on their faces when I walked into one of those executive offices. I always signed my entire name at the end of the query letters that stated my qualifications, and it headed every page of a marketing proposal—Stanley Beckwourth Booker T. Washington Carver— how could they not realize I was an American Negro?

My first round through the automobile industry brought me the best offers I'd had to that date: three assembly-line jobs and even one as assistant to the assistant foreman. I told them that I knew nothing about oiling engines and mounting them into cars. They told me that as bright as I obviously was, I'd have no problem learning. My second week in Detroit the heat wave returned with a vengeance. I purchased my own small fan and spent two nights sleeping under it in a tub of cool water. The other roomers complained to the landlady about my locking the bathroom door and she told me I couldn't stay there running up her electric bill that way. So I bit the bullet, went downtown for a day of shopping, and bought another wardrobe. I told the salesgirls my sister was stout. I left with a simple tailored cotton dress and street jacket.

Dark cotton gloves. A modest straw bolero—no ribbons, no veil—realizing my own hat would make the outfit look ridiculous. For that same reason I was pressed to give up my shoes and socks in exchange for very flat sandals and sheer cotton stockings. That was as far as I needed to go. I could carry my wallet in the briefcase along with other papers and keep the stockings up by twisting them above the knees. When I scrutinized myself in the mirror, the image was a little strange but definitely presentable. And hitting the steaming sidewalks of Detroit, I discovered how blessedly free it was.

Those first blocks to the bus stop were hardly easy, but I kept telling myself to keep my eyes straight ahead and concentrate only on one soothing breeze and then another that kept circulating through the light clothes. I used that bus ride the same way I always did: glancing through the classifieds for any new want ads and then organizing the checklist for my second and third rounds of visits. Sure, the people downtown stared, but then they always had when I was in a business suit. And it also wasn't the first time I received frightened glances from pretty blonde receptionists. The very same ones as only last week, as a matter of fact. And now I'm going to hold a conversation with what I assume are some of your more troubling thoughts about this whole endeavor:

This man isn't really serious. What chance does he have of being hired for such a high-level position wearing a woman's dress?

—What chance did I have of being hired for such a high-level position at all?

But if this company just happens to be the one place that will truly give a chance to any qualified man and he walks in there wearing a woman's dress, he's certain to be rejected.

—But the margin for this company being just such a place—having rejected me before—on just the day that it's hot enough to necessitate my wearing a dress was statistically small. Much smaller than the margin of physical comfort that those clothes offered me.

But he doesn't know that for a fact.

   —It's quite true, I didn't. I was only at fifty-five and still counting. *And then it's possible that the man who offered him the assistant to an assistant something down in the factory might have had a change of heart over the week. It appears he was awfully impressed by that proposal.*

   —While not highly probable, it is possible. And if that was the case, I blew it.

The next day I didn't need those clothes; the day after, I did. I left Detroit at sixty-two and counting. Toledo at seventy-one. Akron at seventy-eight. Youngstown at eighty-two. Cincinnati at ninety. Most of the time I was in my gray flannel suit, but each time I had to put on a dress it was getting easier. As the numbers kept accumulating, any nagging doubts I might have had were put firmly to rest. Those dresses weren't making a *bit* of difference to anyone but me. On the up side, I'd never felt more like a man. With each new town I was growing stronger in purpose, having no excuses for not working from dawn until well after dark. My proposals had started out just being academically sound; now they were sharpened with reference points from like industries in other regions of the country. I could talk as if I'd been working in the field for years with a ring of authority in my voice. I knew more about shoe leather, pork products, steel, cast-dieing, corn flakes, baby formula, heavy machinery, parts and accessories than many of the companies distributing them— and it showed. In the way I walked into an office. The way I leaned toward a desk, flipping open a portfolio. Sometimes forgetting that with French pleats I had to close my legs.

On the down side, it took a lot of fast talking not to get arrested in the streets. Officer, if I intended to be impersonating a female, wouldn't I have done a better job than this? They could smell my aftershave. See the way my hair was closely trimmed. Short fingernails. A heavy briefcase. Then you need some help, pal, ya know? The one time I was hauled in for possible commitment, the judge turned out to be a man who listened with his eyes. To back up my story, I showed him my travelogue.

—Where are you headed next? he asked.

—Pittsburgh.

—Well, good luck.

I did have it, because the weather changed. It was moving into fall, so I could pack away my dresses, but in a funny way I missed them. Pittsburgh was a mecca for what I wanted to do. It served as the raw pulse for what moved most of America. Steel. Iron. Petroleum. Coal. And I even read in the local papers about plans to harness the bomb. Imagine, a whole city of street lamps lit up from atomic energy. But it was that kind of place; *energetic* is the only word for it. Industrial research was old hat there. And if I couldn't make it in a place that small with so much to offer, I doubted if I could make it anywhere. I settled myself into a rooming house overlooking one of the valleys and planned a long siege.

I know I've been talking about the whole ordeal as if it were one big mathematical experiment, but there has to be something a little prophetic about it being my ninety-ninth place. Waco Glass and Tile. An international company with a huge complex of buildings that rivaled U.S. Steel. If You Can Break It, We Make It, said the nameplate facing me on the huge desk. Old man Waco's creed, said the head of domestic marketing. I told him that my father was somewhat of a poet as well. The head of domestic marketing wanted to hear all about that. The head of domestic marketing was extremely interested in my life. The rise from a cotton farm to a scholarship at Stanford. I had already corrected him twice, but the third time he brought up my sharecropping beginnings, I knew to let it rest.

He leaned over the desk and fixed me with a pair of awestruck eyes. My proposal had stunned him, he said, absolutely stunned him. Why, my proposal had been just extraordinary. I sat there wondering how such effusive praise could still feel like a slap in the face. My marketing plans had been . . . well, why, he was simply speechless. In fact, that particular marketing proposal had been quite basic. It was built on a little common sense and what I had observed traveling across the country. Women were having a lot of babies. And with men coming back from the war to an economy that was booming, women were going to be having a lot more. And Waco Glass would be well served to phase out their division in flint-glass tumblers and start producing baby bottles. It was nothing to go from there to a ten-year plan based on target regions for the greatest increase of infant population, working with the factors of socioeconomic levels (the poor are likely to have more children, the wealthy less likely to breast-feed) and throwing in previous census data to back it up. But the head of domestic marketing kept going on and on, and, of course, I kept smiling and saying, Thank you.

It seemed that the marketing division of Waco could use a man like me. Why, he was going to break both of my legs if I tried to walk out of that office. And he bet that this kind of enthusiasm from someone like him sure came as a complete surprise to me. I agreed that it did. Yes, he bet that I was bowled over by his enthusiasm. He just bet that I'd thought he wouldn't see the *brilliance* of this marketing strategy because he wouldn't be able to look past the fact that I was a Negro. (I kept waiting for the other shoe to drop.) But there were decent Americans without an ounce of prejudice in their hearts. And he was the first to admit there weren't enough of them. He had been around Negroes all of his life. He knew that Negroes were some of the finest people in this country. Why, a Negro woman had been like a mother to him—better than his own mother. And she still worked for him and the wife, getting a little old and senile, but hell. (I kept waiting for that shoe.) And not that Hattie was ever easy to get along with—not one of those *servile* Negroes that made some people comfortable—no, she had spit and fire in her. Would talk back to him in a minute, like an equal. (It was ninety-nine, you see, and I wanted to stop counting.) And Hattie had two boys that had turned out pretty well, considering. She had worked her fingers to the bone for those boys and without a breath of complaint about supporting their shiftless daddy—cutest things you'd ever want to see. Why, he would take a bullet for Hattie. If he offers me less, I thought, if he offers me one penny less than the base salary advertised in the *Wall Street Journal,* I'm going home, putting on my navy blue dress, and coming back here to tell him where he can shove Hattie.

But the head of domestic marketing had other things in mind. He wanted me to have lunch with him and another good man working in the company. The second in command at layout and design. He wanted me to hear firsthand how things would be at Waco Glass and Tile. Now, how did I guess that this fellow was a Negro? Yes, they were a progressive company. There would be *two* of us now. And marketing ran his own ship. They tried to give him any flak from upstairs, he'd just shame them with that proposal. I truly believe that I would be employed at Waco Glass and Tile right now if we hadn't ordered lobster thermidor at that luncheon.

I followed him through a maze of hallways and underground passages that connected the various buildings in that complex, hundreds of typewriters thundering around me. He pointed out the offices for domestic production (run by an idiot), international marketing (run by an even bigger idiot), specialized import/export (run by the biggest idiot of them all, but a heck of a nice guy). A boom time for the foreign division, he told me. Just imagine how much glass got broken in the war! They were going around the clock over in the foundries. But he'd save the factories for later; that tour was a day by itself. I started to turn into a large cafeteria at the elbow of one of those myriad Ls on the first floor. A room of spanking white walls, stainless steel, and Formica, and crowded with office boys and secretaries. But he grabbed my arm with a large grin and a wink. No, that's for the proletariat. We're upstairs.

The twelfth floor was another maze of hallways, but carpeted, and with only the faint clacking of typewriters behind closed oak doors. Research and design. The think tank of the whole operation, he told me. They invent it; his division sells it; and the public, God bless 'em, breaks it to keep everybody's mortgage paid. At the end of yet another L was the executive dining room. Muted beige walls, silver plate, tablecloths, and fresh flowers. Never dreamed you'd be eating at the top, huh, Stanley? I still wasn't. There had been another eight buttons on that elevator.

A cloud of cigarette smoke hung over the hunched backs of all those gray flannel suits. And I knew they weren't all the same man because of the ties and pocket handkerchiefs: some polka dotted, some striped, some spitalsfield, some tweed with lattice network. The gray flannel we would be lunching with was waiting for us at a far table, but it took a while to navigate the room because the head of domestic marketing stopped at practically every table to introduce my degrees: My new marketing analyst, a Ph.D. from Stanford. Stanley, meet . . . And as I shook each limp hand: Best damn proposal I ever read; I'll send you a copy. When we finally reached our table, the second in command of layout and design rose and extended his hand first. The grip was firm. The smile sincere. Pleased to meet you, Stanley. You're going to love it here. The head of domestic marketing beamed.

The meal was all clear sailing from there. The head of domestic marketing ordered for the three of us. He told me that I didn't really want the steak; the lobster there was the best in town. The second in command had never bothered to open his menu. It seemed he'd lunched with domestic marketing before. It seemed he and domestic marketing were the best of friends, according to domestic marketing. And we treat you right here, don't we? He agreed that he was treated very well. I had been told constantly on the way to the dining room that this man and I would have a lot in common. But midway through the second martini I was still trying to figure out what it might be.

He was easily ten years older than I and a native of Pittsburgh, having grown up on a crowded street not too far from my rooming house. His father was a cab driver, his mother still alive and active in the Baptist Church. He was one of several children and had gotten married five years ago, just after coming to the company. And they had been five good years at Waco Glass and Tile. Then, perhaps, he had gone to a West Coast college? No, he'd never left the state, had earned a graduate degree in art and design right there from Carnegie Tech. At the top of his class, boomed domestic marketing. Over the top, really, second-in-command whispered in reply; and I knew just what he meant. I mentioned that he'd managed to move up pretty fast in the company, and he looked at me as if I'd made some sort of a nasty dig. Well, second in command of your division is awfully impressive, I said.

The waiter brought our lobsters and a paper bib for each of us. Tie 'em tight, said domestic marketing; this stuff is good but it can get pretty messy. Second in command tied his so that the strings dug into his neck. I wondered how he was going to swallow with it so tight. But he took very small bites. Domestic marketing wasn't wrong; the lobster thermidor was very tasty. And they served it in the middle of a whole lobster with the claws still intact. We were handed silver nutcrackers to start on those after we'd finished the rest. My bib was getting splattered and domestic marketing's even more so because he relished dipping the crisp French bread into his sauce. But it was the paper bib of the second in command that intrigued me the most; it was remaining perfectly spotless. My eyes rarely left it as we talked about the future of glass in America, my future at Waco, rebuilding Europe, the Marshall Plan. The head of domestic marketing had very definite opinions about all of this, and so did I. The second in command had a spotless bib.

I was woozy from the rich food and alcohol and probably wouldn't have noticed it if it hadn't been my focal point during the meal, but after the

dishes were removed and the third round of martinis arrived, the second
in command folded his paper bib into a perfect square in front of him
and began shredding it into tiny tiny pieces. By this time the head of
domestic marketing wouldn't have been aware of a tap-dancing pygmy
in the middle of the table. He'd drunk the lion's share of the wine and
his martinis had all been doubles. A little excess was called for that day,
he told me with a wink; we were celebrating. It wasn't every day that
the best damn analytical mind in the country walked into his office.
Walked right in with just the ticket to save his division's profits. For a
long time he'd known something was wrong and now—thanks to me—
he knew what it was. (When the shoe drops this time, I thought, it's
going to be a biggie.) He was finally going to move Waco into the twentieth
century with this one. Oh yeah, he was going straight to the moon. Buy
stock, boys, he told us. Buy lots of stock. And he could thank all those
prejudiced bastards who had turned me away. They didn't want to hire
a nigger—good for them. It had sent me straight to his door. And he
was proud to be sitting at the table with *two* of us, proud to be a real
American. The second in command never changed that mild and interested
expression. The piles of shredded paper were growing in front of his
hands. Tiny tiny tiny pieces. He did it without ever looking down. He
did it by rote.

The room was beginning to get too close. I removed my jacket and
loosened my tie. I got noticeable glances from the other tables, but it
felt so much better. My plan had been to stay with one of those companies
ten years—top. Build up some assets, the contacts, and experience.
Midway through my interview, I'd even figured that Waco could be done
in seven. The company had a generous profit-sharing plan, and they were
ripe for a new direction. Now I wondered if seven years would be cutting
it too close. So could I get away in five years? Four? The head of domestic
marketing was now talking into his martini, something about the damn
finest people in the world, something about my being a credit to my
race. The second in command frowned slightly at my shirtsleeves and

shook his head ever so slightly more. Then his smile returned as he gazed into the blurred eyes of domestic marketing, who'd raised his head to ask abruptly how things were at layout and design. The second in command said things couldn't be better. Another drink? asked domestic marketing, signaling for the waiter without waiting for a reply.

—Another round for everybody, he said.

—No, thank you, I said; I've had enough.

—Aw, come on, we're celebrating. Aren't we celebrating?

The second in command agreed that we, indeed, were. His knuckles were almost buried now in the piles of shredded paper. I forced myself to look everywhere but there; it was becoming something indecent to watch. Such tiny tiny tiny tiny pieces. I looked down at my own hands. Still calm. Still able to rest on both sides of my martini glass. When I looked back up it was only to lock into the eyes of the second in command:

So you like working here?

Yes, I do. It's a great opportunity.

But you're the only person in layout and design, aren't you?

I was wondering when you would figure that out.

So where to from here?

Do you really need to ask me that?

No, I didn't. The waiter brought the three martinis, although I'd specifically told him that *I* didn't want one. But I let him place it in front of me with his usual flourish. I raised my glass with them for yet another toast—To the best damn proposal in the world—and sipped. When the warm flush ran through my body, I took my tie off completely and put it in the jacket hanging over the back of my chair. I undid another button on my shirt with the next sip. A third button with the next. I finished the drink with my shirt wide open, but the perspiration was still making my undershirt cling to my skin. A heavy buzz rose around the room; eventually every face was turned to our table. The second in command had given me up for dead after I removed the tie. But the head of domestic marketing didn't notice a thing until the buzz escalated into a muted roar as I removed the shirt completely. I folded it neatly over the back of the chair with my jacket.

—What in the high holy *hell* are you doing?

—Getting comfortable, I said.

—Are you frigging *crazy?*

—No, not yet.

It felt like medicine to be out in the brisk air with my shirt open and my jacket hooked over my shoulder. Walking helped to settle my queasy stomach and burn the alcohol out of my blood. I was composing a final letter to my father in my head. Papa, I will say, the language you taught me is wonderful. I have been in small towns and large cities; I have been in clothes of every description. There is no doubt—nor ever will be— that I am a man. And it doesn't bother me that practically no one in this country understands a single word I say. America is growing and changing; we are on the brink of unimaginable possibilities. I have just finished walking through the parks and streets of a city that will shortly find a way to light itself from breaking apart an atom. Change is hope; you've always told me that. I'm a young man; I will see a lot of change. And *that* is what worries me, Papa, because today I had lunch with the future.

The pawnshop was on a narrow back street. The plate-glass window was overflowing with the broken relics of uncountable dreams. Regardless of the lighting, the insides of these places always seem dingy. I peered through the rows of guitars, saxophones, and clarinets and saw an old Jewish man sweeping the wooden floor. His head was bowed low over the broom handle, the black yarmulke frayed around the edges. His tangled and yellowing beard hung to his chest, brushing across his vest with each stroke of the broom. He swept in slow, deliberate strokes as if painting the floor. At the far end of the counter I saw the locked gun case. The revolvers were laid in neat rows on the glass shelves; above the case were shoe boxes filled with assorted shells. I stood outside the window until he had made his way across one end of the shop with the broom. That was when he looked up and our eyes met through the curve of one of the saxophones. He knew what I wanted. Slowly, very slowly, he moved to the locked door, the broom still in his hands, and flipped the sign over. It read: Out of Business. And under it was a red-and-gold arrow that pointed me farther down the narrow street.

In the middle of the block was a squat little cafe. And at the end of the counter was a woman who introduced herself as Eve. And to make a very long story short: after taking one look at me in that gray flannel suit with my open shirt, she offered me a job as a housekeeper with terms that I couldn't refuse.

Miss Maple goes back to regular pants and a jacket in the winter. But he's taken to wearing a wool cape instead of an overcoat. He says he likes the swirl and freedom of it, and it keeps him just as warm. No doubt about it, the man has flair—and courage. And looking at the way he can wear any piece of cloth on his own terms gets you to thinking that maybe . . . just maybe. But no, as hot as it can get over this grill, I can't bring myself to do it. And besides, over the years Nadine has gotten to be a good half size larger than me anyway (throw that pan, darling, and I'm calling the cops).

Miss Maple's brought us in a big bottle of champagne for a midnight toast. He bows at me and pulls it out from under that cape to present it like a magician. Moët. He tells me it's one of the best brands around. I'll have to take his word for it. When you get higher than the shelf where they keep the Jack Daniel's, you're out of my league. He says that if things keep going the way they are, we won't be seeing him by the end of the new year. He'll have saved enough to start his own company. I'm really happy for the fella; he shouldn't have been here anyway. But I guess that can be said for about just everybody, myself included, although

I don't have his brains. And I sure don't have his money. He's earned every penny of it, though, and I don't begrudge him one red cent. A lesser man would have fallen back on what his family had, and from what I gather they're hardly poor. But the champagne he's uncorking is gonna taste real sweet from being bought the way it was.

He's got his job at Eve's down to a science. Unless he and Jesse are feuding and she won't let him into her room, he can pull all the linen, wash and blue it, and have it dried, ironed, and stacked between giving all the furniture and woodwork a good polishing. The rugs are vacuumed every other day, the windows washed once a week. Twice a month there's the heavy scrubbing: walls, front steps, back patio. And once a month the fireplaces. It's all finished by noon—and it's a four-story brownstone—which leaves him free time until six in the evening, when the gentlemen callers start ringing the bell. And it's that free time from noon to six, when he builds on the housework he's been doing all morning, that's making him a prosperous man.

WRITE THE WINNING JINGLE ABOUT SWIFT'S CLEANSER

Just picture it! You—queen of all you survey in your favorite department store—if you're the lucky winner in the great Swift's Cleanser Contest! Buy anything you like—a mink coat, beautiful furniture—outfit the whole family, redecorate your home, get all the wonderfully crazy hats you ever wanted! And *charge everything* —Swift & Company will *pay the bill!* Think of all the household appliances, furnishings, fabulous dresses, furs, jewels, silverware, and china that $5,000 will buy!

Miss Maple came out with third prize in that one. A Westinghouse electric roaster that he sold for thirty dollars—but he was on his way. Oxydol. Chiffon soap flakes. Old Dutch cleanser. Fab. Ajax. Vel. Cashmere Bouquet. The jingle that brought him in the biggest lump sum of cash was the Colgate-Palmolive-Peet's Hundred Thousand Dollar Gold Rush Contest. He took almost five thousand dollars for second prize. But he said his biggest personal satisfaction came from the Chiffon jingle:

I like Chiffon—tender white flakes for a tender white hand.
Even tender enough for my gold wedding band.

You see, when he was in Chicago he'd applied for a job at Armour and Company. The research he'd done for their proposal showed that the new attitudes of American housewives made them ripe for a dishwashing detergent that would leave them feeling both married and sexy. The Ford V-8 he pulled in for that one proved that someone inside the company had taken his numbers very seriously.

Miss Maple has told me that these jingle contests are more than a publicity gimmick; by reading the thousands of entries that come in, a company analyst can tell exactly what their customers want a product to do for them. And they use them to plan future strategies. The winning jingles have nothing to do with their being good; they're just the ones that can be used to spearhead the new marketing campaigns. And since he's already jump started a lot of these places, he already knows what the bulk of those entries from housewives are going to demonstrate. And taking that knowledge, along with the *working* knowledge he got at Eve's from using those very products, he's going to the bank each month. Or to the car dealers. Or to the appliance stores. Or to the jewelry shops. All of it to the tune of close to fifty thousand dollars and counting.

Eve's cut is 10 percent. I'd gladly fork over double that, he says, because the whole thing was her idea—even my name. Instead he gives her tips on what new stocks to buy. There's a sure killing to be made in baby bottles—but avoid Waco Glass and Tile. They're sitting on a marketing strategy that they'll never use because it came from a lunatic. I doubt that she needs too much advice, though; this is a savvy businesswoman from day one. Slave labor is never as productive as the work of a free man—even if he's working for free. And Eve has allowed Miss Maple to be one of the freest men I know.

The bells outside begin to toll for midnight. 1949. He takes his full champagne glass to the rear of the cafe. As I watch from the doorway, he steps off boldly into the midst of nothing and is suspended midair by a gentle wind that starts to swirl his cape around his knees. It's a hot, dry wind that could easily have been born in a desert, but it's bringing, of all things, snow. Soft and silent it falls, coating his shoulders, his upturned face. Snow. He holds his glass up and turns to me as a single flake catches on the rim before melting down the side into an amber world where bubbles burst and are born, burst and are born.

—Happy New Year, Bailey.
—Happy New Year, Miss Maple.

THE WRAP

My old man used to say, Always finish what you start. It's a sound principle, but it can't work in this cafe. If life is truly a song, then what we've got here is just snatches of a few melodies. All these folks are in transition; they come midway in their stories and go on. If this was like that sappy violin music on Make-Believe Ballroom, we could wrap it all up with a lot of happy endings to leave you feeling real good that you took the time to listen. But I don't believe that life is supposed to make you feel good, or to make you feel miserable either. Life is just supposed to make you feel.

When I first got into this business I didn't think that way. I figured that it was gonna be the answer for everybody else, since it had come as the answer for me. But it was Gabe who cued me in to the fact that running this cafe had done no such thing: My puppy, you still stand on that wharf in San Francisco, America. And the world, it still waits to commit suicide by swallowing a ball of fire. We do nothing here but freeze time; we give no answers—and get no answers—for ourselves or the next man. As a Jew, don't you think if there was an answer for what has been done to my people, I would have found it?

Now you gotta understand something about Gabe. When he refers to his people, he doesn't just mean the refugees fleeing from Europe, he means the whole ball of wax. Even little Mariam. And he's going a long long way back. For him Hitler was only the latest punk on the scene. But I served in that war and I can't buy it—pick up a newspaper and they're still finding graves. We're talking about a real monster. But Gabe won't budge on this one. He says, No, we are talking about a human being. I would like to believe you are right, he says; it would allow me to sleep at night since I am confined to this earth. And many do sleep believing that they have arrived at a reason for the unthinkable. They can place this demon they need so desperately to create with the other unthinkable horrors that arise out of their nightmares. They can feel some cleansing as they shed their tears over the photographs of our children who survived with eyes that are beyond saving. I would love dearly to do the same. And Gabe will pull at the edge of his beard then, forgetting that I'm even there as he travels to somewhere that I can't follow. No, my friend, he was no more than a man. And Hitler had help.

He means a lot of help. A world of help. Which is why he has trouble sleeping. And Gabe believes life is much too complicated to start pointing fingers; we wouldn't have enough of them. If that makes him a better man than me, so be it. Having fought in that particular war, I'm entitled to my opinion about the maniac who started it, but on other things dealing with Gabe's people I let him have his say. The way he lets me have mine.

He's a Russian Jew. I'm an American Negro. Neither of us is considered a national treasure in our countries, and that's where the similarity ends. We don't get into comparing notes on who did what to whom the most. Who's got the highest pile of bodies. The way I see it, there is no comparison. When most folks come out with that phrase, what they're really saying is that their pain is worse than your pain. But Gabe knows exactly what I mean: they're two different ball games.

And that's why we can honestly talk to each other or even get into full-blown arguments on subjects that other people wouldn't dream of bringing up in mixed company. I don't pull in his pogroms when he may dispute me on some point I've made about lynchings in the South, and he doesn't pull in Jim Crow when I don't agree with everything he says about the quotas on Jews. Because there is no comparison. But there are many long afternoons in his pawnshop when two very different people can look each other in the eye over glasses of strong tea and learn. There's a lot of lip service going around about the brotherhood of man, which is a crock of bull. This man is *not* my brother. My only brother left home close to forty years ago and I haven't seen him since. This man is simply

someone who doesn't have to run around trying to guess what I really
think about him because I *tell* him so. And if you're finding that heart-
warming and refreshing, it shows you how far the world still is from
anything that even looks like peace among men.

None of us here had the answer for what was to happen when Mariam's
baby came due. Her situation was a first for everybody. I'm afraid that
Eve let her heart rule her head on this one. I'm not saying that Mariam
shoulda been kicked back out into Addis Ababa and left to starve, but
Eve knew she couldn't stay here in limbo forever. And we had no idea
what an actual birth would do to this street. It's nothing but a way
station, and the choices have always been clear: you eventually go back
out and resume your life—hopefully better off than when you found
us—or you head to the back of the cafe and end it. But how can Life
itself ever begin here? A little snip of a girl bringing a really big question
like that, because she got herself born black and a Jew.

Gabe tried to use his little bit of savings to pay one of his cousins to see
that she got passage to Israel. And he's come down pretty hard on the
new government for not allowing her into the country under the Law
of Return. So she has no knowledge of the Talmud? Moses didn't know
Talmud. Elijah didn't know Talmud. Would they be barred as well? People
who should be our leaders sit over there and play these ridiculous games.
Jerusalem was more than a dream come true for them; it was the one
chance in the life of civilization for the setting right of at least one wrong.
If only there had been a way for the Jews to be given a homeland while
the politicians got left where they were. I'm still friends with Gabe because
when he starts in on his own people, I don't take sides, one way or the
other. And on this one, he was off and running. And banging down old
radios and flinging used overcoats into boxes and sweeping up a dust
storm. Puppy, cover your ears, a goy shouldn't be hearing these things.
But they're worried about the Arabs? Paper will destroy the country.

They have a chance to do something good for all Jews and they're going to drown themselves in paper. In their own stupid prejudices. And then he started sputtering about chickens peeing on their heads, which I guess was some Russian way of saying they were pretty low-down.

I know that Gabe's frustration comes out of love for his people and his belief that they have a God-given responsibility to be better than others. A light for the world. But I can afford to be more objective about the whole thing. People are people. And government is government. And Israel isn't gonna be run any differently from any other country. The first order of business is to make sure they can survive at all, since they got plunked right down in the middle of new neighbors who aren't gonna be knocking on their front doors with lemonade and pound cake. But inside those borders it's the same old story: You got your haves and your have-nots. You got those who are gonna be considered inferior to others because of the type of Jew they are, the color of Jew they are, or whatever. But above all, the groups who are in power are going to do whatever they can to stay in power. And that means dancing to the tune of whoever can bring in the most votes—or make the most noise. And there are none of Mariam's group in there right now who can do either. But I don't believe that a government like that can afford to keep ignoring protests like Gabe's—if only to avoid embarrassment. The one thing politicians hate more than a knowledgeable voter is bad press.

But we knew we didn't have time to wait for that to happen. Gabe kept trying until he found out about somebody named Rabbi Matthews, who lives in New York. He has other Falasha people in his congregation up there in Harlem, some who still speak her language. And for a while it looked like we'd found someone to adopt her and give the baby a home. And this is where I can get so mad I start sputtering. Gabe is right: When I walk out of this cafe and leave this street, I'm still in San Francisco. He's up in the Caucasus Mountains. And Eve is in New Orleans. You see, it's whatever life we've come from. And since we can't ever leave our businesses for any length of time, we're thinking that the easiest thing is to get some of the regular customers who happen to come in here from Harlem to take little Mariam back out with them. And what I heard is too ignorant to believe. And just guess who I heard it from? (Sister Carrie and Sugar Man, in case you need a hint.)

—That Matthews is nothing but a fraud. Whoever heard of a colored rabbi? Instead of misleading the Negro people he should bring 'em on to Christ.
—There's no such thing as a black Jew. Ain't being one or the other bad enough?
—I'm not messing with those people; they . . .
—I don't trust those people; they . . .

It was more than disheartening; it broke your heart. I wanted to tell the both of them to get the hell out of my place—and don't come back. Except it's not really mine. No, I'm just the fool who's forced to stay in here and serve people like that. But I'll fix their butts. By the time they get through eating their next meal in here, they'll be in the bathroom yelling for anybody's god who'll listen. None of which was going to help little Mariam, and then it got too late to matter. We only had a few hours to wait.

A lot of things didn't happen that day. The sun didn't shine. The pilot light didn't catch under the grill. The jukebox went totally on the blink. And not one person complained. It was as if they expected it to be a day unlike any other. Eve brought Mariam in about noon. She was all stomach with those little thin arms and legs. It made you sorta sad, what oughta be a woman's body topped with such a blank young face. Her complexion was a lot healthier, though, than when she first came to us, and she tried to waddle along as best she could as she was led to the rear of the cafe. She seemed almost eager. She'd been crying for days, asking for her mother. And Eve had told her she was going to her village again, and in a way she was.

Earlier that morning Eve had set everything up. The eucalyptus trees. The juniper. A steep-sloping mountain in the background. The air drifting from the back smelled like damp moss and thin lines of sunshine filtered in under the doorjamb. All of that effort drained her and, I guess, so did the worry of what lay ahead. Eve had hunched over a cup of coffee, looking older than I've ever seen her.

    —I had no choice, Eve said; she can't do it for herself. And I think I have it all about right.

But I wondered if she was going to deliver the baby out in the open countryside.

    —No, but the last is something only she can do. I'll just have to try and time it so she's back there by the first contractions, and then that hut she needs will appear. But all of this is so tricky, Bailey; I'll have to cut her before her water even breaks. You know, she's sewed up like a . . .

I knew and didn't want to hear about it. I'm sorry I was so abrupt with Eve; nobody else had the courage to take this job on. And for all we knew, when that baby gave its first cry, this whole street could have just faded away. Sure, we'd have been thrown back to those same hopeless crossroads in our lives, but she'd have been doomed out there in endless space. And there I was only dreading the thought of having to hear Mariam screaming.

    —No, this girl has been through enough, Eve said. I can't do anything about the blood, but there's a way to alter the pain.

I never dreamed that she meant lights. Sparkling. Shimmering. Waves of light. We could see them even from the front of the cafe. Besides the few customers, everyone who lived on the street was gathered inside. And I mean everyone, even strange little Esther. She'd squeezed herself into the darkest corner of the room, sitting on the floor with her arms wrapped around her bent knees. But even her face was in awe. Silvers. Pearls. Iridescent pinks. They now sprayed out into the sunless room and hit the ceiling. The walls. The floor. Glowing copper. Gilded orange. And all kinds of gold. Sequins of light that swirled and spun through the air. Cascades of light flowing in, breaking up, and rolling like fluid diamonds over the worn tile. Emerald. Turquoise. Sapphire. It went on for hours. I looked over and there were tears streaming down Gabe's wrinkled face: God bless you, Eve. And finally only the muted glow of a cool aquamarine. Then we heard the baby's first thin cry—and the place went wild.

Nadine hugged me so tight she almost lifted me onto my toes. Then Gabe grabbed me, whirled me around, and we started to dance. He could kick pretty high for an old goat. Miss Maple took his other hand and the three of us were out in the middle of the floor, hands raised and feet stomping. People were up on tables and cheering. Someone was banging on the counter with my spatula. Someone tore open a sack of rice and was throwing it into the air. I didn't give a damn. Jesse had her skirt raised in the throes of a mean flamenco. And, wonder of wonders, Esther smiled. But I think it was Peaches who started to sing. I know she has the best voice, and the spiritual started off high and sweet. You could hear it even above the mayhem. As everyone could still hear the lone cry of new life.

> Anybody ask you who you are?
> Who you are?
> Who you are?
> Anybody ask you who you are?
> Tell him—you're the child of God.

One voice joined in. Another voice joined. And another.

Anybody ask you who I am?
Who I am?
Who I am?
Anybody ask you who I am?
Tell him—I'm a child of God.
Soon we were all singing, a bit ragged and off-key. But all singing.
Peace on earth, Mary rocked the cradle.
Mary rocked the cradle and Mary rocked the cradle.
Peace on earth, Mary rocked the cradle.
Tell him—was with the child of God.
You see, folks, that's why almost a whole hour passed without it dawning on us that we hadn't found out if it was a boy or a girl.

It turned out to be a boy. A little frail, but they both made it through fine. As it was her custom, she kept the baby out there with her until today. Eve brought him into the cafe this morning because it was time for him to be circumcised. Gabe made sure we did the whole thing to the letter. He placed a clean pillow on the counter for the baby. He was standing in as the father, and he was to perform the operation. I thought my days of being a *mohel* were over, he said and winked. I had to stand in as the honorary *sandek*, the godfather. And Miss Maple took the role of the other male guests to help me respond to the blessing. Don't worry, Gabe said; God will forgive you for not being Jews. As the old man looked down at the baby, his face became solemn and his words echoed deeply inside of me. Only an absolute fool would have missed the point that this ceremony was about survival:

—I am ready to perform the commandment to circumcise my son, even as the Creator, blessed be He, hath commanded us, as it is written in the Law: And he that is eight days old shall be circumcised among you, every male through the generations.

The foreskin was taken very quickly. But he's a feisty number, and did he squall. You can tell this boy is gonna be a fighter. After Gabe cleansed the wound, he continued:

—Blessed art Thou, O Lord our God, King of the universe, who has sanctified us by Thy commandments and has commanded us to make our sons enter into the Covenant of Abraham our father.

And then we had been rehearsed for our part:

—Even as the child has entered into the Covenant, so may he enter into the Law, the nuptial canopy, and into good deeds.

I'm gonna tell you, it was really touching. And that's what I like the most about Gabe's faith: nothing important can happen unless they're all in it together as a community. After that I felt like this baby was really a part of me. Like I had a special responsibility to have him grow up a decent and good man. As his honorary godfather, I couldn't think of him having a better start than to give him my own father's name. But it turned out his honorary papa was planning on doing the exact same thing. And with personalities like ours, there was no way we could have come to a compromise. Somebody's name would have to be *first*, now wouldn't it? Before Miss Maple had to separate us from fisticuffs, Providence stepped in; it seems both of our fathers were named George.

So the baby's arrival didn't make this street disappear. I still have this place and it looks like I'm going to keep it for a while. But with the celebrations over and things settling down, we had a chance to reflect on what it all means. The times they are a-changing. If the world outside is becoming such that life itself can be brought forth in limbo, then one day, much too soon, I'm gonna start seeing young children walk through that door. Children who have lost their futures. *(The children who survived with eyes that are beyond saving.)* I don't know about you, but I shudder at the stories they'll have to tell.

And believe me, there's nothing I'd like better than to give you a happy ending to what happened today. I want to wrap it up by saying that after we gave George his name we took him back to his mother, and after Mariam follows her custom by staying out there with him for a month, she and the baby will eventually make their way to Rabbi Matthews. She'll meet kind and patient people who understand her ways and who know that she will need guidance to raise her son. So they'll find her a man in her faith to marry. A man who'll take the boy as his own, love him as much as his own; because they will go on to have other children. Mariam and that man won't have a perfect life together—no life is perfect—but it will give them the most that you can expect from any marriage. Someone to grow old with in comfort and peace. Yeah, I'd almost cut off my right arm to be able to say something like that. But after Eve tried to return the baby to Mariam, she was met with a wall of water. In Eve's absence Mariam had tried to create a running stream to bathe in. And the void out back produced exactly what her childlike mind called up: endless water.

Of course, we won't be raising the baby on this street. And if our prayers are answered, once he leaves us we'll never see him again. I have a customer who shows up occasionally, every six months or so. Irene Jackson runs a shelter for homeless boys. She takes her work so much to heart that whenever she can't turn a child around, it drives her close to the brink. She's a hard woman, but decent and fair. She'll make something worthwhile out of this boy—or break both their backs trying. But Wallace P. Andrews isn't run like a prison. Doesn't look like one either. You'd mistake it for a college campus if you didn't look too close. Gardens. A baseball diamond. I know it sounds like I'm trying to convince you that we're doing the right thing, but I'm really trying to convince myself.

You see, I know what Irene Jackson thinks of what goes on at Eve's. She falls into the camp that believes it is *not* a boardinghouse. And when she finds out that's where Mariam was living, and that we don't know the identity of the father, no matter what else we say she'll come to one conclusion. And it bothers me that the little boy will grow up thinking that about his mother. He should know that when he was born the world lit up with lights. But what else can we do? The whole nature of this place runs against a customer ever walking in here who'd be in a position to adopt him. What we have here is your classic damned-if-you-do-and-damned-if-you-don't. A perfect situation for this place, huh?

And that's how we wrap it, folks. It's the happiest ending I've got. Personally, I'm not really too down about it. Life will go on. Still, I do understand the point this little fella is making as he wakes up in the basket: When you have to face it with more questions than answers, it can be a crying shame.